Blizzard in August

by Sydney Duncombe

The Unlikely Candidate (1999)
Blizzard in August (2001)
Freedom County (2002)

Enduring Faith (2000)

Blizzard in August

Sydney Duncombe

2nd Edition
with a foreword by Rod Gramer

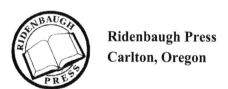

Ridenbaugh Press
Carlton, Oregon

This novel is a work of fiction. The names of cities and lakes are real. However, incidents, the names of people and corporations and their characters, are the products of the author's imagination or are used fictitiously, and their resemblance, if any, to real-life counterparts is entirely coincidental.

BLIZZARD IN AUGUST

Copyright ©2001 by Sydney Duncombe

All rights reserved. No part of this book may be reproduced or transmitted in any form, by any information storage or retrieval system, without written permission from the publisher, except in case of brief quotations used in critical articles or reviews.

For more information, contact Ridenbaugh Press, P.O. Box 834, Carlton OR 97111.

Printed and bound in the United States of America.

First edition 2001

Second edition November 2016

10 9 8 7 6 5 4 3 2 1

ISBN 978-0-945648-38-3 (softbound)

Front cover photo: by Kevin Poh, 2013

Back cover photo: courtesy University of Idaho

Ridenbaugh Press

P.O. Box 834, Carlton OR 97111

Phone (503) 852-0010

www.ridenbaugh.com

stapilus@ridenbaugh.com

Dedication

To my sons Charles, Bill, and Richard and my daughter and her husband, Dan and Mary Ellen Haley, who shared the joy of backpacking with me to the lake basin depicted in this novel

Acknowledgement

I would like to thank my children and their spouses for reading my novel in its early stages and giving advice. My thanks go to Janet Romanek, Michele Wilson, David and Sally Duncombe and my Thursday critique group for their excellent help in polishing my prose. U.S. Forest employees helped me with information about the 1969 period.

Introduction by Mary Haley

Blizzard in August is based on a real snow storm. It was not as dramatic, but it left my father, Syd Duncombe, with the seeds of this thriller. This book is set in the White Cloud Mountains in Central Idaho but the real event happened in the Sawtooth Mountains. The summer of my thirteenth year I broke my arm, but that didn't stop Dad and me from backpacking to our favorite, no-named, no-trail, fishing lake. The morning we were to go home we awoke to six inches of snow. At least I remember six inches, but like the size of the fish we caught, Dad's snow depth kept increasing over time. It was a difficult hike out. The snow made the steep, trail-less mountain hard to navigate, and Dad not only had to get a one-armed girl down, but the worm box as well.

This book is unique in the three Idaho based books, because it is a psychological thriller. Blizzards in August are not unheard of in Idaho's central mountains, and the characters face this deadly high mountain snowstorm in their own ways. Some have secrets that endanger the lives of others, but many act with a heroism brought out by adversity. One of the gifts of wilderness is the beauty and danger of wild places that bring all of us to a deeper understanding of who we are and what we can be. So come and enjoy some high mountain adventure, and since this is a Syd Duncombe book, there will also be death, and yes, even some sex.

A huge thank you goes to Chris Carlson author of *Cecil Andrus, Eye on The Caribou* and *Medimont Reflections*, who championed the release of this book, it's editing, and forward. Dad would have been thrilled to have such a wonderful writer in his corner.

My brothers and I will give all the family's royalties of this book to the University of Idaho's Syd Duncombe Scholarship which is used to continue to train students to give their very best to our cities, counties, states, nation, and the world.

Mary Haley is daughter of Dr. Syd Duncombe and author of The Great Potato Murder.

Foreword

by Rod Gramer

When I attended the University of Idaho there were a few professors who stood out of the crowd. Their larger-than-life presence was felt strongly both on campus and beyond the city limits of Moscow. Not only was Syd Duncombe one of those professors, he was, in my book, at the top of the list.

Being a Journalism and History major, I did not have the privilege of being one of the many students Syd mentored. My admiration for Syd was more from a distance, like someone admiring a fine piece of art or witnessing a rare triple play.

For me Syd was an imposing figure as he strode across campus, tall, with a strong and memorable face, distinguished by an unmistakable Romanesque nose. Intelligence and wisdom radiated from the man. If one was casting the perfect character for a college professor in a movie, it would be Syd Duncombe.

Even though not one of his students, I still benefited from Syd's incredible knowledge of politics and government in Idaho.

In 1974, the Lewiston Tribune gave me the opportunity to cover the Idaho Legislature with the incomparable Jay Shelledy. I was a wet-behind-the-ears journalism major who had just finished a year as editor of The Argonaut, but still had a lot to learn about both reporting and life. Especially how things worked at the Statehouse.

I took to Boise a book that Syd had written about state and local government in Idaho. Besides the school of hard knocks that I would experience as a cub reporter in the months ahead, that book became my indispensable guide for understanding the complexities of state government.

The book, its pages eventually dog-eared and its spine broken from use, rested on my desk as I graduated from the University and joined The Idaho Statesman, serving first as its local government reporter and then its political editor and Editorial Page editor. I'd like to think I finally mastered the workings of Idaho politics, but I would not have gotten there without the Tribune, Shelledy and Syd giving me a sound foundation. For that, I will be eternally grateful.

But there were students whose lives were touched by Syd in a more personal way. My friend, Ray Stark, tells the story about how, toward the end of his graduate studies, Syd asked him to his office. Syd had recommended

Ray for a job in the Legislative Budget Office and the meeting turned into an interview and a job offer.

"Syd changed my life," Ray told me, never forgetting that Duncombe opened that crucial door for him. Ray went on to serve the Legislature for many years and now manages governmental affairs for the Boise Metro Chamber of Commerce.

If the mark of a great teacher is to not only pass along knowledge, but to infuse wisdom into his students and care about their personal and professional welfare, then Syd Duncombe is the model for that kind of professor.

What Syd did for Ray, he did for countless other students who passed his way.

Idaho is blessed to have so many political, government, business and other leaders who had the chance to be mentored by Syd. Even now, Syd's legacy lives on in the work his protégés are doing to improve our great state.

But who would have thought that Syd was not only an inspiring professor, but also an accomplished novelist?

The book you have opened, *Blizzard in August*, is a compelling story about the struggle to survive in the Idaho wilderness.

The book is set in the sixties when all hell is breaking loose on college campuses, and when mores and morals are undergoing tectonic shifts. Syd uses what was supposed to be a leisurely hike into the White Cloud Mountains to explore these changing values and how they clashed with traditional ones like honesty, respect and human decency.

Blizzard in August reminds me of one of the novels by the great Wallace Stegner, who like Syd was a professor in the 1960s and had a front row seat to those turbulent times. Like Stegner did in *All the Little Live Things*, Syd is attempting to make sense of those topsy-turvy times and demonstrate that some of those old-fashioned values were still the best ones.

It's clear from reading this book that Syd not only knew his way around the halls of the Statehouse, but also around the Idaho backcountry. He describes this adventure in the White Clouds like someone who knows the trail well.

He combines the detail of an experienced back-packer, with the eye of a skilled novelist.

In short, it's a good read.

John Steinbeck once said, "I have come to believe that a great teacher is a great artist . . ."

Steinbeck could have been speaking of Syd Duncombe. Family man. Teacher. Intellectual. Public servant. Mentor. Friend. Novelist. Not a bad life at all.

Rod Gramer is the co-author of Fighting the Odds: The Life of Senator Frank Church, *a novel,* The Good Assassin, *and spent 38 years working as a journalist. He is now president of Idaho Business for Education, a group working to improve opportunities for Idaho's students.*

Chapter 1

Central Idaho, Tuesday, August 27, 1969 – 1:30 p.m.

The dead silence of the alpine slope was broken by the crashing, clattering sound of a boulder, which appeared to gain size and momentum with each bound. Kelli's heart raced. The boulder bounced off one stone after another and, as it tumbled and skidded downward it dislodged a score of smaller rocks. Paralyzed by fear for the moment, she threw her body behind an overhanging ledge to her right. Close! Kelli looked up to see a watermelon-sized rock pass only ten feet from the ledge that had given her cover.

Looking up was a mistake. Kelli lost the grip she had on the rock ledge and began to slide down the forty-five degree slope on her right side. The gray rocks were loose and there was no good place to get a handhold. Five feet, ten feet, fifteen feet; even though she had taken off her backpack a few minutes before, she could not check her descent. Despite the cold, she could feel sweat on her face. Twenty feet, twenty-five, she was going faster now. Looming ahead was the top of what appeared to be a cliff. Panic gripped her.

Kelli reached for a triangular stone but it began to roll as soon as she touched it. She saw a young pine with a trunk the size of her fist growing near the top of the cliff. Would it hold her weight? Slowly, she coiled her body as she slid toward the edge. Composing herself, she uncoiled her body and reached for the pine. The roots nearly pulled from the ground but it held fast. Quickly, she reached out with her other hand and found a handhold in a rock crevasse.

She was safe for the moment, but her right leg throbbed and her right hand and hip hurt. The pain slowly diminished and she quickly assessed the damage. Scrape marks and dirt covered her right hand. She found just a bruise on her hip.

Kelli looked up the steep mountainside with its gray rock outcroppings and loose shale. She half expected another rock to come hurtling down upon her. None came. Warily, she climbed hand over hand back to the place she had left her pack, hearing nothing, but smelling her own sweat and fear. She sat down and stopped to think. Had she almost been nearly a victim of a quirk of nature, a rock nearly balanced on the precipitous slope, suddenly set in motion by a gust of wind or an animal? Or could the rock have been accidentally dislodged from its place by a careless hiker?

Kelli called, "Hello, is anyone up there?" There was no answer except the faint echo off the sharp-peaked ridge across the valley. The ridge was majestic with a crown shaped like the upturned blade of a saw and slopes that plunged almost straight down, gray rock with sharply pointed outcroppings and not a hint of green vegetation. As she watched, a gray cloud moved over the sun giving the peaks a cold, forbidding look.

After washing her wounds with water from her canteen, she applied an antiseptic cream, and covered the wounds with Band-Aids. She looked down at the forty-five degree slope feeling dizzy and slightly nauseous. Kelli sat on the ground hugging her knees to her chest. The next wave of nausea swept over her, and with it came that terrible memory.

A ten-year-old Kelli had been picking her way up a steep rock slope in the Sierra Nevadas, trying to keep up with her eighteen-year-old sister, Melissa, who, as usual, was trying to impress her boyfriend.

"Wait for me!" Kelli had called, but they had not waited. In her rush to catch up with them, Kelli slipped and slid off the edge of a twenty-foot cliff, tumbling over and over, with brush slowing her descent, and her vision a jumble of sky, rocks, and bushes. The scene replayed itself over and over in her nightmares in the hospital as she recovered from a broken leg.

"Why didn't you wait for me?" she demanded of her sister. Melissa had looked down her nose at her. "I told Mother we shouldn't have had to take you along," she said, her voice edged with resentment. "You'll be okay. Just don't try to keep up with me again, that's all."

"But you're my big sister," Kelli called as Melissa left her bedside to meet another boyfriend. But Melissa tossed her head, letting her blond hair fly, and had left the hospital room.

Hugging her knees, Kelli felt the nausea pass, and she considered her current situation. She was thirty-three now, and an elementary school principal, but her relationship with her older sister had not changed much. She was always trying to win Melissa's approval and, despite misgivings seemed to end up doing what her sister wanted. Kelli was painfully aware that it was Melissa who frequently asked her to care for her preteen daughters whenever she and her husband, Richard, went out to dinner; it was Melissa who got her to stay with her teenage daughters when she and her husband went on vacation; and it was Melissa who had persuaded her to take her nieces on this backpacking trip to central Idaho.

Kelli thought again about the rock that came close to hitting her. A backpacker ahead of her might have discharged it accidentally, but she had seen no one except the four members of her party since they left Walter Lake at nine that morning. Pam, Ann, Jason, and Darry were all ahead of her. It

Blizzard in August   3

couldn't have been one of them who dislodged the rock accidentally, or, as an ill-tempered act, meant to scare her. Or could it?

Pam and Ann were her nieces, Melissa's 21 and 19 year-old daughters. They wouldn't want to hurt her, would they? Melissa was concerned about Pam's steamy romance with Darry, the son of a multimillionaire chief executive of an industrial conglomerate. Pam must have been in contact with Darry because when they arrived at the trailhead at Livingston Mill yesterday, they found Darry Baltz and Jason Green waiting for them. Darry and Pam had wanted to share a tent but Kelli, who owned the larger of the two tents, insisted that her nieces share her tent while Darry and Jason slept in Jason's tent. Could this be the reason either Darry or Pam tried to slow her down?

Kelli put on her pack. She had to catch up with her party. The pack felt heavy and she wondered why. Opening it she found four rocks in the bottom neatly wrapped in her underwear and sweatshirts so they wouldn't rub together and feel hard through the pack.

No wonder she had felt so tired. Who would have wanted her to lag behind? Pam or Darry, she thought. She couldn't believe her niece would do that to her. But Darry was not family yet and she didn't trust him. It was essential that she catch up with the others.

As she climbed the slope carefully, but more quickly with a lightened pack, Kelli recognized that she was a more experienced backpacker than either of her two nieces and probably Darry. Jason was the only one of the group who had been into the White Clouds Mountains before, and his knowledge of the area was invaluable. But Jason seemed to be leading the group now and she needed to reassert her leadership.

Melissa had ordered Kelli to keep both of her daughters from sleeping with anyone on the trip. She feared Melissa's waspish tongue and knew that if either girl were seduced on this trip, Melissa would never forgive her. But the chaperone's role seemed outmoded in the era of sexual freedom of the sixties. Why did she agree to do this? Was it a deep-seated habit of always doing what her older sister demanded that dated back to her childhood?

She had to keep Darry and Pam from sleeping in the same tent at night. But how could she keep them apart during the daylight hours?

Reaching the top of the ridge, she sat on a rock composing herself. She was depressed and the rocky, gray landscape reflected her mood. There was little vegetation on the slope and the endless slabs of stone, loose shale, and small rocks seemed harsh, dangerous, and unforgiving. There was a stark beauty in this Idaho landscape, but she sensed a danger for the unwary backpacker. It was over nine miles back to the trailhead if someone was injured.

She thought about Pam and Ann again. She wished her nieces were her own daughters, so she could have guided and disciplined them. Oh, she just wished that Sterling had been able to give her a baby during their three disastrous years of marriage. How many more years would she still be able to bear a child, she wondered? She thought, I like being an elementary school principal but I would like marriage and my own children.

Rested now, Kelli rose and pushed onward. She had fallen behind because of the rocks in her pack and her slide down the mountain. She needed to stride up to the others confidently and regain the leadership of her party. Climbing up the last rise towards the lake she thought she saw someone two-hundred yards to the east watching her with binoculars. She shivered slightly and wondered who it was.

Chapter 2

Cirque Lake White Clouds Mountains 2:00 p.m.

Ann Pettigrew sat on a rocky promontory and looked across Cirque Lake. The deep blue waters rippled under a cloudy sky and she saw a triangular-shaped ridge rising more than a thousand feet above the far side of the lake. There were a few stunted pines clinging to the rocky shore to her right, but she couldn't see a single other tree or bush. The far side of the lake appeared to have no vegetation. The tan color of the bank merged into light gray as the steep rocky slope rose precipitously to the sharp-edged ridge above. To her left, across an arm of the lake, there were a few tufts of grass and another hillside that led to a snowfield that clung to the north side of another peak.

"It's beautiful," Ann said. "I like the strong, stark colors...the cobalt blue of the lake, the off-white of the snow, and the various shades of gray, some with a tan hue, others tinged with a slight touch of burnt umber, yellow ochre, or raw sienna. I wish I had my paints."

Jason Green ran his tanned fingers over his strong jaw. "I'm impressed. I didn't know you painted."

"Oils. But I'm not very good at it," she said. "But you know, something else amazes me … the quiet, the absolute silence … no sounds of people and not even the sound of planes, animals or birds. And the air. It's pure and cold. No haze or pollution like we have in Los Angeles."

A smile creased Jason's face, his dimples showing. "I knew you wouldn't want to miss Cirque Lake," he said. "It's the top one in this basin … over 10,000 feet. It's covered with snow and ice nine to ten months each year." I think this is one of the most beautiful lakes in the world."

Ann smiled back. "I'd have to agree. You know you appreciate the beauty of a flower garden or a mountain lake much more after you paint it and see the subtle mix of colors and the way light shades into dark."

"Are you going to major in fine arts?" Jason asked.

Ann, a student at Southern Oregon College, gave a self-depreciating smile. "No. Oh, I'll take a course or two in painting as an elective. But I'll major in something practical, elementary education. I'm just starting my first semester next week. Who knows where I'll end up? Maybe I'll get into alternative nutrition. You know, macrobiotic diets and such. Do you eat meat?"

"Sure," Jason said, startled by the question. "There's a lot of good beef grown in Idaho."

"Meat is bad for you," Ann said. "Particularly red meat, like steak. You're better off on a vegetarian diet. But fish is good for you, too."

Jason dug in his pack and found his fly rod case and put together a sectioned rod.

Ann studied Jason carefully. She had not expected to meet a man who interested her on this backpacking trip, but was pleasantly surprised at her first impression of him. He had dark hair that bushed out beneath his wide-brimmed green cap and a smile that brought dimples to his cheeks. She had followed him up the steep slope, and he had stopped frequently to give her a helping hand. He had been respectful to Kelli and very courteous to her. She was impressed that he was a senior in mining engineering at the University of Idaho.

"Want to try some fly fishing?" Jason asked.

"Sure," Ann replied. "Can you teach me?"

Jason put on his fly reel and tied a renegade on the tapered line. He stood on the shore with a large flat rock behind him and whipped the fly forward, then backwards over the rocks, and then forward again. The fly nestled on the water.

Ann tried with Jason standing behind her and slowly learned the basic rhythm. Her first casts were not very long, but her sixth cast went forty feet. The fly lit just where the light blue of the shallow water shelved off into deep blue. It sat there a minute and was sucked in so quickly that Ann almost missed it.

"Set the hook," Jason shouted.

Ann pulled back on the rod and used the hand lever to bring in a footlong trout. Jason went to the shore, caught the trout by the gills, unhooked the fly and set the trout free. "Wow! My first trout," she said. "Don't you want a turn?"

"No. It's fun just watching you," Jason told her, draping his long legs over a rock.

Ann had no bites for the next ten minutes. She looked at the gray sky and, feeling colder, said in surprise. "It's snowing. I've never seen it snow in August."

"It's not unusual up here in August," Jason commented. "I've backpacked into this basin seven times with my father and uncle and it's snowed on us at least one day on three of those trips."

Ann's eyes grew large in disbelief. "Do you camp up here when it snows?"

Blizzard in August

"We've done it twice. Once, four inches of snow came overnight and melted off in the sun the next day. The other time, the snow came in the morning and a cold rain melted it during the afternoon."

"And the third time?"

"That was the last week in August three years ago. Three inches of snow accumulated by noon and it was snowing hard. We packed up and moved camp down at Island Lake so we could be on a trail." Jason took off his glasses, wiped them with a piece of Kleenex and looked at the snowflakes descending lazily into the lake. He grinned. "It's not bad so far."

Ann gave the rod back to Jason and watched the route they had taken up to the lake. She couldn't see Kelli. That concerned her.

Ten minutes later, Kelli came over the rise, hiking confidently with long strides. Ann admired her lean, athletic, yet feminine figure. She wished she could work off her own flabbiness.

Kelli sat down beside Ann on a rock, took off her pack, and asked, "How long have you and Jason been here?"

"Maybe half an hour," Ann said. "I was beginning to worry about you. What happened?"

"I slipped and slid down a rocky slope almost to the edge of a cliff. I'm okay. Just some scrapes. It took me a while to climb up."

Kelli's mouth was set in a tight line and her jaw protruded more than usual. She's not beautiful like my mother, Ann thought. She has the same golden blond hair but her chin and forehead are too prominent and her mouth too wide. Her face reflects character and strength, not the perfect oval face of my mother.

"Did Darry and Pam come right up after you?" Kelli asked casually.

Ann wondered what she was leading up to. "No. Pam reached the lake about ten minutes after we did. Darry followed a few minutes later."

"Where are they now?" Kelli sounded irritated.

Ann shrugged. "They headed down to the next lake. Told me they wanted to find a good place for us to camp tonight."

Kelli snorted and Ann looked sympathetically towards her. "They're going to do what they're going to do," she said. "This is the sixties. There's nothing you or Mom can do to stop them. So just relax."

Kelli's shoulders sagged a bit. Ann looked across the lake. The wind was blowing fiercely from the north, whipping the water into white caps. The snowflakes came down more thickly and gray clouds were now obscuring the steep triangular ridge to the west.

Jason pulled in his line, took apart his rod, and put it back in his pack. "I don't like the looks of this storm," he said. "The temperature is dropping fast. This is a dry snow and it's coming down harder now and sticking on the rocks. We may have six to seven inches in this basin before morning."

"What do you suggest?" Kelli asked.

"1 think we should stay at Island Lake tonight. We need to camp at the head of a trail if it snows a lot."

"What about going back down the way we came?" Kelli asked with worry lines around her eyes.

"Too dangerous with this snow," Jason said. "I've heard there's a rough trail somewhere up that slope, but I've never been able to find it. We're safer going to Island Lake. I've taken that route four times." "Show me on the map," Kelli demanded.

Jason took the contour map out of a plastic container he had hung around his neck and opened it. Both Ann and Kelli looked on as he pointed out their position on Cirque Lake.

"We're at nearly 10,200 feet right now," he stated. "Sapphire Lake is the next lake down, it's nearly 9,990 feet. Then, about fifty feet below Sapphire is Cove Lake. We need to skirt around the north end of Cove Lake, cross a snowfield, then it's two miles mainly downward to Island Lake, which is only 9,200 feet. Jason paused. "I think Darry will agree to this. He needs to get to an important meeting in a few days." Ann put on her pack and took a last look at Cirque Lake, wishing she had brought a camera. The wind had shifted to the northwest and the driving snow was obscuring the far shore of the lake. She turned her back to the wind and followed Jason as he picked his way along a rocky cove and over a low ridge. Is Kelli headed for trouble? Ann wondered. Pam and Darry had been sleeping together secretly for at least a month. How would they react to a continued, heavy-handed attempt by Kelli to keep them apart?

Chapter 3

Sapphire Lake, Tuesday, 2:30 p.m.

Darry had found the perfect place for lovemaking, a thin, level area of soft grass between two rocks that hid them from anyone walking along the shore of Sapphire Lake. He spread a blanket on the grass, but Pam dawdled, picking brilliant orange Indian paintbrush flowers and admiring the deep blue waters. Grabbing Pam, half-playfully, Darry wrestled her down to the blanket. Then the first snowflakes began to fall.

Undaunted, Darry doubled the blanket around them and started to undress her. She lay back blissfully and let him proceed. Then, Darry heard voices—they were three to four hundred yards away.

"Damn," he said, sitting up so he could peer over a rock. "They're coming," He said quietly. "Get up. We've got to get down to the lake shore where our packs are before they get there." He pulled up his jeans, buttoned his shirt, and grabbed the blanket. Pam rose more leisurely, pulled on her clothes, and followed Darry down the hill.

Jason, Kelli, and Ann came into view when Darry was more than fifty feet from the shore. He felt foolish to be carrying a blanket, irate at being interrupted, and angry at Kelli. She was the one who had taken Pam and Ann away the previous weekend, when he had plans to take Pam on his father's forty-foot yacht on a trip to Santa Catalina. She was the one he blamed for dragging Pam on this trip to Idaho.

Darry thought he had outsmarted Kelli when he learned from Pam where they intended to backpack. Kelli didn't know that his father owned a mine about forty miles from Livingston Mill, so it was easy for Darry to show up at the trailhead with Jason as a guide. However, Darry's scheme had been thwarted last night when Kelli had prevented him from sleeping in the same tent with Pam. Darry was in no mood to be nice to Kelli.

"Did you find a good spot to lay the tents?" Kelli inquired glancing up the rocky slope Darry had descended.

Darry took instant offense at what he thought was Kelli's emphasis on the word "lay". "What do you mean by that crack?" he said testily.

"I thought you went ahead to find a camping spot," Kelli said. "I just want to know if you found one up on that rocky hillside."

Darry exploded. "I don't like the tone of your voice. What Pam and I do is our business, not yours. We're adults. We don't want or need a chaperone."

"I'm just doing what my sister asked me to do," Kelli commented mildly.

Darry raised his voice. "You're the chief troublemaker. It was you who suggested taking Pam and Ann to Carmel last weekend when you knew I wanted to take her on my father's yacht. And you had a lot to do with planning this backpack trip to Idaho. You're always sticking your nose in when you're not wanted."

Kelli's voice also rose in anger. "Look. I let you come on our backpack trip. You should be grateful." She paused. "I found my pack very heavy today. You know what I found when I unpacked it? Four large rocks. Did you put them in my pack to slow me down ... to give you and Pam more time to ... to find a campsite?"

Darry's anger flared again. "Damn it! Can't you take a little joke? You have no sense of humor."

Kelli's face reddened in anger and she glared at him. "Putting some rocks in my pack may be a joke, but rolling a rock the size of a small watermelon down the slope and nearly hitting me is not a joke. I had to duck behind a rock, lost my grip and nearly slid off a cliff." "I didn't have anything to do with that," Darry asserted angrily. "I was a hundred feet away when that rock slid down the hill. Besides that rock missed you by nearly forty feet."

"Ten or fifteen feet," corrected Kelli. "Look, Darry, you are my guest on this trip and I expect you to behave yourself. I'm letting you know right now that Pam and Ann are both sleeping in my tent tonight."

Darry's mouth compressed with rage but he was silent. He wanted to get Pam alone in the tent and he wanted to get even with Kelli, but how? He followed the others to a little bluff above the shore of Sapphire Lake where he had left his pack.

As Darry and Pam were putting on their gear, Jason said, "The snow is coming down too fast. We might get stuck up here for a while. Darry, you said you had an important meeting in Los Angeles on Friday."

"Yes," Darry said. "A very important meeting. Can't miss it. I'm being considered as head of a Central American division in our company." Darry didn't mention that his father had objected to his trip to Idaho until Darry had promised to get back in time for this all important board meeting.

"You'll head a division! Cool," Pamela gushed.

Darry gave Pam a loving smile and then turned back to Jason. "We can't get stuck in the snow; let's camp lower down."

Blizzard in August

"I suggest Island Lake," Jason said. "It's more than six hundred feet lower, but more important, it's on a trail that leads to Livingston Mill."

"Excellent. Let me look at the map." Darry looked relieved.

Jason traced the proposed route on the map and Darry raised a question when Jason mentioned the snowfield on Cove Lake. "How are we going to get ourselves and our packs up the snowfield?"

"I have rope and some icewalkers I can strap on my boots. I can climb the snowfield and use a rope to bring the rest of you up."

"Good idea," Darry said. Then a plan came into his mind. He said nothing about it. Would his father approve? Of course. He would get to the meeting on time and would also get to sleep with Pam tonight. The ends justify the means, his father had always told him.

Jason started along Sapphire Lake and Darry scarcely noted its deep blue waters. The snow was coming down harder now and there was more than an inch in places. Darry had taken his place as second in line after Jason and had gotten Pam to follow him. The wind rose in intensity, whipping up whitecaps on the lake and causing waves to break over the rocky shore. The snow slanted down on Darry, impairing visibility and biting into his neck and back.

As they skirted around a knobby bluff. Darry kept worrying about what his father would think of his plan. Big Mike Baltz had taken time to come to his Little League baseball games. He had taught him a devious play he could use as a pitcher to pick a runner off first base.

"Is this fair?" nine-year-old Darry had asked.

"Who cares," said his father. "Nice guys always finish last."

Big Mike was a hustling competitor and expected his son to be likewise. He hated softness and once bawled Darry out for pitching underhanded to a short kid with braces on his legs. The opponent's coach told Darry the kid hadn't been up all year, and with Darry's team ahead eight to nothing he could afford to pitch softly. Darry did and the kid lashed the ball down the left field line and the boy who ran for him made second base. This sparked a rally in which the opposing team scored five runs and made it a close game. Darry's team still won, but Big Mike was angry because Darry had given the boy a chance.

"Never let an opponent up when he's down," was Big Mike's slogan. "Never let pity interfere with attaining your objective." This last saying made Darry smile inwardly. They came to a cove on the east end of Sapphire Lake. Jason was pointing out an area with some level spaces among the rocks and trees. "This isn't a bad campsite," he said sitting for a minute on a rock. "I camped here two years ago with my father and uncle. There're some good trout in the cove." Then he pointed to the next lake below. "That's Cove Lake. It's only forty feet lower."

A stream gushed out of Sapphire Lake, but instead of following the stream, Jason led them inland a ways to avoid a shallow pool. Soon they came back to the stream at the point it entered Cove Lake. "This is the best camping spot in the basin," Jason announced.

Darry saw a green backpack tent with a fly that had lots of overhang in front. Looks like someone's camped here. This could be a big help, he thought and made a revision in his plan.

"We cross the stream here," Jason said.

"Why cross here?" Kelli questioned. "Why not go around the northern end of the lake and avoid both this stream and the snowfield?

Let me see the topo map."

Jason brought out the map. "The problem is the outlet stream of the entire lake basin is in the northeast corner of the lake. It's thirty feet wide and too deep to cross. The only place to cross is right here."

Kelli was looking at the twenty-foot wide stream. "How do you cross here?"

"Jump across on the rocks." Jason nimbly used six rocks to cross, took off his pack, and came back to ferry the packs of the others across. Kelli was the last to cross. She slipped on the fifth rock and Darry hoped she would fall in, but instead fell on her side.

"Are you all right?" Jason asked as he stooped down to help her.

Kelli rose slowly, looking gratefully at Jason. "Fell on my good side. I'll be all right in a minute."

Darry did not pause after he saw Kelli rise. He put on his pack, helped Pam on with hers, and they both started along the trail that skirted the western end of the lake. It was a few minutes before the others would follow, time enough to determine how best he could use the snowfield for his plan.

Chapter 4

Cove Lake Tuesday 2:45 p.m.

Hank Barclay sat alone on the west shore of Cove Lake thinking of Susan as he looked at his bobber floating fifty feet off shore. This time last summer he and Sue had spent five glorious, sunny August days camped at the head of Cove Lake. Hank looked at his backpack tent pitched in exactly the same spot it had been last year and for the five years before that. Sue had loved to backpack and thought the White Clouds mountains were the most majestic on earth. Her photos chronicled the changes in colors of these looming ridges and rocky peaks. They gleamed a yellow-orange in the first light of sunrise, a shimmering white in the bright rays at noon, and could almost have a tangerine color in the setting sun. Now, in the overcast sky, they were gray.

The bobber twitched and Hank waited, but nothing further happened. He was thinking. Next year. Sue and I were going to bring the girls. They would be old enough then. Sara would be 13, Julie, 11 and Joanne, 9. It would have been their first long backpack trip as a family.

All this planning was so fruitless now. Hank felt hollow inside just thinking about it. His whole life, so full of joy and hope, was dashed to pieces in a single moment on the Lewiston Hill.

Memories of that terrible day flooded back. It was six on a snowy February evening. Sue had gone shopping in Lewiston and was due back before five. Lewiston was only six hundred feet above sea level and it had been raining down there. There were over a hundred hairpin turns to reach the top of the Lewiston grade at a 2,600 foot elevation. Somewhere in that grade the rain turned to ice and then to snow.

The phone call came shortly after six. Susan's Ford was hit by a man driving a pickup who skidded on a turn coming down the hill, smashing into Susan's car head-on and driving her off the cliff. The patrolman said that her Ford plunged four hundred feet down the slope and turned end over end, bursting into flames. He identified her through the contents of her wallet, which was thrown out of the car.

Hank had gone to Lewiston the next day to identify the remains. It did not help when he learned that the driver was saved from death because hitting Susan's car kept him on the highway. His blood alcohol content was above the legal limit and the police cited him. But that did not bring Susan back. Hank could not fully believe that Susan was dead until after the funeral. All spring he had been deeply depressed, showing little of his usual vitality with his children and spark in teaching history at the University of Idaho.

Now, the first lazy flakes of snow started to come down. Gray clouds were covering the sky and it matched Hank's mood. Perhaps, it was a poor idea to leave the girls with Uncle Ted and Aunt Marge and come back to the White Clouds another year. He had returned to remember Susan, hoping for closure on his time of grief. The backpack trip turned out to be a bittersweet time, full of wonderful memories of Sue's enthusiasm for life, and bitter memories of her life cut short.

His mind drifted back to a pretty, dark-haired girl with green eyes and freckles. It was 1950 and they had been dating for three months. Sue's parents owned four hundred acres of wheat land between Deary and Troy, about twenty miles east of Bovill.

Sue had brought him home for dinner and he had not made a good impression on her parents. As he was leaving, he overheard her father say, "He's the grandson of a logger, he's the son of a logger, and he's a logger during his high school summer vacation. He looks like a logger. He'll be a logger all his life. And you know what that means; hard drinking, hard living, unemployment, and maybe disabling injury." To Sue, her father said, "I don't want you to see any more of him."

Well, they had continued to date. Sue had faith in him. She stuck with him during the Korean war when he was overseas for almost two years. It was Susan's faith and encouragement that had gotten him to apply for college with the GI Bill. Later, after graduation, her parents relented and they were married. Yet the bitter memories of her father's words still rankled Hank.

It started to snow hard. Hank moved down the bank until he could sit under the overhanging branches of a big pine fifteen feet from shore. He cast out sixty feet and propped his rod up on a bush that grew just above the shoreline. He wondered how much it would snow tonight. Perhaps he should pack up and go down to Island Lake even though he had been through a seven-inch snowfall in the basin before. What if I'm snowed in and can't get down?, he wondered. Then morosely he thought, It isn't likely but if it does happen, I'll just see Susan in heaven before I expect. He could picture Susan in his mind now; the radiant smile, the twinkling eyes, the musical laugh. How he missed her faith, her joy, and her kindness. He began to cry softly. His life was without meaning. He needed somehow to try to overcome his grief, if just to be a better father to his girls. But he knew he would always remember Susan.

Out of the corner of his eye. Hank saw five backpackers stop at the stream crossing near his tent. He wondered momentarily whether they were thinking

Blizzard in August 15

of joining him at his campsite, then he saw them begin to cross and he shifted his attention to his bobber.

Sitting twenty feet from the shore under a tree limb, he could see the backpackers pass in front of him without being obvious to them. The man in the lead had red hair, an expensive green pack, and top-of- the-line hiking boots. The woman who followed wore designer jeans and a stylish blue jacket. Her cameo face was framed with hair the color of light gold. He guessed they were wealthy, style-conscious, and not experienced hikers. He could catch snatches of conversation as they approached.

The man said, "Your aunt drives me crazy. If she has her way, I won't be able to sleep with you tonight."

The woman said, "She drives me bananas too. She's so dowdy, such a prude. I wish we didn't have her with us."

The man said, "Maybe I can do something about that. I have a plan. I have an idea she won't make it up that snowfield over there."

The couple continued to talk, but Hank couldn't hear the rest of their conversation. A few minutes later, three other backpackers approached. A lanky, darkhaired man with a tan backpack led the way. His pack and clothing were inexpensive and well-worn. He's had a lot of backpacking experience and he knows this basin. Hank decided as he heard him telling about Island Lake to a shorter blonde girl who followed.

Finally, there was a woman who was probably in her thirties. She strode along with determination and a lengthy stride. Not a beautiful woman, he decided, but she had an athletic figure and was probably a good hiker and backpacker. Her clothes and pack showed that she was not as wealthy as the redhaired man and the two blonde girls. She looked in his direction, spotted him and said "Hello."

"Howdy," Hank replied without moving.

As she hiked along the shore of the lake towards the snowfield. Hank wondered whether this was the aunt that the redhaired hiker was talking about. Getting up the snowfield with freshfallen snow is going to be tricky, Hank thought. It will be interesting to see what happens; see what, if anything, the redhaired man plans.

As the backpacking party approached the snow slide, Hank realized that he missed human contact. This was his fourth day camped at Cove Lake and these were the first people he had seen.

Chapter 5

Cove Lake Tuesday 2:50 p.m.

Kelli looked up at the snowfield that covered much of the north end of Cove Lake. She saw no way around it, for it not only came down to the edge of the lake but hung out over, it making it impossible to get around the shore. Snow was falling faster now and Kelli could barely see the top of the two hundred foot snow slope. Her spirits plummeted. "There's a way around this," Jason was saying as Kelli approached. "But it'll take more than an hour to backtrack in this snow storm. I'm going to climb this slope with my ice walkers and take a rope up with me."

Jason put the ice walkers on his boots and attached a rope to his waist. She wished he had crampons. He made slow progress, testing each step as he angled to the right, away from the overhang. He finally made it to the top. His wave was barely visible through the densely falling snow.

Jason let the rope down. Darry tied it on first his own pack, then Pam and Ann's. Kelli sat on a rock to watch as Darry attached the rope to Pam's jeans with a clip and told her to hold on tight. Jason hauled her up without incident. Jason let the rope down again and Ann ascended. Now, it's my turn, thought Kelli as she took off her pack. But this time, when the rope was lowered it was Darry who used the clip and his arms while Jason pulled him up. "What about me?" yelled Kelli but there was no immediate answer. Darry shouted something at Jason and the tall Idahoan started hiking along the edge of the snowfield searching for the trail ahead.

"Don't leave me! Lower the rope with the clip," Kelli ordered with a hint of panic in her voice.

There was no answer. Two minutes later. Darry's head appeared at the top of the snowfield and he let down the rope without the clip. "Hold on to this tightly while I pull," he ordered.

"Where's the clip?" Kelli yelled up the slope.

"Lost in the snow," was Darry's reply.

"How about taking my pack first?" Kelli countered.

"No time. We've got to be on our way. There's almost two inches of snow on the ground up here. Jason is having a difficult time finding the trail. The girls are freezing. We've got to get down to Island Lake before we get lost in this blizzard."

Kelli wasn't sure she was strong enough to climb the slope with a pack and hold on to the rope. But she wasn't going to admit that to Darry. She was not sure she trusted him.

"Can you get Jason to help you with the rope?" she yelled.

"He's too far away," Darry yelled back. "We're wasting time. You can make it. You're as strong as a horse. You aren't scared, are you?"

Fear played around the corners of Kelli's mouth, but Darry had issued a direct challenge. She couldn't admit her fear, besides she didn't want to be left behind. She yelled, "I'm coming up."

She gritted her teeth, put on her pack, looped the rope around an arm, and held on with both hands. Climbing, with Darry pulling on the rope was more difficult than she thought it would be.

Darry hauled her up slowly, moving to the left towards the overhang. When she was fifty feet from the top, the rope suddenly dropped to ankle level. She started to fall and put a hand out to protect herself Then the rope pulled upwards with a jerk and came out of her hands. She felt herself sliding down the ice field faster and faster, out of control.

I don't want to die.

It was Kelli's last thought before she hit the ice-cold water.

Chapter 6

Cove Lake Tuesday 3:00 p.m.

Damn it, that was deliberate, Hank thought as he saw the woman go sliding fast down the slope and into the freezing water. He knew she was in serious trouble.

The woman screamed as she hit the water. The shorter of the two blonde girls yelled, "Aunt Kelli! Oh, my God!" Her voice carried across the arm of the lake.

The taller blond girl called, "Darry, Jason, help her.. .look Kelli is standing up … she'll be okay."

"She's going to drown," wailed the shorter blonde. "It's Darry's fault."

"No. She let go of the rope. It's her fault. She'll be all right. Remember I wasn't hurt when I fell in a California lake last year," the taller girl yelled.

"Please do something," begged the shorter girl.

Neither the redhaired man nor one of the blondes slid down the slope to help. The tall, darkhaired man came racing back along the trail. Hank reeled in his line quickly and hurried towards the snow slide with long, rapid strides.

The darkhaired man reached the top of the snow slide and took off his pack. "Hold the rope, Darry, as I go down," he yelled and then he slid to the edge of the snowfield, which extended ten feet out in the lake. He paused to check the speed of his descent and dropped into the freezing water beside the woman.

That takes guts, Hank thought as he rounded the last bend of the trail before he reached the snow slide.

The darkhaired man had his arm around the woman. They were standing chest high in water. Slowly he was leading her to shore as she put nearly her whole weight on him. Hank arrived on the shore just in time to reach out a hand and pull both over the bank up to dry land.

"Thank God," yelled the shorter blonde from the top of the snowfield.

The woman sat on a rock and let the darkhaired man take off her soggy pack. Her face showed extreme pain. Stoically, she said. "I think my left ankle is broken."

Hank introduced himself. The darkhaired man was Jason Green and the woman was Kelli Johnson.

Blizzard in August

"I'd suggest you take your boot off right away," Hank ventured. "If your ankle is broken, your foot will swell. It will make wearing your boot very painful and you'd probably have to cut it off."

"Good idea. Do it." Kelli said.

As Hank took off the left boot he thought, thank God this woman doesn't panic in an emergency. Why don't those three at the top of the snow slide come down here to help?

"We've got to get her out of her wet clothes into dry ones as soon as possible," Hank found himself saying.

"You're right but the clothes in her pack are probably wet and she's soaking." Jason responded. "We may have to dry her clothes out by a fire. I wish we were closer to Island Lake."

"It's two and a half miles. She can't make it on her ankle," Hank's face looked grim. "She's in danger of hypothermia if she is out in the cold too long." Hank looked up at the three people on the top of the snow slide who stood immobile and asked Jason who they were. "Get down here and help," he roared angrily. "She's your aunt," he yelled accusingly at the two girls.

"Why should we come down?" the redhaired man flung at him. "We had a hard enough time getting up the slope. And we need to be on the way to Island Lake."

"And leave this woman here? She may die." Hank wanted to climb the cliff and throttle the redheaded man, but the rope had been pulled up, so he shook his fist and bellowed.

"She won't die," the redhead retorted. "You look strong enough to carry her to your campsite. You must have room in your tent for another person." His voice could be barely heard above the rising wind.

Hank yelled at the top of his lungs, his face getting red. "I do have space in my tent. But she doesn't have a dry sleeping bag or dry clothes." Hank paused. "The best way to save her is for you three to come down and we'll all hike over to my camping area. We can set up all the dry tents." Hank turned to Jason. "And we can get dry clothes on you, too."

"That's the best way," agreed Jason. "By camping together we can pool our dry clothes and rations."

"Then let's do it now," Kelli urged. She yelled up to the top of the snowfield. "Pamela. Ann. Come on down with your packs."

"No," the redhaired man yelled back. "I'm leading this backpack trip now and I say we go on to Island Lake. Get up here, Jason," he ordered. "You're going to lead us."

"I should stay," Jason yelled up at Darry.

"You've got to stay and help, Jason." Kelli was pleading for her life and her voice showed it. Anger and fear framed her mouth and cheeks.

Jason looked up the snowfield at Ann. She took three steps towards the steep slope. Then Darry restrained her and she called "I'm afraid to come down the snowfield alone."

"Ann and Pamela, you come down here, now. We're going to set up camp near this man's tent." Kelli yelled her order up the slope in a voiee tinged with desperation.

"You don't give the orders any more," Pamela yelled putting a restraining arm around her younger sister. "Darry gives the orders now."

"And I'm ordering you up the slope," Darry yelled at Jason. Hank glared in anger at the redhaired man and he turned to see how Jason would react.

Jason's face looked tormented but his voice showed some defiance. "What if I don't?"

"Your uncle will be sorry. His contract comes up in a month," Darry shouted down. "And it will cost you any hope of a job at the mine after graduation."

Anger flashed momentarily in Jason's eyes, but he said nothing. A minute passed and the hard set to his jaw seemed to sag.

Darry yelled above the rising wind. "You have one of our tents in your pack. We need it tonight at Island Lake."

"Stay," pleaded Kelli. "You need dry clothes, too."

"I'll give you some of my clothes when we get to the top of the divide," Darry shouted. "You were hired by me to be our guide. If you desert us, your uncle will lose his job."

"Your duty is with us," Pam echoed.

Jason wavered and then broke. With anguish in his eyes, he turned to Kelli and said, "I have to go and lead them. I was paid to do that. My uncle is very special to me. He'd have a hard time finding another job as a mine foreman at his age."

Hank turned towards Jason. The hard lines of his mouth softened. "You have a tough choice. It's a hard decision. Darry is Big Mike's son, isn't he?"

"Yeah," said Jason. "You know him?"

"I've written about him," Hank said. "Never met the bastard in person. I suppose his son is a bastard too."

Hank looked up the slope and called again. "Let Jason stay with me. Let down his pack so we can have a second tent."

"Hell no," Darry roared. "We'll need that tent at Island Lake and we'll need Jason to lead us there. Jason, get up here. You're our paid guide."

Jason's jaw sagged and he looked defeated.

Then Darry threw down the rope and Jason grabbed it. A few minutes later Jason was on top and the party of four headed towards Island Lake.

"Are you going to leave me here?" Kelli asked Hank.

"Hell no. Not unless you want me to." Hank was too angry to speak further, angry at his luck of having to save a woman he knew almost nothing about, angry at her two nieces, and, most of all, angry at Darry. He turned to Kelli and said, "I know you don't like this any more than I do. I just can't let you freeze to death."

Kelli looked at Hank with a strange expression. She evidently had mixed emotions about depending on him. Then she said, "Thanks for not deserting me. I suppose we'd better start towards your camp at once."

She seems to have an inner strength and courage in a crisis. Hank thought. We'll need it to survive.

Chapter 7

Cove Lake – Tuesday – 3:15 p.m.

Kelli took a long look at Hank as she heard the voices of her nieces receding into the distance. She knew nothing about this man except his name. He did pull her from the water, took off her wet boots and didn't abandon her. For this, she was grateful.

With his shaggy brown hair and full, stubble beard, and six-foot-five-inch frame Hank could have been a 19th Century Mountain Man with the fur traders of Jackson Hole. His strong jaw, impassive blue eyes and massive shoulders disturbed her in a way she could not identify. With his war-surplus green poncho, he seemed more like a tramp than a backpacker.

Oh, Lord what have I gotten myself into, she thought.

Hank stood there a minute, perhaps having second thoughts himself then he said, "The first step is to carry either you or your pack to this side of the stream between Sapphire and Cove Lakes. Which would you prefer I carry first?"

"Me," said Kelli.

Hank bent down so she could put her arms around his neck. He put one strong arm under her knees and another around her lower back and hoisted her into his arms. She hung on to his neck but not tightly since he had her securely in his arms. Incredible, she thought. He can lift a hundred and twenty-three pounds without straining.

The trip along the shore to the stream was made with three stops so Hank could put her down on large rocks and rest for several minutes. He was always gentle as he lifted her and put her down but he never talked. He was very careful and sure-footed as he picked his way along the slippery trail near the shore. Kelli was in awe of his strength and once, during the carry, had a little fantasy that he was a cave man carrying his new mate into his lair.

Hank put her down on a rock beside the stream and said, "I'll be back as quickly as I can with your pack." He returned five minutes later.

"Now what?" Kelli asked.

"I've a problem," Hank replied. "I can leap across on the stones carrying your pack and my fishing gear. That's easy. But I'm just not strong or sure-

Blizzard in August

footed enough to leap across with you on my back." She grimaced. "So what are you going to do?"

"Well, I won't leave you here, if that's what you're thinking," he said with a smile. "It's going to take me a minute to figure the safest way for you and me to wade the stream together. We don't want you to make your ankle worse, and we want to avoid getting swept down into the lake."

Kelli watched the stream boil through the narrow twenty-foot opening, a frothy green-blue torrent. She saw the lake shelve off quickly to more than ten feet. "How are we going to do it?" she asked.

"We'll go on the up-stream side of the rocks. I'll get some rope from my pack to tie between two trees—rope we can hang on to. And I'll get my staff from the campsite. I'll try to keep you off the rocks on the bottom as much as I can, but where the water is really swift, you'll have to be on your feet."

"Please do it," Kelli said. "I'm feeling really cold."

It took five minutes for Hank to get his staff and tie the rope to two trees. Then he stripped naked except for his underpants, and piled his clothes under his rain suit. "Sorry, ma'am, I can't risk getting my clothes wet when I wade. You're already wet so it doesn't matter so much whether you get another soaking."

Kelli tried to look away but couldn't ignore those strong arm-muscles, huge shoulders, and the flat stomach above his boxer shorts. He picked her up and carried her out into the shallow edge of the stream and set her down in front of him. The water on her ankles and lower legs was frigid.

They moved cautiously, one step at a time. He picked her up with one arm and moved her across the bottom a foot and lowered her so her feet would touch the rocks on the bottom of the stream. She stood on her right foot, holding on to the rope with both hands. Some of the rocks on the stream bottom were covered with moss, and sometimes she slipped, putting her left foot down to steady herself, causing pain in her left ankle. Her security was the rope and the pressure of his arm around her waist.

Then when her footing was firm, he felt ahead for footing with his staff, and then moved her ahead another foot. Where the big rocks broke the water-flow downstream, the going was relatively easy, but in the gaps between the rocks, the force of the water against Kelli's legs was frightening. It was then she heard the swishing, gushing sound of the stream and felt most the pounding of her heart.

The deepest part of the creek proved to be the four-foot gap between two rocks near the far side. Hank lifted her into the middle of the gap and she felt herself sinking to the middle of her stomach. She put both feet down but couldn't keep her footing. "Grab the rope hard," Hank commanded but her feet kept coming out from under her. Hank abandoned his staff and kept one arm around the rope and the other around Kelli's waist. He forced Kelli's legs down and then inched forward one small step at a time until the water became shallower. Kelli was shivering violently and was very tired as she reached the other side and collapsed on the snow. How wonderful it would be to go to sleep in a nice warm bed at home, she thought.

Without offering to pick her up, the nearly naked Hank crossed the stream on the rocks and put on his clothes, poncho, and logger boots. When he returned, Kelli felt delightfully warm and was drifting in and out of consciousness.

Hank looked into her eyes. "Are you still shivering?" he asked.

"No, it's wonderful. I feel warmer," she said. "Isn't this snow beautiful on the pines? It's like Christmas. Are you going to light a fire for us?"

"I'm worried, very worried, Kelli." Hank said. "You sound like you are in the early stages of hypothermia. I've got to get you dry and warm as quickly as possible. It will take too long to get a good, hot fire going."

"'Chestnuts roasting on an open fire'...'I'm dreaming of a White Christmas'" Kelli sang, her words mingling with the wail of the wind down the gorge by the stream.

Hank picked her up and gently shook her. "Listen to me! You're close to hypothermia ... you're getting close to losing consciousness and dying. I'm going to take you in the fly of the tent and take off all your wet clothes."

Hank's words quickly revived her. "No, you're not."

"All right," he said and there was a faint smile on his lips. "You undress yourself under the tent flap and take everything off, even your underpants. Then unzip the flap of my tent and get the towel that's hanging near the door. Dry yourself off hard, even the soles of your feet."

"Then what?" Kelli was making sense again and Hank grinned.

"Leave your wet clothes and towel outside and go into the tent and slip into my sleeping bag. You'll find dry, warm clothes there. Put them on. Curl up in a ball and try to get warm."

"And where will you be?" Kelli asked, wondering if he might be planning to take a peek or two through the fly to catch sight of her in the nude.

"I'll be up on the hill gathering firewood for the morning," he said. "But I'll ask you how you're doing every few minutes. And if you're slow in getting your wet clothes off. I'll come in to help you."

"Don't you dare!" she shouted over the wind. But his warning spurred her efforts as she took off the wet clothes under the large tent flap, dried herself, and entered the tent. It was still light enough so she could see the opening of a very large sleeping bag, and she quickly crawled in. She found a flashlight near the pillow, brought it into the bag, and located the clothes wadded at the bottom. She slipped on an undershirt, feeling its tightness on her breasts. Then she put on a flannel shirt, a wool shirt and a bulky wool ski sweater. To cover her legs and bottom, she used a pair of his undershorts and a long-legged pair of wool pants. "I'm in the sleeping bag and dressed in your clothes," she yelled to Hank.

"Do you feel warmer?" His voice sounded thirty feet away.

"I'm beginning to," She paused and for the first time had some concern for him. "When are you coming into the tent?"

"Not for a while. It's still light enough out here to gather firewood." He paused. "I found a hatchet in your pack and am using it. I hope you don't mind."

"No. Go right ahead." Kelli said and changed the subject. "Do you think the others made it to Island Lake?"

"It's only been an hour since they left us," Hank said. "If they take the valley route, they'll be struggling to get over some big rocks right about now."

"After they camp, will they send someone back to get us?" Kelli wondered.

"It will be well after four-thirty before they'll have set up their tents. Jason will be the only one with the will and ability to make his way back. His toes may be frostbitten by then. I hope he doesn't try to come back tonight. He would probably freeze to death trying."

"What's it like out there?" Kelli asked.

"The snow is driving down from the sky in white sheets. Everything is covered, even the tent flap. I'd say there are three inches of snow on the ground already."

"Ever been in this much new snow up here?" Kelli asked.

"Four or five times. I once woke up at dawn to find eight inches of new snow on the ground. The sun came out the next morning. The sight of new snow on the spires of the peak across the valley and the way they gleamed pink in the first rays of the sun was awe-inspiring. I took some good pictures."

Kelli felt reassured. Whatever else he was, Hank was an experienced backpacker and he had lived through snowstorms in this 9,900 foot high lake basin before. She heard him up the hill using her hatchet. She was getting sleepy and just before she fell asleep she wondered what was happening to Pamela and Ann. With a pang of remorse, she remembered that she was supposed to be their chaperone.

Chapter 8

Cove to Island Lakes – Tuesday – 3:20 p.m.

Darry Baltz was having a few misgivings about leaving Kelli at Cove Lake. Stopping at the top of the low divide separating the Cove Lake and Island Lake drainages, he scanned the end of Cove Lake to locate Kelli. The fisherman—what was his name—was carrying her along the shore. The fisherman would take care of her; he could give Kelli dry clothes and share his tent. There was no sense in going back now; Kelli and the fisherman had almost reached the man's campsite.

Reaching in his pack, Darry found a dry set of clothes for Jason. Thanking him, Jason disappeared behind some pine trees to change.

As Pam and Ann caught up with him, Darry said, "Kelli will be fine tonight. As a matter of fact, that fisherman may keep her nice and warm ... if you know what I mean."

Ann was shocked, "You mean, he might try to rape her?" "Seduce her," Darry smiled. Ann was much more traditional than she would admit. "I think your Aunt would welcome his advances..."

"It would do Aunt Kelli good to have a little sex," Pam interjected. "She's so unbending, such a prude." Darry turned to look towards Island Lake. He was in command now and he needed to banish concerns about Kelli and think about getting down to Island Lake. Jason returned from changing into dry clothes and, seeing Pam and Ann still looking back at Cove Lake, tried to get them to go back and camp with Kelli and Hank, the fisherman.

"Kelli will be okay," Darry said firmly. "We made a decision to go on to Island Lake and we're going to stick to it. You can go back to get Kelli this afternoon or tomorrow morning."

There were hard lines around Jason's mouth but he kept quiet. Surveying possible routes towards Island Lake, Darry pointed to a gradual descent with a small stream running down the middle. "This is the way to go, isn't it?"

Jason disagreed. "You get into some big boulders and downed trees that way," he said. "It's better to slant along the hill to gain elevation. There's more brush that way but you save having to go over the big boulders."

Darry had to make an executive decision, and he made it. "We take the valley route," he said.

Blizzard in August

On the way down, Darry wondered what his father would think of him now as he led his four-person team. Big Mike Baltz had been a tough construction worker in his youth and had climbed over the backs of his co-workers to become first supervisor and then owner of a large construction firm. He became wealthy in the postwar housing boom building tract houses and then branched out to purchase lumber mills, a hardware chain and other industries that provided raw material for his growing construction firm. By the early 1960's his financial genius was recognized by Wall Street and he was referred to as a "rising captain of industry."

The International Mining Company, one of Baltz's holdings, owned five firms. The Williams Creek mine had the fewest employees. But to Jason and to the people of Challis, fifty miles to the north, the Williams Creek mine was very important. Jason depended on it for his summer employment, his uncle hoped to work there until retirement, and the people of Challis saw the mine as an important prop to their economy. Darry understood this and he could, and would, use this to give himself power. Men were basically motivated by money and economic power. The theory that employees were also greatly influenced by non-monetary considerations such as loyalty to one's firm or pride in one's work was hogwash according to Big Mike. And he must be right because he was so successful.

There was a time Darry felt differently about Big Mike. He hated his father at age eight—how he hated him. As Darry picked his way down towards Island Lake, he remembered a painful scene from his childhood.

"Darry, what are you doing upstairs on a nice day?"

"Reading, Dad,"

"Reading what?"

"Poetry."

"Poetry is for wimps and perverts. Come down this minute." An eight-year-old Darry descended the stairs to see his father red-faced. "I like to read."

"But you should be out on a nice fall Saturday afternoon playing football. You know I was quarterback on our high school team. That's where I learned leadership."

"You told me twenty times." Darry was angry now. "Last spring I was interested in baseball. You said you would help me learn, but you were working late ... you helped me only once all spring."

"That's because your mother was always getting drunk. Then she ran off the road and was killed."

"You were never around, Dad. You were always working late. You didn't love Mom and you don't give a damn about me."

"Stop your sassing. You're lying." Big Mike advanced and Darry could smell liquor on his breath.

"You drink worse than Mom did."

Mike slapped him hard and knocked him down. He pulled Darry to his feet and hit him again saying, "Can't you fight back, boy?" But Darry couldn't fight and Mike rained blow after blow to his face and body. Darry cringed in the corner of the room with an arm over his face but it did no good. He was terrified, expecting his father, in his anger, would kill him. Then suddenly. Big Mike stopped and started to cry. "You're the only child I've got. What am I doing?" He looked at Darry, crumpled in a heap in the corner and said, "Stay here." Darry was too hurt and terrified to do otherwise. He could hear his father splashing water on his face in the bathroom and rinsing his mouth. He returned, picked Darry up gently, and carried him out to the car. As he put Darry in the passenger seat, he said. "I ain't never going to do that again if you don't sass me, hear."

"Yes." Darry was too terrified to risk his father's rage any more. "And when we get to the hospital you're going to say you fell down the stairs."

"Yes, Dad."

"And next spring I'm going to spend most of my weekends at home and I'm going to learn you baseball."

"Yes, Dad." Darry paused, not believing a word, and then he suddenly said, "Really?"

"Really. You got to grow up to be a man. Because some day you're going to be an executive in my business."

Darry had not believed his father, but Big Mike had changed, not all at once, but over time. He drank less. He was there next spring to teach Darry to pitch, catch and bat—and to tell many stories about when he was his high school's star pitcher. And Darry did become a pitcher on his little league team and took his turn on the mound in high school. And his dad was there to watch most of his evening and weekend games.

Darry had a love-fear relationship with his father then and now. He loved his attention and the way he would shower Darry with gifts and love if he was successful in sports and his studies. He feared his father's wrath more than anything in the world. It was partly physical fear; his father was still bigger and stronger than he was and still had a violent temper. But as he came to appreciate his father's enormous wealth and power, he realized that if he could be the kind of man his father wanted, and if he didn't cross him, his father could make him an executive and he could follow in his father's footsteps.

As Darry trudged on, letting Jason have the lead now, he realized that it was power he sought, more than wealth. He enjoyed eating at fine restaurants with his father but also liked it when the headwaiter greeted him and his father by name. He liked the fine clothes he wore and the new red Jaguar his father bought him, but even more important were the appreciative stares and smiles of the pretty girls who realized he was rich. Wealth could sway people and attract beautiful girls. With his red hair, smile, good looks, and the charm he seemed to naturally possess, he could have his way with them.

Pamela was a case in point. He thought of kissing her white full breasts in the sleeping bag tonight and then climbing on top of her for a long, languorous time of making love. She was an enthusiastic bed partner, the best lover he had ever had, but lately she was getting too demanding—too insistent on talking about marriage.

Darry's memories ended when they reached the top of a crest and could look down on Island Lake. "Where's the best camping spot on the lake?" he asked Jason.

Jason stopped and turned back towards Darry. "On the north shore by the stream outlet," he replied.

Darry looked at his watch. "It's four-thirty and time to set up camp," he said. "It's too late for anyone to go back to Cove Lake for Kelli tonight. It would be suicide." The snow was slanting in from the northwest and there was at least three inches of snow on the ground. They were lucky to be on Island Lake tonight with a good trail leading down to Livingston Mill. He had an important appointment Friday in Los Angeles that he needed to keep.

"What about tomorrow?" asked Jason. "Should we send a party back to get Kelli? I'm really worried about her."

"What's the big deal? Kelli gets a little dunking in the lake. It's August. I've swum in California alpine lakes in August. Kelli will be all right once she dries off and rests her ankle." Darry's voice was reassuring but a concern momentarily plagued him.

"This is Idaho, not California," Jason said. "The weather is colder and backpacking can be more dangerous. I'd feel better if you and I went back to get Kelli tomorrow morning."

"We'll consider it." Darry changed the subject. "How are your feet, Jason? You thought they were beginning to freeze a ways back."

"I may have some frostbite," Jason said beginning to unroll a ground cloth.

Darry waited until Jason had selected a level site and then he and Pam picked a good site forty feet away where they would be largely out-of-earshot. It was obvious that he and Pam would sleep together in the larger tent tonight leaving Ann and Jason in the smaller tent. He wondered whether Jason would take advantage of the situation but doubted it. Jason was a Boy Scout and a follower. That was why he would never become a hard-driving corporate executive as Darry would.

Chapter 9

The Log Crossings – Tuesday – 3:40 p.m.

Three miles east of Cove Lake and a mile and a half northeast of Island Lake, balding, overweight John Peterson was facing a crisis. His face was flush, he was short of breath, and he felt pressure increasing in his upper chest. He had none of the other symptoms—nausea, dizziness, or pain in his upper arm. But, with high blood pressure, he feared he might be having a heart attack. "Let's stop for a minute, Edna," he called to his wife.

"Paul, Loreen. Find a log. We're resting for a minute," Edna called to their eight-year-old twins. She sat beside her husband on the log and put an arm around him. "Are you all right?" she asked.

"Just tired," he lied. "It's been harder than I thought carrying both my pack and those of the twins. Three inches of snow doesn't make it easier. Luckily, most of the way is down hill."

"I wish we had left Walter Lake before noon and not at two," Edna said.

"But we didn't see snow until about two," John said, wishing now he'd taken his wife's suggestion that they leave that morning, a day early. Big flakes of snow slanted down between the pines, and it was hard to see more than a hundred yards ahead on the trail. He looked at his watch. Three-forty. They couldn't camp here. The next good camping place was a mile and a half away at Five Mile Meadows.

John felt his heart beat more slowly and the pressure subside in his upper chest. "Rest is over," he announced. "Paul. Loreen. You need to carry your own packs for a while. I'm pooped."

"Nuts. My shoulder's sore," Paul protested.

"You'll both do what your father wants," Edna said. "He's been carrying both your packs for more than two miles. Can't you see he's terribly tired?"

The twins put their packs on grudgingly and John took the lead. It was easier now that he just had his own pack to carry and he had rested, but he set a slow pace. The trail was level for a while and then plunged steeply downward. He could hear the rushing waters of Big Boulder Creek to his right. Five minutes later they reached the first log crossing and he called a halt.

"How are we going to cross this time?" Edna asked. "Are you going to wade the stream as you did on the way up?"

"It's not a sunny day. I can't afford to get my feet and legs wet." John paused looking at the two-foot diameter log that spanned the stream four feet above the rushing waters. "The safest way," he said, "is for me to cross the log on the seat of my pants with my pack on my back. It's too slippery now just to walk across it."

"How are you going to get the packs across?"

"I'll leave my pack on the other side, come back for the twins' packs, and finally return to take yours across." "How about the twins?" "I'll take one at a time. They'll sit in front of me as I cross. I think they can straddle the log okay."

"I can slide over with the first twin," Edna said. "Do you have time to make all these trips across on the logs? There are a number of these log bridges."

"Seven," said John. He looked at his watch again. We're going to run out of daylight before we get to Five Mile Meadows, he thought.

It took nearly half an hour to cross the first log bridge and reach the second crossing. John felt the pressure rising in his upper chest again. They sat in an opening in the trees with the snow driving in on them. John needed a fifteen-minute rest but he couldn't afford it now. They still had an outside chance of reaching the Meadows before it was too dark to see.

Suddenly, he heard someone talking behind him on the trail. When they came into view he recognized the three graduate students who had also camped at Island Lake.

"Hey, Paul buddy. Practicing that Frisbie throw?"

A large man with wild, black hair shooting up in all directions approached John's eight-year-old son.

Paul smiled, recognizing the three men. "These are my buddies."

John sprang into action, all smiles. "Glad to see you. I wondered whether you'd be packing out this afternoon. Don't think I introduced myself at Walter Lake. I'm John Peterson from Boise. This is my wife Edna, and my twins, Paul and Loreen. You already know Paul." John paused not knowing exactly how to proceed, then asked, "Are you camping at Five Mile Meadows tonight?"

"We might. By the way. I'm Pat," said the backpacker with the long, black hair.

"We hoped to get farther," the thin backpacker said.

Blizzard in August 33

"Shawn, buddy. Five Mile Meadows is as far as we can go tonight, Patrick said. "It's another two miles beyond the Meadows before we get to another good site. Don't you agree, Isaiah?"

Isaiah, the black backpacker with the orange poncho smiled, "Yeah." He turned to John Peterson. "What Patrick is leading up to, I think, is an invitation to join us?"

Patrick grinned. "Right on, buddy. These good people are going to have problems reaching Five Mile Meadows before dark—what with all those packs and kids. We can help get them across the log bridges and down the trail."

Each of the three men took a pack with Patrick carrying the heaviest, Edna's, and Shawn taking the lightest. John crossed the second bridge on his seat with his own pack.

Once on the other side, John shook the hands of all three men. "You may have saved our lives. Thanks. Where are you guys from?" "Pocatello," Patrick said. "We're graduate students at Idaho State. We're all Irish," he said winking at Isaiah. "I made Isaiah here an honorary Irishman for the trip."

"Next Sunday, you're coming with me to the African Methodist Church," said Isaiah. "With that hair they'll think you're a soul brother."

The good-natured banter went on between Patrick and Isaiah as they all continued slowly down the trail. John relaxed and his chest pain eased. He was quite sure that he and his family would be safe tonight. There must be a wilderness ranger at the Meadows. Tomorrow, the ranger could lead them all the five miles to Livingston Mill.

Chapter 10

Clayton Ranger Station – Tuesday – 4:30 p.m.

"Joe, are you there? How are things in Stanley?"

"Sure, I'm here, Ray. Where else would I be, you old fart?" Joe's raucous voice blasted through the phone line. "Course I wouldn't mind a cushy Boise highway engineering job instead of running the Sawtooth road operation."

Ray Winters could never understand why Joe Brezinski and he were best friends; they were so different. Joe was a 250-pound, beer- guzzling, cigar-smoking Pole with thinning dark hair and an irreverent wit. Ray was a meticulous, thin, white-haired career Forest Service employee who neither drank nor smoked. Despite their differences, they trusted each other and their wives were good friends. Ray respected Joe's intuitive judgment and appreciated having a pipeline to his department's weather sources in Boise. He had been transferred two years ago from Arizona and wasn't used to central Idaho weather and politics.

Ray decided to lead into his concerns slowly. "It's beginning to rain here. Course we're less than fifty-five hundred feet. One of my men fighting the Panther Creek fire north of Clayton reports light snowfall at the seven thousand foot level. What's it doing in Stanley?"

"It's raining, but a cold fain," Joe said. "We're sixty-two hundred feet about thirty-three miles west of you. Some of the mountains around Stanley are beginning to show white. It's all come in the past two hours."

Joe drew in a breath and Ray imagined him puffing away on a cigar. Ray asked, "Do you expect snow on the Galena Summit tonight?

"Sure. It's eighty-seven hundred feet," Joe said. "My department has a hotline. The two o'clock forecast predicted snow above 7,000 feet tonight in central Idaho. I called my three graders back from working on the Pettit Lake Road. The lake, you know, is nearly that elevation and I don't want them to get stuck before I can put on chains and plows."

"How much precip do you think we'll get?" Ray asked with pencil and paper in hand.

"Maybe three or four inches of snow at the 7,000 foot level and at least eight inches on Galena Summit. I may have a hard time keeping Galena open throughout the night so vehicles can take Highway 75 south to Ketchum and

Blizzard in August 35

Twin Falls." Joe paused. "Why are you asking? You don't have any roads to plow."

"Well, I may have." Ray chewed on his eraser, wondering how much he should confide in his friend. "You know the Panther Creek fire?"

"Sure. Did you finally get a fire line around it?"

"Not yet," Ray admitted, "Well, this morning when I heard the news of the cold snap coming, I put everyone on it, including all my wilderness rangers from the East Fork area. I wanted to get a fire line around it while we had the advantage of cold weather and maybe some rain. You know we could have another heat wave in a few more days."

"That makes sense," said Joe. "So, what's the problem?"

Ray looked up at a wall map above his desk. "Suppose my road up there gets buried in snow? The fire is controlled all right, but it'll be hard as hell to get my crew out." He sighed. "I didn't have this problem during summers in Arizona."

"You worry too much," Joe told him, puffing on his cigar. "You can handle six inches of snow with plows on the front of some of your jeeps." Joe had not offered to help him plow out and Ray was disappointed. He couldn't blame Joe, for he had the responsibility for keeping Highway 75 open from Clayton nearly to Ketchum, a stretch of 84 miles.

Joe hung up and Ray did worry. He looked up at the large personnel assignment chart on the wall. Mitch Davidson, Ed Grant, and Vito Morelli were three of his four wilderness rangers on the east side of the White Clouds Mountains. They were now on the fire lines. Jean Arnold was home in Ketchum on a week's leave. Ray turned to Stan Oxley, his assistant. "Stan, did you contact Jean?" he said. "Will she come back to her base at the Germania Creek guard station before her leave is up?"

"She has the flu. It'll be another week." Stan replied.

"Darn." Ray said. "I don't want to bring back the others until the fire is fully contained."

"Could Jim Watkins at the Redfish Lake Ranger Station spare a wilderness ranger for a few days?" Stan suggested.

Ray phoned and reported to Stan. "No. He can't spare a man. He's got over two hundred backpackers out there in the Sawtooth Mountains including forty scouts at Toxaway Lake. If it snows a lot tonight he's going to need them. Toxaway Lake is over eighty-five hundred feet."

The top lake basins in the Big Boulder Creek and Little Boulder Creek drainages are a lot higher than Toxaway Lake, Ray thought.

He pulled out a map. Cirque, Sapphire and Cove Lakes were over 9,800 feet; Walter, Island and the Goat Lakes were 9,000 feet or more. He hoped any campers up there had sense to leave there at the first sign of snow. Tomorrow morning he would try to find out how many backpackers were still up on the lakes on the east side of the White Clouds Mountains. The west side of the White Clouds and the Sawtooths were the responsibility of Jim Watkins at the Sawtooth National Forest ranger station.

Ray turned back to his Panther Creek map. His first priority now was the Panther Creek fire.

Chapter 11

Up From Goat Lake – Tuesday – 5:00 p.m.

At the time Darry Baltz and his group reached Island Lake in safety, Herman Wagner and his family were trying to find a camping spot a mile away. The Wagners had stayed at Goat Lake the night before and were desperately trying to reach the trail that led from Island Lake to Livingston Mill.

Pain shot through Herman Wagner's right leg. He had tried to get to his knees but the pain was far too intense. It felt like a bone in his lower leg was broken and there was a gash where the sharp end of a tree branch had pierced his jeans and skin. Thank God it had happened this afternoon when Trudy and Tom were there and not this morning when he was fishing the upper Goat lakes.

It was ridiculous that he should fall within three hundred yards of where they were going to camp for the night. Perhaps he had been overconfident because he had been able to carry his pack and three-year-old Emily up the steep slope from the first Goat Lake. He trudged over the crest of the trail as it was getting darker and just didn't look where he was going. Snow had drifted between two fallen logs and he had slipped on top of one log with his left foot and his leg came down between two logs less than a foot apart. A sharp-edged branch impaled his leg and his momentum caused him to fall over both logs. Twisting his leg, and feeling a bone crack.

Trudy came running, concern etched in the worry lines around her mouth, and tears at the comers of her brown eyes. "Are you all right? How's Emily?" she asked.

Herman had held Emily when he fell, and to avoid crashing on top of her he twisted so he cradled her on his chest. Emily was frightened but unhurt. He released her now to her mother and Trudy asked eight-year-old Lisa to watch her for a few minutes until they discussed what to do.

"I can't walk even with a cane or crutch," Herman said. "It's worse than when I broke my leg on our ranch five years ago."

"Could we build a travois? You know, one of those things that Indians used to use to transport sick or wounded people," Tom said.

"Good idea," Herman said, "but there's no time. We've got to set up the tent before dark. Trudy, I want you to take everyone down to the creek. I think it forms two branches at this point, but don't try crossing tonight. Find a good spot, take the ground cloth from your tent and get it ready to put down. Tom, after you've left your pack at the creek, come back here. You're going to have to carry my pack down to the camp area. You're man enough to do it. I've seen how you heft bales of hay."

"What's going to happen to you?" Tom asked. "How are you going to get to the campsite?"

"Crawl or slide down hill on my butt."

Herman saw his family leave through the densely-falling snow. He hoped Tom would think of bringing back a flashlight because it was getting much darker under the overhanging pines. The pain intensified for a few minutes, and he remembered the time as a boy when he had broken six ribs and a collarbone falling off his horse. He was on his father's ranch in northern Custer County—a ranch Herman owned just forty miles from where he now lay. The pain had been intense for six hours; then his father found him and brought him home with a tractor and cart. Now, he reflected, he was in the White Clouds Mountains in a snowstorm eight miles from the nearest road.

He could no longer hear or see his family. They were swallowed up in the swirling snow. He started inching his way downhill on his rump, feet first. He hit a small log, tried to ease over it, and pain shot through him again. How did we get into this? he wondered. I should never have taken the two girls backpacking. Trudy was right. They're too young. And I should have come down from the third Goat Lake at the first sign of snow. He had slipped on the way down and twisted his left knee this morning—not badly—but enough to slow him down some.

Trudy had sent Tom back to look for him. They had met as he reached the shore of First Lake. Then, as he and Tom walked along the edge of the lake, disaster struck again. Emily leaned too far over the lake to catch sight of her father and fell into the cold water. It was deep there and Trudy jumped in after her. Trudy rescued their little girl, but both were soaked and were very cold even after they put on dry clothes. Emily now had a cough and this worried her father.

Herman could hear his son calling his name through the trees and answered. "Couldn't go more than twenty feet before a log stopped me."

After helping his father over the small log, Tom put on his father's pack. "Stay a minute and help me if I need it," Herman told his son.

"Sure, Dad."

Blizzard in August

Herman looked at Tom's face. He saw strengths handed down through three generations of central Idaho ranchers—a strong Jaw-line, large mouth, blue eyes that seemed to see through you. "This is your chance to become a man," Herman said.

"What do you mean?"

"You're going to have to take over lots of things I normally do—like putting up the tent with your mother, building fires, and sitting by the trail hoping that someone comes by."

"Won't Uncle Rudy know where we are and come looking for us if we're not back by Thursday?" Tom said.

"Sure, we're due at his house for dinner in Challis. He'll go to the signboard half a mile from the trailhead at the caretakers house at Livingston Mill and see where we signed in." Herman stopped crawling and clapped a hand to his head. "I put down Frog Lake first...then I mentioned the Goat lakes. Remember, we met a man who had such good fishing at the Goat Lakes? Rudy and I have been to Frog Lake. He'd go there first, not Goat Lake. Son, no one knows where we are."

It suddenly hit Herman that he and his family would have difficulty getting out. He couldn't crawl out; he couldn't get over those seven log bridges on the way to Five Mile Meadows. If someone tried to rescue them, they would probably go to the wrong lake. As he looked up at the snow falling thickly through the beam of Tom's flashlight, Herman knew they were in serious trouble.

Chapter 12

Cove Lake – Tuesday – 6:00 p.m.

Hank Barclay looked across Cove Lake in the direction of the snow slide. The slanting snow had turned gray in the dim light, and the wind still riffled the waters. But the howling noise of the wind had subsided and even the rushing waters of the stream seemed muted. It's settling down to a serious, steady snow, he thought. I don't see anyone coming towards us from Island Lake. It's time to go in the tent.

Hank measured the snow on the ground using his hunting knife. The blade was six inches long and the snow went a width of a fingernail beyond the blade. If it kept snowing at this rate, the snow could be a foot deep by morning. He picked up the two smooth sticks he had been cutting and polishing and brought them and his hunting knife with him to the tent fly.

With a tent fly that covered the entire tent and extended three feet beyond the front of the tent, Hank had a space that was partly protected against the wind and snow. It was a little like a carport with sides that went part way to the ground. Knowing that the weight of too much snow could collapse the tent fly. Hank gently brushed off the snow. He then entered the tent with his hunting knife, the two sticks, and a package of gauze from his pack. He zipped up the mosquito netting and tent fly and sat down near the door to carefully remove his poncho and boots. The air in the tent was warmer than the air outside, but it was still bitterly cold – probably close to freezing. He had to wake Kelli.

Gently, he placed a hand on Kelli's shoulder. "How do you feel?" he asked.

Kelli stretched, still groggy, and Hank repeated the question. Kelli sat up and said, "I'm rested, but my ankle is throbbing now." She turned to Hank. "You must be frozen."

"I am," he said. "The air outside must be in the low twenties, and the air in this tent is probably just above the freezing level." He paused. "We need to splint your ankle now."

"But how? You don't carry a splint in your pack do you?"

Hank smiled. She evidently had never had the experience of splinting a limb in the wilderness. "I've been whittling two sticks just the right size and

Blizzard in August   41

have removed the bark. I've gotten a roll of gauze from my pack. But you have to get out of the sleeping bag a minute for me to do the splinting."

Kelli grimaced in pain as she pulled herself out of Hank's sleeping bag and pointed her feet towards his lap. He gently lifted her legs, cut a strip of gauze with his hunting knife, fitted the two sticks in place, and wrapped the gauze around. Cutting additional lengths of gauze, he wrapped the entire splint and tied it securely in place. "Are you a doctor?" Kelli asked.

"Hardly, but I've splinted the ankle of an experienced logger who told me what to do." He paused. "We're going to need to elevate and cushion your ankle tonight."

"How?"

Hank was leading up to a moment he was dreading. How would Kelli react to his proposed sleeping arrangements? It would be better if she consented willingly. "I think I will take an old sweater I keep in the corner of the tent and wrap it around your ankle." He added almost offhandedly, "You know we both need to fit in my sleeping bag. I don't have blankets, and anyone outside the bag will freeze to death before morning."

"You mean you'd crawl in this sleeping bag with me?" Her voice was incredulous.

"We should be able to fit," he said. "My wife and I used to fit, but it's not a full double bag." Hank paused and added in a persuasive tone. "With both of us in the sleeping together, we would be a lot warmer tonight. The bag would retain our body heat."

"Not on your life," Kelli said indignantly. "You might....You might...."

"Take advantage of you?" Hank laughed. "If we both fit, and I'm not sure we will, there won't be much room for lovemaking." He paused. "No offense ma'am. But survival is on my mind tonight, not romance. I'm a widower who is still grieving the loss of his wife. I'll make any promise you want just so we can try getting in the same bag together."

"No sleeping on top of me," said Kelli with a warning tone that let Hank know she would put up a fight if she had to.

"Agreed," Hank replied equitably. "And although you're lighter than I am, it would be hard for me if you slept on top of me. It would be better if we both slept on our sides."

"Not facing each other," Kelli said warily.

"Any way you wish," Hank said. "You make the decision and I'll abide by it."

Kelli paused to consider her options and then said. "I'd like us both to lie on our right side facing forward. I'll lie behind you and face your back."

"That's fine with me," Hank said. "You'll be keeping my back warm. You'll have the sweater wrapped around your broken ankle to keep it protected and elevated."

"What about us both sleeping on our backs?" Kelli asked.

"We can try, but my wife and I didn't have room for it and she was smaller than you."

Getting into the sleeping bag with Kelli proved difficult, even when it was unzipped halfway down. Kelli got in first with Hank's old sweater wrapped around her broken ankle. Hank slipped his feet and legs in easily; with some tugging, his hips and stomach went in. But he couldn't get his shoulders in without keeping the top three inches of the sleeping bag unzipped. Both he and Kelli were wearing sweaters and he hoped those would keep them warm.

Movement of any kind was very difficult, and Hank was afraid of hitting Kelli's sore ankle with his feet. "I've got to keep my feet and legs from hitting your sore ankle," he said. "Let me know if I hit it accidentally." His concern for her ankle seemed to relax Kelli, and she started to ask questions as she lay behind his back.

"I know nothing about you except your name," she said. "And that you're a widower. When did you lose your wife?"

Hank paused for a long time, not knowing what to say, not wanting to open up all the old wounds. "This February. She died in a car accident. Drunk driver. Lewiston Hill." Hank choked up, unable to say more.

"I'm terribly sorry," Kelli said, "I know it's hard to talk about it." She paused. "Do you have children?"

"Yes. I have three. Sara is twelve now—almost a teenager. She's organized and responsible like Susan was. But she misses her mother terribly. They were almost like sisters." Hank's voice broke again.

"And the other two?"

Hank focused on their faces. "Julie, she's ten. She's got black hair like her mother ... and she's a tomboy ... loves fishing and sports." Hank lapsed into silence again. "Joanne is eight. We call her Jo. She has brown hair like I have. Loves to read. Likes to dress up. She can be a little princess. We almost lost her when she was a baby." Hank remembered how Susan had cried in the hospital waiting room, and tears formed now in the comers of Hank's eyes.

Hank knew Kelli wanted to learn more about him but he wanted to shift the conversation to a less emotional subject. "I grew up in Elk River," he said.

"Where's that?" Kelli asked.

"About fifty miles east of Moscow," Hank replied.

"Russia?"

Blizzard in August   43

Hank laughed. "No. Moscow, Idaho."

"Where?" Kelli wanted to know.

"Moscow's about ninety miles southeast of Spokane, Washington."

"What did your father do for a living?"

Hank was startled that Kelli would probe into his family background so quickly. "My father was a logger and a very good one. He died in 1938 when I was six."

"I'm sorry." Kelli said. "How?"

Hank's face reddened in anger as he remembered the incident, and his voice was harsh. "One of his work crew came on duty drunk and felled a tree poorly. The tree toppled in the wrong direction and a big limb crushed my father's chest." Hank paused. "To this day, I won't go into the bar that served that man."

"What did your mother do?"

Hank paused as he remembered his father's funeral. "She grieved a lot at first. She was really close to Dad." Hank paused again, remembering the two months that his mother sat curled up like a ball in bed most of the day while her funds and food stocks dwindled. "Then Uncle Ted...he's from Bovill, twenty-five miles away ... he came and helped her get on welfare ... Aid to Families with Dependent Children they called it."

"How many children did your mother have?"

"Four," Hank replied. "I'm the youngest. Clarissa is 37 and now lives with her husband in Texas. Clark is 39 and owns a little restaurant in Ontario, Oregon. The oldest died during the Depression...pneumonia and malnutrition." Hank could remember the funeral of his oldest brother. There were others who died in Bovill that cold winter.

"Didn't welfare give your mother enough money to feed your family?" Kelli persisted.

"Not hardly. But Uncle Ted would get a deer and elk each fall and give us some of the meat. I caught some fish and we had a small garden. And we would get school lunches and, later, food stamps." Hank lapsed into memories of going to bed hungry after skimpy dinners. "We survived and became a close-knit family."

"Your mother," Kelli said. "She must have been a remarkable woman."

"She was," Hank said. "Very strong, very loving, and very determined that her children would have a better life than she did. But I went to work as a logger for the money during summer vacations while I was in high school."

"I thought you looked like a logger." There was a touch of condescension in her voice that annoyed Hank.

"Well, I'm not," he said, slightly miffed. "I'm an Associate Professor of History at the University of Idaho."

"I'm impressed," Kelli said. "How did you do it?"

Scenes of trench warfare flashed before Hank's eyes and he could see white-clad Chinese soldiers charging through the snow. He said simply. "I was in the army during the Korean War. Afterwards I got the G.I. Bill. I went to college and found I enjoyed the academic life and was good at it."

"Did you ever go back in the woods?" Kelli wondered.

"In college at the U. of I. and graduate school at Washington State, I worked every summer as a logger to help pay college bills not covered by the G. I. Bill." Hank paused. "It's hard work, but I like it. You know I'm proud of my logging background. And coming from a small town helps me relate well to the many students I have who come from rural areas."

It seemed to Hank that Kelli thought more highly of him now she knew he was a college professor, and it amused him. What were her stereotypes of a logger? He would have liked to explore this, but she had asked all the questions. It was time he expressed an interest in her life. He asked, "What type of work do you do?"

"I'm an elementary school principal in Garden Grove—that's just outside Los Angeles."

"And you're unmarried. Or I don't see a wedding ring on your finger." Hank didn't want to pry, but he was curious.

"Divorced." Kelli's voice sounded bitter as she continued. "I was talked into marriage by my mother and older sister. They thought it was a good match. Sterling was a very handsome, gallant man in his thirties who never worked a day in his life and lived off what my mother thought was an enormous inheritance."

Kelli paused, obviously wondering how much she should say. "My mother grew up lower middle-class and used her beauty to better herself financially in marriage and so she thought that marriage to Sterling would make me rich. Does that shock you?"

"No," Hank said. "But I don't get a very good impression of your mother." He toyed with changing the subject but then asked.

"How did your marriage turn out?"

"Poorly." Kelli sounded angry. "Sterling was a snob and an alcoholic. We quarreled and he used to hit me when he came home drunk."

"Did you call the police?"

Blizzard in August 45

"No. I had taken some judo classes and laid him out cold one night on the living room floor." Kelli laughed. "He wasn't that much bigger than I was, and I'm afraid I enjoyed taking him down hard and humiliating him."

Hank grinned. He admired a woman with spirit and he could see Kelli had backbone. "And did that break up your marriage?"

"In a way. He was a coward and a wimp. He filed for a divorce, but before it came through, he became drunk one night and died in a car accident. I must admit I didn't grieve long."

"But he left you a fortune." There was an edge that Hank couldn't keep out of his voice.

"No, he changed his will after he filed for the divorce...damn him... left his sister what little was left of his estate."

"And you had to raise little kids like my mother did?" Hank could visualize Kelli with two small children preparing a meager dinner in a two story walk-up apartment.

"Sterling was sterile." Kelli sounded bitter again.

"So you became an elementary school teacher."

"Yes. I taught fourth grade...then I earned my principal's certificate ... and last fall became principal." There was pride in Kelli's voice and Hank admired her for it. "I can see you are tough and determined. We're going to need this to survive this storm."

"Survive? What do you mean?" Kelli sounded alarmed. "There will be more than a foot of snow on the ground by morning," Hank said. "We can't break camp and get even to Island Lake without help. And if we did get to Island Lake, there'd be two sets of clothes too wet to sleep in, leaving just one dry set."

"But won't Darry come back for us tomorrow morning?" Kelli asked.

Hank scoffed. "Darry ... he's a bastard ... you know he deliberately caused you to fall into the water."

"Deliberate? I thought it was an accident."

"I had a clear view of what happened," Hank said. "When you neared the top, he dropped his arms, right to nearly snow level. That's why your rope went slack."

"Yeah, it did go slack. And then the rope went suddenly tight." "Yes, he pulled in hard and brought the rope up so it would be nearly impossible for you to hold on. It's called snapping the whip. There was a kid who did that to me once in grade school. I pounded him so badly he ran away crying with a bloody nose."

"Then you don't think Darry will come back for us?"

"No. Darry got what he wanted, the chance to sleep with Pam tonight. He's not going to get you back and have you act as a chaperone again. You ought to have heard what he and Pam said when they passed me on the shore."

"I have to admit that I don't have too high an opinion of Darry either, Kelli said. "He put four rocks in my pack earlier today to slow me down. He admitted that. And he may have sent a rock rolling down the slope in my direction. That he won't admit."

"I'm not sure I'd trust Darry if he did come back for us."

"But Jason's different. He won't leave us." Kelli's voice turned up as though she was unsure of what Jason would do.

"Jason seems like a good backpacker and a nice guy," Hank said. "Normally, he would come back for us. But you heard Jason obey a direct order from Darry this afternoon to come back up the slope and lead them to Island Lake. I don't think he'll buck Darry tomorrow. Moreover, his feet may be frostbitten enough so the main thing on his mind will be getting down the trail to Livingston Mill."

"What will they do tomorrow then?" Kelli asked.

"Pack up, if there's not too much snow, and go as far as they can. They could probably make Five Mile Meadows by late afternoon tomorrow."

"And when would they reach Livingston Mill?"

"The day after tomorrow. And the road may not be plowed out from Livingston Mill by that time. Kelli," he said grimly, "If the storm keeps up we may need to survive in this camp three or four days until we're rescued."

"What about my nieces?" Kelli said. "They won't let us down." "I'm not sure." Hank said. "I don't know that much about your nieces. Pam seems like she will do what Darry wants. She followed his lead at the top of the snow slope." Changing the subject he asked, "Did you see anyone camped at Walter Lake when you were there?".

"I saw just two groups of campers—a family with grade school twins and three college-aged men."

"I saw the same groups. I hope they started to hike out today. It's going to be hard to get those twins over the log bridges this side of Five Mile Meadows. But the group I'm most concerned about was the one I saw headed up the Island Lake trail.. .a man, a woman, and three children.. .the youngest about three. I'm going to be praying for all of us up in the White Clouds tonight." He paused again. "Now, tell me what you enjoy most about teaching, and then let's go to sleep. We are going to have a very hard day tomorrow."

Kelli relaxed and described the joy she found as a teacher and then a principal. She had countless stories of helping children with reading, math, and other subjects. Bone tired, Hank went to sleep while Kelli was in the middle of one of her stories.

Chapter 13

Stanley – Wednesday morning, August 28th

Joe Brezinski sat at his cluttered desk at the state highway shop close to Stanley with an unlighted cigar between his teeth. He was tuned to a Boise radio station and heard the newsman say, "Central Idaho from the upper Snake River plain to the Clearwater River is paralyzed this morning in the wake of a freak August snowstorm. Cold rain fell in the Snake River plain and it froze in areas above forty-five hundred feet. The Interstate system is free of ice or snow from the Oregon border through Boise, Twin Falls, and Pocatello. But icy pavement is reported north of Idaho Falls to the Montana border. Highway 55 is reported closed north of Cascade, and Highway 95 closed north of Council. McCall is reporting nine inches of snow on the ground."

"What's the weather forecast?" asked Joe's deputy.

"Hasn't got to it yet." Joe motioned for Ed to keep quiet, took the cigar from his mouth, and listened.

"Highway 75 is closed from Ketchum through Challis with eleven inches of snow reported on the ground in Stanley. Highway 93 is closed from Arco nearly to Challis."

"Damn, we're not alone," Joe said. "Every single north-south route through central Idaho is closed. Doesn't that frost you? At least those damn Boise bureaucrats won't be on my tail because Galena Summit isn't open."

Joe looked at the wall map of the area his highway shop was supposed to maintain. His main responsibility was Highway 75 from Prairie Creek fifteen miles north to 8,750-foot Galena Summit, then nearly forty miles down the Sawtooth Valley to Stanley. Then he had the thirty-three miles northeast on Highway 75 to Clayton and twenty miles west of Stanley on Highway 21 to Cape Horn. Joe's entire road system was closed and he was worried about it.

"Get Vince and Terry out on their snowplows. It's six-thirty," Joe said.

"Where do you want them to plow first?"

"Down river to Clayton. That way when the Challis district plows up-river to Clayton, we can have the 57-mile stretch open to Challis." Joe looked at the snow falling outside his window and shook his head. This was going to be a bad day.

The phone rang; Joe answered it. "Galena Summit is not open," he told his supervisor in Boise. "I kept it open until nearly ten then I pulled the plows back to the valley floor. At two in the morning I pulled my plows back to Stanley. I had to tow the old one in ... been working on it all night and it still isn't fixed. Sure could have used the new one you took out of my budget." There was an edge to Joe's voice. His eyes were red, his temper short, and he enjoyed sticking his supervisor with a little needle.

"How many plows do you have operating now?" the supervisor asked.

"Two. They're headed down river to Clayton." Joe switched the subject as he heard the motor of one snowplow-grader just starting. "What's the weather report for today? A heat wave, I hope."

The supervisor laughed. "We had a heat wave all summer long...temperatures over a hundred for ten straight days in Boise in early August ... and now you want it back. Well, the Arctic front is still going to be with us for a few more days."

"Hell."

"When are you going to open Galena Summit?" the supervisor asked.

"When my two working plows get back from Clayton, I'll send them south of Stanley on 75 up the valley to Obsidian and Smiley Creek store. There are stores, gas stations, homes and a campground along the highway that need to be linked up to the supermarket and other businesses in Stanley. Then, sometime this afternoon we'll try to plow Galena Summit. How about having Ketchum plow north to the Summit so I don't have to plow down to Prairie Creek?"

The supervisor in Boise made no promises and hung up. Joe turned to Ed. "Boise wants us to plow Galena Summit right away. Told him my two plows were on the way down to Clayton, and when they get back we'll plow the valley route to Smiley Creek store. Then we'd get to Galena Summit. We got the highest damn pass in the whole Idaho highway system and he expects us to open it as soon as possible." "What about the side roads to the campgrounds at Alturus, Pettit, Redfish, and Stanley Lakes?" Ed asked.

Joe wiped his forehead with the palm of his hand and then took a sip of coffee. "That's low priority. We'll give it a try after we get the main roads and the summit clear."

"How about the road access to trailheads in the White Clouds and Sawtooths?"

"No way can we get to them for a few days. Especially those on the east side of the White Clouds." Joe gave Ed a worried look. "We may have some starving people on our hands if this storm keeps up too much longer."

"What help can we get from the Forest Service?"

"I'll find out," Joe said, and he called first Jim Watkins at Redfish Lake, Ira Smithers at Champion Creek, and Ray Winters at Clayton. Then he went out in the shop to find Ed with his head back under the hood of the old snowplow.

"Jim and Ira can't help us," Joe reported. They're trying to get plows attached to a few of their jeeps. Maybe they can get the roads to Redfish, Alturas, and Pettit Lakes open by late afternoon but not the roads to most trailheads. There are over two hundred backpackers up in those lakes. We're going to have some people running completely out of food and may have campers needing urgent medical attention." "What about Ray Winters at Clayton?" Ed asked.

"He's in worse shape. He's got most of his men trapped up the Yankee Fork in more than a foot of snow. He has a fire line around the Panther Creek fire but he can't get supplies in or men out. He's rigged up two jeeps with plows but it's going to take a day to plow that twenty miles of road with jeeps. He wanted me to help but I said, 'No way.'" "How about the road up the East Fork of the Salmon?"

"They can't plow it and neither can we," Joe said. "I worry about Livingston Mill. It's seven miles up that windy, one-lane dirt road from the East Fork Road. No telling how long that'll take to plow. Hope the caretaker at the mill has supplies. The Livingston Mine is two miles beyond Livingston Mill on a dangerous jeep track. I hope no one is trapped at the mine."

"Does Ray have wilderness rangers in the White Clouds to handle emergencies?" Ed asked.

"Not one damn ranger," Joe said. "He pulled them for the fire line. There're about twenty backpackers up the Little and Big Boulder chains that have to fend for themselves. No telling how much snow there is above the nine thousand foot level."

"That's serious," Ed said.

"Yeah. No way of knowing how quickly some of the backpackers will run out of food." Joe looked out at the falling snow. "I'm glad I did my backpacking two weeks ago."

Chapter 14

Cove Lake – Wednesday morning

Kelli slipped into an uneasy sleep that night and woke at seven with her arms wrapped tightly around Hank's lower chest. She released her grip a little and heard a momentary change in the pitch of his snore. It took a minute for her to bring the events of the past day into focus. She was sleeping in the same sleeping bag with a man she hardly knew—a man who could wake up at any moment and try to make love to her. No, that wasn't true. He was a gentleman, a college professor. But he was also a logger and everyone knew loggers were very physical men. And Hank, with his scraggly beard, broad chest, and flat stomach seemed very much like a logger.

Kelli tried to understand what Hank was really like. He had some sort of code of ethics that wouldn't allow him to abandon Kelli even though staying with her endangered his life. He probably would have tried to save anyone in that situation—a child, a grown man, an old woman. Her life depended on this unwritten code and she was supremely thankful for it. He was willing to save her when the other four in her backpacking party left her freezing beside Cove Lake.

She wondered if Hank was a Christian. Probably. He might have also been a Boy Scout as a youth. But he was also a logger, a man with a quick temper and strong biases. He beat up a schoolboy who cracked the whip on him and might have thrown Darry in the ice-cold water if he could have reached him. Was he dangerous to be around?

Kelli slipped back into sleep and awoke shortly after seven when Hank began to inch his way up to the top of the sleeping bag.

"What are you doing?" she asked anxiously.

"I have to get up to water a tree," he said. "I can't hold it any longer. I'm going to dress in my 'outside' clothes. Please turn your head for a minute."

He slipped his "inside clothes" back in his sleeping bag after he dressed. And then he went outside. He returned after a few minutes and lightly brushed the snow off the tent fly. "There's about 14 inches of snow and its almost stopped snowing."

"Should I get up?" she asked.

"It looks as though the sky is a little lighter in the west. The snow may let up or slow down. Try to stay in the tent as long as you can. It's vital you don't get any of your clothes wet."

"But I'll need to go to the bathroom soon. And it's not as easy for a woman."

"You can go in my metal wash basin and I can carry it up the hill so it won't pollute the lake." Hank paused. "Would you give me permission to go through your pack? I want to see if you have any dry clothes and any food we can add to mine."

"Do it and let me know what you find." Kelli commanded. Hank shouted through the tent a few minutes later. "Everything is wet, but you have two pairs of panties and a bra that might be dried in half an hour. As for food, you have two cans of applesauce, two cans of peas, four freeze-dried dinners, a box of granola bars, and four small packages of freeze-dried vegetable soup."

"How much food do you have?"

Hank came under the outer tent flap and gave Kelli an exact count of the food he had remaining. "We have enough food for a minimal diet for three or four days. We ought to be able to extend that two or three more days if we catch enough fish".

"And by that time we'll be rescued," Kelli said confidently.

"Sure," said Hank, but the tone of his voice seemed to indicate that he was worried.

When the snow stopped about ten o'clock, Hank carried Kelli out and placed her on a stump near the homemade fire pit that he had constructed. She grimaced in pain as her ankle and foot touched the ground.

He lit a fire using some dry firewood he had kept under the outer flap of the tent. In a little more than an hour, they managed to completely dry three of her underpants, an undershirt, a bra and two pairs of light socks. He also dried for himself an extra shirt, underpants, an undershirt and a pair of wool socks— clothes he had worn on the way up to the lake four days ago and put away slightly damp. They had made significant progress in increasing their store of dry underclothes but had not completely dried any of Kelli's jeans, sweatshirts or sweaters. Still, it was a good start.

It started snowing again lightly at eleven-thirty. Hank completed the drying of Kelli's poncho and gave it to her. She put it on and asked Hank to move a rock closer to the fire for her to sit on. She talked mainly about her childhood during the time they were sitting around the fire. She had been born in Los Angeles in the San Fernando Valley in 1936. Her father sold new and used cars for Fortune Chevrolet. He was a tall, pink-faced Swede with blond hair and a mustache, who was genuinely interested in his customers' needs and was usually well liked by his co-workers and clients. He was a heavy social drinker who became an alcoholic in later life.

Hank sat beside Kelli listening with interest. "What was your mother like?" he asked.

"She had some Irish and German blood in her. She had darker blonde hair —almost light brown—and was very pretty. She was more ambitious than Dad. She wanted more than their modest two-story, green and white ranch home in the Valley. She liked better clothes than we could afford and liked to dine in expensive restaurants. Every year on her birthday and on Mother's Day, Dad would take her to a really plush restaurant in the Hollywood area. Mother looked forward to that all year."

"Did your folks have a good marriage?" Hank asked.

"Probably at first. There was a great physical attraction between them. But when I got to be ten or eleven, I could see the tensions grow. My mother wanted Dad to quit his car sales job and take a job that paid better. She thought he would be a good insurance salesman and pushed him into an insurance course he hated. She tried to push him into selling real estate and he balked. Mother felt frustrated and complained about her dowdy house and clothes. Dad was angered at each attempt by Mother to interfere in his life. Gradually, they drifted apart and Dad went to a local bar more often after work."

Hank looked out at the gray, placid lake and was pleased that Kelli was so open about her family. "I'm surprised that your mother didn't go to work herself to earn more money for your family."

"She did in 1946. I was about ten at the time. She took some courses in real estate and became a saleswoman. From the start, she did well. The Los Angeles area was booming and it was not difficult to find customers for the new houses that were being built."

"This must have raised the family income," Hank observed. "It did. Mother made almost as much in her part-time job as father did at the car dealership. Dad was of the old school and was hurt that he no longer was the only breadwinner in the family and that Mom was using her income to change the family's style of living. She bought more expensive clothes for herself and her two girls. We ate in restaurants once a week and we bought a two-story home in a nicer neighborhood in the Valley. As a girl, I welcomed the changes, but Dad grumbled that he now had to commute twenty minutes to the car dealership."

The sun came out briefly at noon but ten minutes later was back under leaden, gray clouds. Hank asked, "What was your sister like as you were growing up?"

Kelli looked at the dying fire and tried to remember clearly. "She looked a lot like Pamela does now—long, beautiful blonde hair that she combed into long curls at her neckline—a pert snub nose, cameo face, a high, exciting Swedish cheek line, and a slim but full figure. She dreamed of Hollywood stardom, as many of the pretty girls in the Valley did in those days."

"Did she try to get into the movies?"

"She had a screen test. She failed it. Mother filled her head with another, more easily attainable dream. She was to go to college, find a wealthy successful man and marry him. Mother was trying to give Melissa the future she wanted and never would attain. It was sad in a way."

"How did Melissa react to this attempt to manage her life?" Hank asked.

"There were mother-daughter battles in high school over who Melissa went out with and when she came in from a date. Mother certainly did not want Melissa to become pregnant. Mother saved enough for Melissa to enter U.S.C."

"And did she find her wealthy man?"

"Amazingly yes. Mother saw to it that Melissa was well dressed and could afford to live in a sorority. She met Richard Pettigrew when she was a sophomore and he was a junior. He sat next to her in a college real estate class and she was impressed with his intelligence and knowledge of the field. She asked him to explain how bankers decide which homes to finance and how they set interest rates. On their first date she learned that his father owned a bank, his mother was in the Social Register, and that his parents lived very comfortably, but not ostentatiously, in Santa Monica. On subsequent dates, she learned that he did not smoke, drink to excess, gamble, or appear to be a womanizer. He was obviously ambitious and very intelligent."

"But did he show signs of being a caring, considerate husband and good father?"

"Yes, she thought so, and Melissa proved to be a good judge of character. Richard has turned out to be all that she expected as a banker and a surprisingly good husband and father. He is deeply in love with Melissa and dotes on their two daughters."

"She's fortunate. Sounds as if Richard Pettigrew is the type of man that your mother wished she had married." Hank observed.

"There's a lot of truth in that." Kelli winced in pain as she stood up to turn over a drying sweatshirt on a stick near the fire. "My mother welcomed Richard into the family with open arms. My father liked him but never felt very comfortable with him after Richard turned down a night of drinking with him at a local bar."

Blizzard in August 55

"And what did Richard's family think of Melissa?"

"They were not enthusiastic about her, of course. Theirs was an old Hartford family with English ancestry and inherited wealth. They lived well, employed servants, and owned a sprawling ranch house towards the foothills. Melissa was beautiful, well-mannered, and intelligent so they posed no objection to the marriage."

It started snowing a little harder now, but Hank was still curious about Melissa's husband. "What is Richard like now?" he asked. "The same capable, intelligent banker that he was a decade ago but slightly busier than at an earlier stage in his career. He still appears to love Melissa deeply but gives in to her whims a little too much. He loves his daughters but spoils them. He is a nice, caring person. I think you'd like him."

It began to snow harder and Hank began to gather up the clothes drying near the fire. He put the completely dry clothes in one bag and the partially damp clothes in another. "I'd like to learn more about your nieces," Hank said. "But it will have to wait until we're together in the tent." He paused. "I want to apologize for what I said about your nieces last night. I tend to make snap judgments based on too little information and I did that last night."

"You were angry at the way my nieces left me and didn't want to camp at your campsite," Kelli said. "I don't blame you. But I think the fault lies with Darry, not my nieces."

"Let's talk more about that later," Hank said. "But first let me carry you in the tent before you get your dry clothes wet."

As Hank picked her up, Kelli asked, "How long are you going to stay out in the storm?"

"I need to stay out for another hour or two just to make sure that Jason and Darry aren't coming back for us. If I can see them. I'll call out so they can locate us better."

"You still don't think they'll come."

"No," Hank replied. "But it doesn't hurt to watch for them as I gather firewood and fish."

"Fish?"

"Yes, that'll be our supplementary source of food. A nice fat rainbow trout will taste good for dinner, won't it?"

"Oh, yes. I hope you catch two or three." She paused. "Do you use flies?"

"I use flies when the fish are rising to the surface in the evening, but this time of day I use a night crawler on a hook and a bobber. Now, don't ask me where I keep my night crawlers." He smiled. "That's my secret."

It was nearly one when Hank put Kelli down on the ground cloth under the extended tent flap and she crawled back into the tent. She wiggled into the sleeping bag. Her ankle was still hurting but there was pain only when she put any weight on it. She could hear Hank gathering firewood for a while and then he went under the tent flap. He's probably getting his worms, she thought. She was beginning to feel comfortable with him, as comfortable as she felt with Richard, her sister's husband.

Chapter 15

Down from Island Lake – Wednesday

In his dream, Darry Baltz was creeping through the jungles of Vietnam. The night encompassed him – hot, humid, and inky black. As point-man of his patrol, his flashlight illuminated bushes, tree trunks, and a faint trail. Darry was shaking inside but vowed not to show it to others. He crept forward straining to see the slightest movement. Suddenly, the staccato of automatic weapons fire broke the stillness. Darry felt sharp pains in his shoulder, leg and stomach. "Medic," Darry yelled, but no one answered.

Awakened by the dream, Darry lay in his sleeping bag in the darkness of the tent. What brought on the dream? He had never been in the army or in Vietnam. Then he remembered; he was due to report for a draft physical in eight days. His days of college deferral were over and even his father could probably not get another temporary delay. Darry broke into a cold sweat. He could not, would not, be drafted and go to Vietnam. The war was immoral— our country should not be involved. His skin tingled and he broke into a sweat when he thought of night patrols and jungle firefights.

Dim light came through the top of the tent as Darry thought of how he could avoid the draft. He might suddenly get married in the next week. Pam would probably agree to this; she certainly hinted at it after they had made love last night. But would this get him deferred? Racking his brain, Darry could not remember the Draft Board rules on a marriage deferment. And did he want to marry Pam?

She was a sexy bitch all right, but a little too possessive and too eager to marry a rich husband.

There was another alternative to the draft—leave the country—not like the draft card burners who surreptitiously crossed the border into Canada—but legitimately as an American executive abroad. If his Board approved, Big Mike could place Darry in charge of the Central American resort division of Swinging Fun, a fast-growing corporation, and part of the large conglomerate his father managed. His responsibilities would include managing three resorts in Mexico and one in Costa Rica. But it all depended on his being at the Friday meeting. He had promised his father he would be there and it was imperative that he make it.

Darry saw that it was getting light outside. Slipping out of his sleeping bag, he dressed quickly without waking Pam. Once outside, he was startled to see at least a foot of dry snow on the ground and snowflakes drifting through the trees. If they started early, they probably could reach Livingston Mill by nightfall. That gave him Thursday to reach Los Angeles by plane and time Thursday night to prepare for the Friday meeting.

Suddenly, Darry remembered Kelli. It was stupid for him to crack the whip on her; he had no idea she would hurt her ankle. He felt a momentary pang of remorse—a sharp prick of conscience that quickly disappeared. Kelli had deserved it and Darry had gained both sweet revenge and another lustful night with Pam. Should he and Jason go back for Kelli today? It would take a whole day to struggle up to Cove Lake and bring her back. Then Kelli would slow them so much they could not reach Livingston Mill until sometime Friday— the date set for the crucial meeting. Darry's mind focused on the Los Angeles board meeting, becoming a corporate executive, and leaving for Mexico. Returning to the tent, Darry could see Pam stirring in her sleeping bag. "Good morning my sweet," he said.

"We were made for each other," Pam said. "That was twice we made love last night."

"You were very exciting," Darry said. "I love you very much."

There it was, Pam thought. He really loves me very much. Now's the time to hint at marriage to Darry she said, "It'll be nice when we can live together openly."

"Yeah."

"Or we might even get married. You know we could be married by a Justice in Idaho and go back to LA as man and wife." Pam's mouth turned up in a charming smile.

"That's rushing things a bit," Darry said. "I have to be in Los Angeles for a corporation board meeting on Friday. I can't consider marriage until after that."

"What's so urgent about the meeting?" Pam asked, her voice showing disappointment.

"Remember, I told you about Dad asking them to put me in charge of the Central American Resort Division … responsible for four resort hotels."

Pam beamed. Darry would be an executive. He wouldn't just be a rich dilettante. "That would be wonderful. I'd be proud to be the wife of an executive...and I suppose we'd get to stay in the resorts you managed."

"Yes. You'd be sort of a hostess. But I have to be there Friday and get the job. The Draft Board is acting on my deferment next week; I need to be in

Blizzard in August 59

Mexico when they meet." Darry paused, "Pam, I don't want to go to Vietnam. It's an immoral war ... I don't want to be killed. You need to help me."

"How?"

"We can't let anything delay us from reaching Livingston Mill today."

"How about Kelli?"

"Especially Kelli."

As she dressed, Pam pondered her feelings for her aunt. Kelli was the dour chaperone – the dragon lady – a woman who she disliked. Yet, she was her aunt. What could she tell her mother if she returned to Los Angeles with Darry, not her aunt? She said, "Who will rescue my aunt?"

Darry's voice was reassuring. "We will be at Five Mile Meadows by noon. There's probably a wilderness ranger there ... he can go back for her. If not, we will be at Livingston Mill by nightfall ... they can radio for help."

"Right," Pam said but she wondered if it would be as easy as Darry had said.

Pam joined Darry, Ann and Jason in a quick breakfast. She smiled to herself. Her Darry was a good leader for this group.

"Are you and I going back for Kelli?" Jason asked during breakfast.

"She might hurt her ankle further if she tried to walk out to Island Lake ... it would take an entire day ... she'd get cold and wet. She may be having a romance with the fisherman and might not want to come." Darry paused and gave Jason a concerned look. "Are your toes frostbitten?"

"Yes, a little. But I'm willing to try to help get her." Jason limped a little as he walked towards the fire.

Outraged, Ann said, "We can't leave her there."

"She'll be better off if we hiked down to Five Mile Meadows and got a wilderness ranger. He'll know what to do."

Within five minutes, Darry, with Pam's support won the argument. Darry thought Jason looked subdued; perhaps his frostbite was worse than he thought. Darry had Jason take the lead, breaking a trail through the foot of snow. Ann came next, stepping in Jason's footsteps where possible. Pam followed Ann at a distance of twenty feet and Darry brought up the rear. Periodically, Darry would stop to listen but, of course, he heard nothing but the faint rustle of pine boughs in the wind.

The snow was beautiful on the dark pines and the trail led through a shallow valley of crunchy snow. Darry could hear a stream rushing fifty feet to the right. He could hear Jason talking to Ann when he would have her stop while he hiked ahead a hundred feet or so to make sure he was on the trail.

Jason was proving to be an excellent guide; Darry would need to have his father reward him.

About nine o'clock the snowflakes fell more slowly in lazy circles and Darry yelled, "I think it's going to stop snowing."

Darry called a halt about nine-thirty and he cleared snow off a log with his glove and distributed trail mix from his pack. They talked of stores and restaurants in Los Angeles and surfing near Pacific Palisades. Jason sat quietly but did say he would enjoy trying to surf. Darry got them going again after twenty minutes. Pam was sure now that he was a born leader. Only a born leader could have made the tough, executive decisions he had made the past two days. Pam compared Darry to her father and found in Darry the same qualities her mother must have found in her husband.

Behind a successful business executive was a strong, brilliant woman and her mother was all of that. Pam could follow in her mother's footsteps. With her help Darry could become, after his father's death, the chief executive of one of the world's largest conglomerates. As she hiked down the snowy trail, Pam was picturing a resort hotel at Acapulco, a summer home on a lake in Maine, a condominium at Aspen, as well as a mansion among the Beverly Hills rich. She would entertain lavishly and wear all the latest Paris fashions.

Preoccupied with her own thoughts, Pam did not hear the sound off to the right. Jason and Ann heard it and stopped but could not identify it. The valley had widened and the creek had split into several meandering branches. "I heard something," Jason said. "It could be someone calling."

"I heard it too," Darry commented. "It sounded more like two tree branches rubbing together in the wind. Look, Jason, why don't you leave Ann here with your pack? She looks winded. You can explore the trail ahead while Pam and I go back and find out what's making the noise."

Leaving their packs, Darry and Pam crossed one of the branches of the creek and walked back a hundred yards. It was rough going through downed timber. They were about to give up the search when Pam saw a boy of about eleven sitting on a log across the stream. Periodically, he would call out in a loud voice, "Help. He-l-l-p."

Darry moved closer but stayed nearly hidden under the branches of a pine. "What's wrong?" he yelled.

"My father broke his leg," the boy yelled back. "We need a doctor."

Darry took off his ski cap, ran his hand over his red hair, but he stayed where he thought he could not be seen. He seemed to take the request under serious consideration. "We have no doctor or nurse in our small party. But we'll be at Five Mile Meadows by about one o'clock. I'm sure the Forest

Service will have a wilderness ranger there, and he can organize a party to bring you out and provide you with the medical attention you need."

Darry turned to Pam. "We better leave now. The quicker we get to Five Mile Meadows, the sooner these folks can get help."

Darry turned and motioned Pam to follow him. The boy chased them on the other side of the creek yelling, "Come back. Come back and help us."

Pam followed Darry away from the stream. He stopped, out of earshot of the boy and said, "You know there's nothing we could have done for them. We don't have any special medical knowledge, we need the food we have to get back to Livingston Mill, and we're short of time. The best we can do is to get where we can call help as quickly as possible."

"We might have gone closer," Pam said. "We might have talked to the mother and father." Her lips tightened in concern; sometimes Darry seemed hard-hearted. But she did not want to oppose him now and jeopardize the marriage she desired.

Darry stopped her again and said, "That kid never did get a good look at us did he?" He paused again and said, "You know, Pam, we shouldn't mention this to Ann or Jason. They would want to go back and do something crazy like try to move them to Five Mile Meadows. Can you see us trying to get a man with a broken leg over those seven log bridges? We don't have a stretcher to carry him safely and we wouldn't make it to Five Mile Meadows ourselves today."

"What do you want me to say?" Pam asked.

"That the noise was two branches rubbing in the wind."

The wind had risen by the time Darry and Pam returned to where Ann was standing by the packs with Jason. "The noise was just two branches rubbing in the wind," Darry said, and they all put on their packs.

In another hour, they had reached the point where the Walter Lake trail joined the Island Lake trail. They stopped for another snack of trail mix, and by eleven they were at the first of the log bridges. On the hike up, the logs were dry and they could each walk across the logs without a pack, leaving Jason to ferry the packs across. Now, the logs were too slippery to cross by foot. They crossed each of the bridges by sitting on the log and sliding forward on the seat of their jeans until they reached the other side. Jason carried his own pack over and recrossed each log bridge three times to bring the other packs.

The log crossings took longer than Darry had anticipated, and it was three-thirty by the time they reached Five Mile Meadows. To Pam's great disappointment, the Meadows were empty. There was no one to whom Darry could relay the boy's message. They trudged to the middle of the Meadows, where three great pines provided shelter from the wind, and lay down their packs and ate a long-delayed lunch. There were only eight inches of snow on the ground, but the wind sweeping down the valley was cold and it had started to snow again.

"Do we set up camp here?" Jason asked Darry.

"I'd like to get farther by evening and camp at a lower elevation," Darry said. "Is there another good camping place about two miles ahead?"

"Yes. Of course that big party that tramped the snow down by the pines might be camping there now. But I think they camped here last night and left this morning for Livingston Mill."

"Are you game for another two-mile hike before we camp for the night?"

Pam was relieved that Jason was willing to go on. She was not over-tired herself and the farther they could go that night, the sooner they would reach the Livingston Mill trailhead the next day.

The last two-mile hike of the day was the easiest for Pam. The trail led downward most of the way and it was well broken in by the large party that had camped at Five Mile Meadows. After two miles, the trail ran between the creek and a stand of lodge pole pines spaced far enough apart for tents to be placed among them. Prior campers had cleared tent spaces making setting up camp easier. It was disappointing that there was no wilderness ranger there who could help the boy she had seen across the stream.

To Pam, their last night backpacking was almost enjoyable. Jason made a fire and they ate up the last of their freeze dried-dinners and had hot chocolate. Pam retired to her tent early and found Darry to be a skillful and passionate lover. She put any concern she had about Kelli and the boy out of her mind and fell into a deep, satisfying sleep.

Chapter 16

Up from Goat Lake – Wednesday – 7:45 a.m.

Tom Wagner had difficulty sleeping that night in the family five-person tent. His mother, Trudy, and baby sister, Emily, were coughing all night, probably the result of being chilled by their plunge into Goat Lake. His father, Herman, thought he had broken his leg and periodically he would wake, cry out in pain, and then start snoring again. At age eleven, Tom had a room of his own in the Wagner's sprawling ranch house only forty miles from where the family was camped and he longed to be in his own bed in his own room.

If he woke up at home in the middle of the night, Tom would go to the bathroom and then sit up and read until he became tired. His sixth grade teacher said he read very well for his age and his tastes ran from children's science fiction to adult fantasies like Dune. Before eight that morning, Tom slid noiselessly out of his sleeping bag and pulled his current book out of his pack. He was fully dressed and needed to slip on his boots and put on his jacket to go outside. He unzipped the tent hoping to leave unnoticed.

His father opened his eyes and stuck out a hand. "Going out to read?" he asked.

"Yea, it's too noisy in here," Tom replied.

"Don't wander off and get lost," his father whispered. "You're the oldest well person in this family and we're going to depend on you today."

"I won't go far. Just to find a sheltered place so I can read and be by myself."

"I understand." His father put a hand on Tom's arm. "And watch the trail. If you see some people coming down from Island Lake, or going up there, let them know that we need help and tell them to come to the tent so I can talk with them."

It was snowing hard when Tom stepped outside the tent. Where there was no overhanging pine, the snow came to the tops of his high- topped hiking boots. Close to the base of the pines, the snow level was only a few inches and the whirling flakes were blocked out. Tom selected a large, brushy Norway pine and cleared the snow from its base. It was light enough to read and he quickly became immersed in his book.

Gradually, the sky grew lighter and Tom could take a better look at the surrounding terrain. They were camped at the base of a small trail leading to Goat Lake. The trail crossed the stream from Island Lake and a hundred feet upstream from the campsite but the log must be now covered with snow. The Goat Lake trail then joined the main trail from Island Lake down to the Livingston Mill trailhead. It would be difficult to see anyone coming down that trail from where he sat, but Tom was sure he would hear them well. Backpackers talked a lot as they walked.

The book was getting exciting but snowflakes driven by the wind kept landing on the pages. Herondes, the eleven-year-old hero in the book, had just landed his hovercraft on the fifth moon of Jupiter. His parents and little sister had crashed there a week ago and Herondes was determined to find them. Walking through the brush, Herondes was attacked by a swarm of avandanti, six-inch long mosquito-like creatures. He swung his light saber in an arc and a dozen fell at his feet. One got through....

A large wet blob of snow fell from the tree and hit the page bringing Tom back to reality. What would Herondes do if he were in his situation? Tom wondered. With a hovercraft, of course, he could transport his father to a hospital to have his leg set and transport his mother and Emily to doctors. It was simple to save people in sci-fi books. But this was for real. His big, tough, rancher father couldn't walk. He couldn't even crawl well. How were they going to get back to the trailhead near Livingston Mill?

Tom thought of his mother. Did she have a cold or was it something worse? Could she walk back to Livingston Mill? Or wouldn't she think she had to stay to nurse Emily who was even sicker than she? Her mother was good at cooking, cleaning the house, and helping Tom with his homework but she was not a strong hiker. She could carry only a thirty pound pack and tired easily. Could she get back to Livingston Mill and bring help for her husband? She wouldn't even try, Tom decided.

As Tom sat staring into the whirling snow beyond his refuge, he fantasized himself into a hero's role. He would be the one to save his family. He pictured himself slogging through snowdrifts, his hands and feet freezing, and saw himself pounding on the door of the mill caretaker's cabin. Then the door would open and he would stumble across the floor more dead than alive. Of course, he would tell the caretaker of his family's location and plight. The caretaker and a friend would rush out on snowmobiles and save his family. Tom, in his fantasy, would become a hero.

"Tom," It was his father's voice from the tent.

"I'm here," Tom yelled back. "Just under a tree about fifty feet away."

"Come over near the tent. I need to talk to you."

Blizzard in August

65

Tom came close to the tent.

"How much snow is there on the ground?"

"A little over a foot," Tom said.

"My leg. It's a bad break. Just below the knee. I can't make it out without a stretcher. Maybe if you tied some big pine branches together like a travois, you could drag me a ways, but I would be very hard to move and I couldn't cross any of the log bridges."

"Why don't I go for help?" Tom said. "If I started early, I could get to Livingston Mill by tonight. I walked out of here last year with you and we got to the trailhead by five."

"You didn't have a foot of snow on the ground and could walk the log bridges. With snow you have to straddle the log and inch across. It's too dangerous. You'd freeze to death."

"What does Tom want to do?" His mother's voice broke in.

"Try to hike through to Livingston Mill in the snow to get help," his father said.

"Nonsense. He'd die trying. Besides, we need him here to get firewood, build a fire, and help move this tent. There was a low spot in my comer and both Emily and I got soaked last night."

"Who's going to know where we are unless someone goes to Livingston Mill?" Tom asked, his dream of glory deflated.

"There must be a party at Island Lake coming down today. You just stay where you can see the trail and tell them to stop."

"But suppose no one comes down the Island Lake trail?" Tom asked.

"We're better off staying where we are and waiting for a rescue party," his father said. "We put Goat Lake as a secondary choice of destination on the sign-in board about a half a mile from the trailhead. When we don't sign out, they'll know we need help. I agree with your mother. We've got to stick together and we've got to have you here." Tom actually felt a little relieved. He could understand the reasons his parents wanted him to stay. In the next hour he was busy. He had firewood to gather and a fire pit to make. His mother came out of the tent with Lisa, his eight-year-old sister. He cleared a place on a log for them to sit. His father stayed in the tent but would stick his head out every once in a while to see what was going on.

It was difficult to get dry firewood, but Tom knew that the underside of pine trees had small, dead branches that broke off easily. With the small branches and a bit of paper Tom was able to start a fire. However, the larger branches were not as dry and the fire never became hot enough to dry clothes and heat more than one pot of water. Nevertheless, they had enough water for two packets of oatmeal apiece and for his parents to each have a cup of coffee.

After breakfast Tom moved downstream a hundred feet where he had a little better view of the Island Lake Trail. The stream had a deep three-foot pool at this point. There were no log bridges near, but the sound of the rushing waters was more muted than upstream by the campsite. Tom sat under an overhanging pine and periodically called, "Help." It all seemed useless.

Then, someone yelled across the creek, "What's wrong?" Tom explained that his father had broken his leg.

"What do you need?" the voice asked.

Tom's hopes soared. "A doctor," he yelled back. So they were going to be rescued after all.

The man came out from under a branch and took off his ski cap. He had bright red hair and the kind of green sunglasses that some famous skiers wore. But he was about seventy feet downstream and Tom could not see his face clearly. The red-haired man yelled, "We have no doctor or nurse in our party, but we'll be at Five Mile Meadows by one o'clock. I'm sure the Forest Service will have a wilderness ranger there and he can organize a party to bring you out and provide the medical attention you need."

The red-haired man turned to the blonde young woman and said something Tom couldn't hear. Then both moved through the woods out of sight.

Tom was furious and yelled, "Come back. Come back and help us!"

Dejected at being unable to stop the couple, Tom walked slowly back to the tent and told his parents. His mother was optimistic that the couple would contact a wilderness ranger at Five Mile Meadows. "They could have someone here to help us by the afternoon," she said. Tom's father thought the couple could only get help when they reached Livingston Mill. "They'll have to camp overnight at Five Mile Meadows," he predicted. "It'll be tomorrow afternoon before the Forest Service knows we need help."

Tom reproached himself. "I should have waded the creek."

"You did just right, boy. We need you healthy until rescue arrives." Herman Wagner said. "Now we all need to help move the tent a few feet to higher ground."

The snow had nearly stopped and the sun momentarily gave the branches a glistening, white hue. Tom's spirits were buoyed. He was still rankled by his inability to get the backpackers to come to his father's tent, but the storm seemed to abate and they might be rescued tomorrow.

Chapter 17

Cove Lake – Wednesday – Afternoon and Evening

Hank Barclay sat on a log and cast his bobber eighty feet into Cove Lake. He had set the bobber two feet above his sinker and three feet above his hook baited with half a night crawler.

The water was a medium blue where the stream from Sapphire Lake entered Cove Lake but the blue kept getting darker as the lake bottom shelved off into deep water. Hank looked across the lake to the snow slide. He could barely see it now with the snow slanting in from the northwest. The rugged peak he had called the Emperor was completely obscured by the falling snow. Hank remembered that on a clear, sunny day this peak gleamed white in the noonday sun and a yellow-gold-tan in the setting sun. The scenery in this upper lake basin was magnificent, the most colorful and majestic Hank had ever seen. That was one reason he kept coming back year after year.

There was no wind but the cold crept under the sleeves and legs of his rainsuit. To keep his fingers warm, he put on his gloves after each cast. Hank looked westward down the shoreline towards the end of the lake but couldn't see the far side. Turning his head to look up the rocky slope beyond his tent he could see clumps of twenty-foot pines bent from years of bitter wind and driving snow. Somewhere near the ridgeline he saw a momentary movement. Was it a bear, a man, or his imagination? He wondered.

Hank lost track of his bobber momentarily. Was it under the water? The line began to play off his reel and he smiled. He waited, waited until the fish was swimming away from him and gave the line a sharp tug to set the hook. The fish ran and jumped a foot in the air and Hank set the drag on his reel loose enough so his line would not break. Slowly, with great care, he brought the fish towards him, let it run, then brought it in some more. Finally, he had it in his net and then measured it. A fat 14 inch rainbow will provide the protein for a good dinner, he thought.

For two more hours Hank fished the bank without getting another bite. It was two o'clock. If Jason and Darry were coming back for them they would have arrived by now. Hank thought of starting a fire but he wanted to save his firewood for drying clothes.

So Hank took the easy way out. He filleted the trout, arranged slices in a small fry pan and put them on his one burner gas stove. He had two canisters of gas left unused, but would have to conserve his use of the stove in the future.

When the fish was cooked, he threw the carcass out in the lake. Normally he buried the carcass, but the ground was frozen and leaving it in the snow would provide a scent that a bear might follow to his campsite. He then rinsed the pan and put the fish on two plastic plates. He brought the plates, a can of applesauce, and a large square of graham crackers into the tent. Kelli climbed out of the sleeping bag and sat with him on the other side of the tent. She was hungry and Hank gave her a little more than half the food.

"What's it like outside?" she asked when she had eaten her last bite of fish.

"Snowing hard. No wind," Hank reported. "The fire pit is covered with four inches of snow. There must be sixteen to eighteen inches by now in most level spots."

"How much will accumulate by tomorrow morning?" she asked, her voice showing curiosity, not concern.

"At least two feet I'm afraid; maybe two and a half feet." Hank was deeply troubled by the depth of the snow but tried to keep that concern from showing in his voice.

"You know. I've never seen that much snow before," Kelli said with an excitement that startled Hank. Didn't she realize that their chances of survival diminished with each foot of snow on the ground? Of course not, she was from Southern California, not the northland. He would have to talk plainly to her about survival tonight without scaring her.

They sat, side by side, talking about their jobs for a while.

Hank learned that Kelli had been an enthusiastic grade school teacher, eager to try new teaching methods, and tireless in getting to know each of her students. She seemed to know the names of dozens of former students and could recount heart-warming stories of their problems and how she helped them. He looked at her, bubbling with enthusiasm over her efforts to teach one black second grader to read, and Hank realized that she was beautiful in her own way. He had a sudden urge to kiss her but he suppressed this and asked, "Do you think that being an elementary school principal is as satisfying as being a teacher?"

"No, I miss the hands-on contact with the kids." she said. "But I see more of the broad strategy of education and can implement some of the policies I believe in. I have joined some educational organizations—The Phi Delta Kappa education honorary, for example." "Phi Delta Kappa," he exclaimed. "I belong too."

"But you're a professor of history. How did you get into Phi Delta Kappa?"

"I'm on doctoral committees of education students, and two of my friends who teach in the Education Department urged me to join and gave me an issue of the Phi Delta Kappan to read. There was an article on new directions in public education that I found was just the thing I needed for an article I was writing. Then I realized that I could improve my own classroom teaching by hearing and reading about new teaching techniques used in public school classrooms."

"Did you try any new teaching techniques as a result?"

"Oh, my yes. I wore different hats and cloaks to put on a Lincoln-Douglas debate in the classroom. Then I was Grant and Lee meeting at Appomattox, and an Indian chieftain and army colonel discussing U.S. policies towards Indian tribes, and even Teddy Roosevelt expressing his buoyant philosophy before his famous charge up San Juan Hill. My students were excited by my dramatic presentations and I soon got them to develop their own." Hank felt his spirits lift in a way that had not occurred since Susan had died. Here was a vibrant professional woman with the same ideals who he could share his thoughts with on an equal basis. He looked at Kelli with a new level of respect.

At five. Hank went out under the overhanging tent flap to get another large square of graham crackers, two granola bars, and a chocolate bar. That was their dinner. They each used the wash pan as a urinal and Hank tossed the contents as far uphill as he could. The wind was rising and it was snowing even more heavily. Hank was deeply worried. He had cut their rations today but they could run out of food after several more days.

When they were both snug and warm in Hank's sleeping bag, Kelli again brought up the subject of Susan, Hank's former wife, and their three children. "I was sorry to hear about your wife's death. It was so sudden. It must have been a terrible shock to you and your children." Hank said nothing at first. He had a difficult time focusing on Kelli's questions. But he needed to be polite. Maybe it would help to talk about his feelings.

"Susan's death was a terrible shock," he said, tears forming in the comer of his eyes. "She was so beautiful and alive that Wednesday morning in February. She was going to Lewiston—that's thirty-three miles south of Moscow—to buy Julie a birthday present and do some other shopping. It was overcast that morning when I drove to the University and I remember hoping that it wouldn't snow. It was snowing when I returned from work. The phone call came just after six." Hank's voice broke. It was all still too real. He felt his world collapsing around him again. Tears flowed down his cheeks.

Kelli waited patiently, not saying a word except, "I'm sorry." After a few minutes, Hank was able to continue, disjointedly giving her the barest details of the phone call, the crash site, the identification of her body, and the agony of telling his daughters that their mother was dead. The retelling did open old wounds and Hank could barely keep from sobbing. "You loved Susan very much, didn't you?" Kelli said.

"Yes." he said quietly and began to sob softly. How could he describe his disbelief that cropped up periodically for days—his sense that Susan would walk in the door any minute—his inability to comprehend that he would never see her alive again? How could he describe his anger—not at Susan—it wasn't her fault—but at the drunk driver that killed her—and drunk drivers in general? And then there was the deep depression that lasted beyond the funeral—which he felt to the present day. He could not put into words his whirling emotions, so he said nothing.

After a few minutes Kelli said, "Did your children take it hard?"

"Yes, they cried and I comforted them for weeks. Even last week Joanne asked me what I thought her mommy was doing in Heaven."

"You're close to your children, aren't you?" Kelli asked.

Hank's eyes grew misty again. "They're three wonderful girls and we have a lot of fun together … picnics in the woods, fishing from the bank of Moose Creek Reservoir near Bovill, church every Sunday, and a long story time each night. I really like being a father, but it's lonely not having Susan to share the joy with."

Hank had opened his heart more than he intended. He didn't resent Kelli's questions, but he felt the need to move the conversation to safer ground. He changed the subject. "Do you go to church?"

"About five or six times a year. The Lutheran Church, the church of my father." Kelli paused. "It's such a big downtown church that I feel almost lost in it."

Hank responded softly. "I went to the Bovill Presbyterian Church for years with my mother, brother, sister, and Uncle Ted and his family. We were there every Sunday rain or shine and knew every member of the forty-member congregation—shared potlucks with them every month, Bible study every Tuesday night, and attended many a wedding, baptism and funeral. We were just loggers, small "stump" farmers, truck drivers, and a few tradesmen. No wealth in the congregation but a lot of sharing, caring people. We were poor in money and sometimes hungry during the Depression but rich in spirit."

Hank saw the comer of Kelli's eyes moisten. Something he had said touched her. She said, "I'm sorry what I said about loggers yesterday. I have some stereotypes."

Hank led the conversation back to her family. "Tell me more about your two nieces," he said. "The oldest, Pamela, sounds a little like her mother and grandmother."

Blizzard in August 71

"Yes, Pam is very beautiful as you know ... much prettier than I am. She's twenty-one and very used to getting her own way. Her mother favors her over her younger sister, Ann, just as my mother favored Melissa over me. She's completed her junior year at U.C.L.A. this spring and seems to be head-over-heels in love with Darry."

"Does his wealth have anything to do with that?" Hank tried to keep an edge out of his voice but couldn't.

"She's physically attracted to him," Kelli said. "She admires his decisive, take-charge manner and yes, she's greatly impressed with his lifestyle and obvious wealth. He represents a big step up the social ladder and she means to take it."

"Does she know anything about Big Mike Baltz and his business dealings?" Hank thought of telling Kelli about his research on out-of-state corporate raiders and their impact on Idaho, but he suppressed the desire.

"She's seen Big Mike a number of times. He seems pleasant to her and laughs a lot. Is he important?"

"Yes, it's important if Darry models his behavior after his father. Darry is leading a group of three people who will probably do exactly what he wants. Our lives are in his hands."

"What do you mean?" Kelli was instantly alarmed.

"We have food enough for two or three more days on short rations. We can stretch the food out longer by catching enough fish. Darry, one of your nieces, or Jason has to take the time to tell the Forest Service of our situation and the Forest Service has to act promptly." "Of course Darry or one of my nieces will inform the Forest Service. They're probably at Livingston Mill now phoning them."

Hank coughed. "They're probably camped at Five Mile Meadows tonight or just past it. There are too many log bridges to be slid over for them to get all the way to Livingston Mill tonight. But tomorrow they should reach the Livingston Mill trailhead if there's not too much snow and no one gets hurt."

"And then they will phone the Forest Service and we will be rescued the day after," Kelli said.

"Yes," said Hank. He had the sinking feeling that the phone might not be working at Livingston Mill but didn't have the heart to mention it.

"I hope we get some sun for drying clothes tomorrow," Hank said.

"And you catch lots of fish." Kelli said.

They gradually drifted off to sleep.

Chapter 18

Stanley and Clayton – Thursday morning – August 29th

Joe Brezinski was bleary-eyed as he sat by the phone at six-thirty Thursday morning. The field operations supervisor at the Highway Department was not encouraging. "This storm is going to continue two or three more days. The Arctic air is mixing with the moist Pacific low, and the frigid, moist air is swirling around central and southern Idaho. It could snow another foot tonight in Stanley."

"Can the Ketchum District plow out Galena Summit? I lost a snowplow last night and can't do it with two." Joe wiped a greasy hand over the black, two-day-old stubble on his cheeks.

"Ketchum can't do it. They've had a hard enough time plowing out the Wood River subdivisions, Sun Valley and the road south through Hailey," the supervisor said.

"How about sending some equipment and men from Shoshone, Gooding or even Twin Falls? Surely, you don't have two-foot drifts down there." Joe's voice showed his exasperation.

"No, but we had a big ice storm last night throughout that area. Sheets of ice cover the interstate and there are cars stranded and off the pavement all over. It made the national news. We've made clearing the interstate top priority and have a big sanding and towing operation going on right now."

"Damn," Joe exploded, pounding his fist on his desk. "You're leaving us completely isolated with two feet of snow on the valley floor and God knows how much more at higher elevations. I had to shut down operations at ten last night and bring both remaining plows in for service. Ed and I have been working on one grader most of the night but still can't get full power out of it. I can't plow out Galena Summit without help so Highway 75 is plugged from the south."

"Can you clear a route east on Highway 21 to Lowman? Our Garden Valley District might connect up with you," the supervisor suggested.

"Are you kidding?" Joe said. "Those drifts are awful on the way to Cape Horn. We haven't been able to plow out the seven miles to the entrance of the Stanley Lake Road. We've got a bunch of campers penned up there."

Blizzard in August 73

"How about Challis? Can you plow down the Salmon as far as Clayton and Challis?"

"We did get our two remaining snowplows to open up a route the 33 miles to Clayton yesterday afternoon, and we must've had forty RVs convoyed behind us. We picked up another grader in Clayton and opened up the rest of the 24 miles north to Challis." Joe said.

"Then you're unplugged."

"The hell we are," Joe's voice crackled over the wire. "Highway 93 is covered with two foot drifts from the outskirts of Challis nearly to Arco, and Highway 93 is blocked north to Salmon. Those forty RVs we convoyed out of Stanley yesterday are sitting in the middle of parking lots and fields in Challis and there's a hell of a lot of bitching going on. State Senator Wagner is mad as hell and says you don't give a damn about his county."

Joe pictured the concern on the faces of a couple in an Arizona camper. The elderly wife was unable to buy interferon locally, a. drug she had to have to control her leukemia. How could he impress his supervisor with the urgency of the situation? "Look, the side roads to Petit, Alturas and Redfish Lakes are blocked. There are people in campgrounds on those lakes that have to get out. We're going to have people running out of food in the next few days. Starving people because the state won't release a few snow plows. How will that play on national television?"

The supervisor paused. "1 see what you mean," he said. "We'll try to get some snowplows to Ketchum to open a route up the Wood River and over Galena Summit." He paused. "Let Senator Wagner know what we're doing and try to keep him satisfied. He's a member of the Senate Finance Committee." He paused again. "And see if the Forest Service can do some of the plowing," the supervisor said. Then he hung up.

"Damn the Boise bureaucrats," Joe muttered. Couldn't they see that some of the stranded people were in need of food and medical service? But calling the Forest Service was worth a try.

At seven that morning, Ray Winters was cursing the weather and his luck. His decision to use every available man to throw a line around the Panther Creek fire seemed reasonable at the time. But it had backfired. The big fire was nearly out, and two feet of snow would have controlled it even if he had just the normal fire crew. Now the snow made it difficult for him to get his men back from the far-flung fire lines, and snow clogged the narrow Yankee Fork Road, his lifeline for supplies.

The phone rang and Ray picked it up. "Good to hear your voice, Joe," he said. "I was just about to call you for a favor."

The way Joe grunted, Ray guessed he was in a foul mood. "I know you're going to need Highway 75 open. If you could spare one of your grader-plows for a few hours, you could open up a lane up the Yankee Fork. I have all these men and equipment bottled up at my fire camp forty miles north of here. If you could help me get them out, I could get two jeep graders plowing the access roads to campgrounds in the White Clouds and Sawtooths."

"No," Joe's voice boomed over the phone lines. "I can't spare a single grader-plow. I have to keep open the lifeline along the valley floor and down the Salmon to Clayton. I was going to ask you for a grader but I see you can't spare one."

Ray motioned for his deputy to get him another cup of coffee. Joe ranted on about his problems for a while. Despite his own troubles, Ray listened sympathetically. Joe was a hard-working field official, just as he was. They were over-worked, under-appreciated, and caught in the middle between desk-bound higher administrators and an angry public. "It's a bitch," he said, "The pressures we're under and the hours we have to put in."

"You said it," Joe said. "You're okay, Ray. Sorry to light into you."

Joe's phone call was followed by dozens of others during the course of the day—many from his fire camp reporting men missing or injured and equipment stuck in the snow. The most difficult calls were from relatives or friends of missing campers or backpackers. The worst phone call of all was from Senator Wagner.

"I need a favor," the Senator asked.

"Be happy to help if I can, sir," Ray responded.

"I'm worried about my brother, Herman. He took his wife and three children backpacking four days ago in the White Clouds. He should be out by now. I called his home but there was no answer."

"Do you know where he intended to camp?"

"I think he was going to start at Livingston Mill. He mentioned possibly going to Frog Lake, but he could be anywhere in the Big Boulder Creek drainage."

"What do you want me to do?" Ray asked apprehensively. "Send your wilderness ranger, what's his name, Mitch...Mitch Davidson, to read the sign-in sheets. See if my brother is signed in to go to one of those lakes and then find him."

"Mitch isn't there. He's up north of here fighting the Panther Creek Fire."

"What about that other guy? Ed, wasn't he? Ed Grant?"

"He's up at the fire too. And so is the guy who normally mans the Germania Creek guard station. They're all stuck until we can get the road to the fire plowed out."

"And the other wilderness ranger?"

Joe marveled at how much the Senator knew about his operations. "She's sick," he said.

"That's great!" The Senator's sarcasm ripped through the phone line. "You got suckered into this like we got suckered up to the China border during the Korean War—suckered up to fight a fire with all your troops when you should have held some back to help out the campers and backpackers."

The Senator was right, of course, and Ray felt he had failed terribly. "I'm sorry," he said in a low, contrite voice. "I know how you feel. I was an Army officer in the Korean War and had to fight my way out of the Chosin Reservoir area just as you did." He paused. "But who could have predicted a blizzard in August? The best I can do now is to get my wilderness rangers back to the White Clouds as soon as possible."

There was a long pause. "I didn't know you had to fight your way out too. I'm sorry I landed on you so hard. I've got pressures from constituents as well as worry about Herman and his family." He asked. "Can you get a helicopter up for a look-see?"

"Not with the snow falling this hard. We're short-handed with helicopters and pilots. It's the war in Vietnam, you know. There's an old chopper based at the Smiley Creek airstrip. I'll see what can be done, but it's attached to the Sawtooth National Forest District, not my Challis National Forest District. They'll have their own priorities. I'll give them a call."

"Please do that," the Senator said. "And I'll phone the Governor. Maybe he'll call out the National Guard. But don't count on it."

The state Senator hung up and Ray refilled his coffee cup. It had been a long day.

And it wasn't over yet.

Chapter 19

Cove Lake – Thursday morning

Hank slept poorly. For the past two nights he had slept on his right side with his back to Kelli and her arms around his chest. His right side, particularly his hips, began to ache and it was difficult to lie hour after hour in the same position. Kelli evidently had the same problem for her arms and hands would occasionally stray down from his chest, to his stomach, and below his stomach. He didn't want to wake her up but she had inadvertently started to get him excited in the middle of the night. He had to fight the urge to turn in the sleeping bag, throw his arms around her, kiss her, and then make love.

At first light, Hank slipped out of the sleeping bag and saw Kelli smile then stretch out on her back. She must prefer sleeping on her back, he thought, rather than on her side. She went back to sleep and he put on his clothes and went out into the storm. Snowflakes came pelting down at him in the dim light. The snow was now waist high; another twelve to fourteen inches had accumulated during yesterday afternoon and last night. The tent flap swayed downward under the pressure of the snow, and Hank gently brushed the snow off.

He brushed off the log at the end of Cove Lake and looked across the lake. He could see only dense white flakes slanting into the slate-gray water. He got his spinning rod with the plastic bubble and fly attached and tried flipping it out in the lake. No bites. This cold snap probably sent the trout deep. Perhaps he would have better luck at midday on worms.

Becoming more depressed as the early morning wore on, Hank realized that his life and that of Kelli depended upon someone in the Forest Service knowing they were trapped at Cove Lake. Darry was in control of the other backpacking group now. His party should reach Livingston Mill today. Would he tell the mill caretaker? Would the caretaker have a phone or radiophone that could get through to the Ranger District building in Clayton? Would Darry really want to see them rescued? Or would it be more convenient for him if they were found dead in each other's arms?

Darry wasn't trustworthy, the self-seeking bastard. Pam was too in love with Darry to oppose him. Hank's life then could depend on what Ann and Jason did when they reached Livingston Mill.

Blizzard in August

At nine Hank put away his fishing rod and rummaged through his pack under the outer flap until he found a square of graham crackers and a package of dried apricots. He went inside the tent and woke Kelli. "What it's like outside?" she asked.

He gave her a full report and added, "At least the temperature hasn't gone anywhere near zero."

"How do you know?" she asked.

"There's no sign of the lake freezing, even near the edges. That would be very serious. We couldn't fish."

"Is it likely to get that low?" Kelli's voice showed both curiosity and concern.

"I don't know how cold it gets here at ten thousand feet," Hank admitted scratching the stubble on his face. "But during the Depression we had a week in which the temperatures dipped to twenty below zero."

Kelli winced. "How did you survive?"

"Stayed indoors and kept the wood stove stocked. We had one wood stove that heated the house and it was a good one," Hank replied. "You heated with wood in the twentieth century? Surely, you had an oil or electric heater as a backup," Kelli's voice showed amazement.

"We did have a small electric plug-in heater for our downstairs bathroom, but no oil heater. We depended on the wood we cut in the fall, chopped up, and stored in a shed next to our house. Most of the loggers in Bovill heated with wood while I was growing up. My mother and Uncle Ted still do today," Hank said.

"But you're using up the forests around Bovill," Kelli protested.

"Wood is a renewable resource," Hank said, "despite what some extreme environmentalists think. There's forty inches of rain a year and our white pine grows particularly well."

"But aren't the big timber companies doing a lot of clear-cutting in northern Idaho? I read an article by a former forest ranger claiming that vast swaths of the Idaho Panhandle are being clear-cut and not replanted."

Without thinking, they had slipped into a subject where they had serious differences. Hank tried to explain how the company he had worked for never used clear-cutting on hillsides and used only small clear-cuts on level ground. Whenever Kelli described what she had read in an environmental magazine, Hank responded with what he had seen as a logger. Not being able to convince Kelli that loggers had an important stake in the environment. Hank moved the discussion to the war in Vietnam. Again, there were sharp differences. Kelli thought that "the War" was immoral and was horrified by all the dead and wounded shown nightly on television. Hank had fought in the Korean War to keep Communist North Korea from conquering South Korea. He was much more accepting of the fact that war brought casualties.

"But wasn't our involvement in the Korean War sanctioned by U.N. resolutions?" Kelli asked.

"That's true." Hank said. "Our actions in the Korean War did receive much more international support and more troops from other nations. That was a difference."

Kelli pressed home her advantage. "And isn't it true that the South Koreans fought much more effectively for their cause than the South Vietnamese?"

"You're probably right," Hank admitted. "Our division fought beside the South Korean Capital Division as we pushed northward from Taegu. They were a crack division—probably a lot better than any South Vietnamese division."

"Perhaps the Vietnamese are ambivalent about winning and we shouldn't be in there messing in their civil war."

Hank thought about this for a while. "Perhaps you're right," he said. "I don't like how the War is dividing this nation." He paused and then asked, "How are Pam and Ann reacting to anti-war sentiment among the young?"

"Ann is against the War but she talks a lot more about the environment. She is greatly concerned about saving our forests, saving the beaches from oil pollution, and, most recently, saving the whales. She is nearly a vegetarian and feels that male aggressiveness is enhanced because men eat too much meat—particularly red meat. But Ann has a sense of humor and humility and she doesn't express her views in an obnoxious manner."

"And Pam?"

"She expressed anti-war views very strongly her first two years in college. I think she attended some protest rallies. But when one of the rallies she attended was broken up by police, she became much less active. She told me she didn't want to get a police record. Since she met Darry she has privately opposed the War—since Darry could be drafted, but has not, to my knowledge, been an active protester. She tends to follow Darry's lead now on the War."

"And how about Darry?" Hank tried to keep his voice from showing the importance of his question.

"Well, he is against the War but doesn't seem to be too concerned about being drafted. Pam told me he could get out of the United States...find work in one of his father's businesses abroad. In fact, he told Pam in my hearing he

Blizzard in August 79

had some sort of meeting this Friday which could land him an executive job in Mexico."

Hank grimaced. This might be another explanation why Darry didn't want to take the time to come back for Kelli yesterday. Hank didn't want to worry Kelli so he kept this concern to himself. They discussed safer topics the rest of the morning but Hank learned that Kelli had wide-ranging interests, read widely, and had an excellent mind. They could disagree on issues and not let the disagreements drive large wedges between them.

At noon Hank went out and reported the snow had nearly stopped. He cleared off Kelli's log near the fire pit and she sat there while he scooped snow out of the fire pit and brought some firewood. Hank had kept the firewood dry under the large extension of his tent flap and the small pine twigs started easily. The dry sticks burned quickly and the heat began to catch the larger pieces, which were still partially wet. With Hank making many trips to a wooded area for dead branches and Kelli feeding the fire, they soon had a good-sized fire going and were making headway drying Kelli's jeans, shirts, sweatshirts, sweaters, and ski socks. By three o'clock, she had two complete sets of dry clothes. She no longer needed to wear Hank's clothes. She asked Hank to help her back into the tent, and she emerged triumphantly in jeans, a blue sweatshirt and a red ski sweater that molded to her upper body.

Hank whistled appreciatively.

Kelli smiled. "Don't get ideas," she said. "You have some fish to catch for dinner."

Hank grinned and brought out the box of night crawlers and his second spinning rod. In the next two hours, he landed five rainbow trout, one sixteen inches long.

Kelli sat beside him on the log reading a novel with her leg stretched out. Periodically she would put the book down, look across the lake at the mountains and make comments like, "I've never seen a mountain so gleaming white in the sun" and "it's so beautiful that it takes my breath away ... you almost feel you're in the mountains of Alaska." But her remarks about the beauty of the landscape were interspersed with remarks like, "It's so majestic, but so cold and forbidding ... like the mountains are looking down their noses at you and just tolerating your existence."

After finishing his fishing. Hank filleted two of the trout and cooked them in a pan over the hot embers along with a can of peas, which he put close to the ashes to heat. It was a delicious dinner. Hank topped this off with some freeze-dried vegetable soup, which he heated in a pot.

"You're the only man who serves soup for dessert," Kelli joked.

"When you're hungry, it all tastes good," Hank responded. "Well, this has been a good day. We've dried two sets of clothes for you and we've added three fish to our outside freezer. And, perhaps, we've seen the last of the snow for a few days." Hank grinned.

Kelli's lips turned up in a broad smile, which showed to advantage her soft lips and dimpled cheeks.

Hank was entranced but said nothing.

"By now Darry will have gotten through to a Forest Ranger and told him our location," Kelli said.

"I hope so," Hank said without conviction.

The snow began to fall again at five, lightly at first, then with driving force. They re-entered the tent in a more somber mood.

Chapter 20

Livingston Mill – Thursday

Darry woke at seven. He had made love with Pam last evening but was now sated. He had much more important things on his mind—the meeting before the board in Los Angeles tomorrow morning, the meeting which could result in his appointment as executive of the Central American Resort Division. Nothing must interfere with his getting there on time. If he hiked to Livingston Mill by noon today, he would have less than twenty-four hours to get to an airport in Idaho Falls or Salt Lake City and take a commercial flight to Los Angeles.

Pam turned on her back smiling, pulling up her sweatshirt to expose the whiteness of her breasts, inviting another languorous session of lovemaking. Darry found himself a bit disgusted instead of enticed. Beneath that cameo face and luscious body, was there the sexuality of a tart? Darry didn't have time for it this morning. "We have to get up, darling," he said. "We need to get to Livingston Mill as soon as we can."

"Why?"

"Remember, sweets, I have to be in Los Angeles by tomorrow morning for that important meeting. You want me to become head of the Resort Division, don't you?"

"Oh, yes. I want you to get the job. You'll have your name on the door, won't you?" Pam asked.

"Yes." Darry dressed quickly and urged Pam to dress as soon as she could. Darry then unzipped the tent and walked out into the deep snow. The drifts were nearly three feet in places. He hadn't counted on that. He walked over to Jason's tent and told him and Arm to rise quickly. "There's a bonus in this for you, Jason, if I can make my big meeting in LA on time."

With pressure from Darry, the four backpackers ate a hasty breakfast, packed up their gear and were on the trail by eight. It was snowing hard at the time and Jason had difficulty finding the trail as it crept snake-like down grassy hillsides. They all fell several times in the soft snow, got up, and plowed on. As trail-breaker with the heaviest pack, Jason was beginning to wear out after two miles when they came to a log crossing. "Only a mile and a half to go," Jason said. "We're almost to where the Frog Lake trail joins us."

They crossed the stream, with Darry helping Jason to ferry the packs, and pressed onwards. A half-mile up the hill from Livingston Mill, they walked by the sign-in box set on a wooden post. "Shall I sign us out," Jason asked.

"You push ahead with the girls," Darry said. "I'll sign us out."

When the others were well past, Darry swung open the hinge on the wooden box and looked at the sign-in sheets it contained. The Peterson family had signed in on Saturday, August 24th for Walter Lake and signed out at five yesterday afternoon. Three men from Pocatello had signed in Friday the 23rd and evidently came out with the Petersons yesterday. Henry Barclay signed in last Wednesday afternoon, the 21st, for Cove Lake and had not signed out. He was probably the huge man that remained at Cove Lake with Kelli.

Two other entries received Darry's attention. A Herman Wagner and family had signed in for "Frog Lake—maybe Goat or Island Lakes." Could it have been a boy in that family that he and Pam had seen? Darry looked at his map. They could have camped at Goat Lake and then came up the trail that intersected the Island Lake trail. Darry worried momentarily about them, but five members of the family signed in—enough to go for help when the snow melted a little. He would make a call to the Forest Service on them when he had time today, but he didn't feel as responsible for them as he did for Kelli. After all, the boy could not have recognized or identified him.

The last entry on the sheet was made by George and Wilma Anderson who signed in for Frog Lake on Tuesday morning the 27th. The day of the first snow.

Darry looked again at the sign-in sheet. It would be very useful to anyone trying to find Hank Barclay, Pam's aunt, the Wagner's, or the Andersons. If he tore it off and put it in his pocket, he could produce it at the right time and be praised. But did he want Barclay, Pam's aunt and the Wagners to be located too soon after he reached the mill. Mightn't someone want him to go back to rescue them with a search party—and that would mean he couldn't reach Los Angeles on time. It might be better to produce the page just as he was about to leave the mill. Darry needed to keep his options open. He tore off the top page and put it in his back pocket.

It was one o'clock before Darry got to the parking lot near the caretaker's log house. He was greeted by a stocky, dark-haired man with a frown who was digging a path for his suburban to turn around. "I'm John Peterson," the man said. "We got here about five last night but they haven't plowed out the dirt road from the mill to the East Fork. The mill caretaker thinks none of the twenty-mile length of the East Fork Road has been plowed either. We're going to be here a while." "I might be able to help," Darry said. "I need to get on the phone with my father. Is the caretaker's phone working?"

Blizzard in August

"It's a radio-phone and it works fairly well for distances up to about forty miles." Peterson said. "We've been trying to get the Highway Department to plow us out all morning. We reached the Stanley highway shop, but they were too tied up to help us."

Darry strode into the caretaker's home with confidence. "I think I can get action to clear your road if you let me make some phone calls."

The caretaker readily agreed and Darry found himself phoning the Wilson Creek Mine and asking for Jeff Fielding, the superintendent. In a slight nasal twang that annoyed Darry, Fielding told him that his father was urgently trying to get in touch with him. Tomorrow morning's meeting would begin at nine. It was urgent that Darry be there.

"Can you telephone my father," Darry said. "Tell him we're snowed in. There may be thirty miles of unplowed road between Highway 75 and the Livingston Mill. Then I've got to drive all the way to Idaho Falls or even Salt Lake City to take a commercial flight to LA. Can't Dad move the meeting back to Saturday or, better yet, Monday morning?"

Darry paused. "If he can't delay the meeting, can he get some of the trucks from your mine to clear the roads?" Darry hung up and stayed near the phone. Twenty minutes later Jeff Fielding called back. "Your father can't delay the meeting. He ordered us to plow the roads. We're putting snowplows on three trucks now."

"When do you think they will get here?" Darry asked, looking at his watch.

"Between four and five this afternoon," Jeff answered. Darry smiled momentarily, but other problems occurred to him. "It may be six before I get out on Highway 75," he said. "How do I get to a major airport and book a flight to LA. Hell, I may have to go to Salt Lake City tonight to get a flight to LA. If I'm unlucky in getting plane connections or getting a seat, I still may not get there on time."

Jeffs voice was crisp but tart. "Your father made getting you to LA top priority. I'm to drive you to Idaho Falls. Your father is sending a corporate jet to the Idaho Falls airport. If that airport isn't clear. I'm to drive you to Pocatello or even Salt Lake City to hook up with the corporate jet. Hell, this must be a damn important meeting." "It is," Darry said. "I'll tell my father you went all out for me." "Thanks," Jeff said. "Is my cousin, Jason, okay?"

Now was the time for Darry to be magnanimous. "Jason was a terrific guide and carried more than his own share of the weight. His toes are a little frostbitten, but he's fine. I want him to be rewarded for his work."

Jason's uncle muttered his thanks and hung up. Darry was ecstatic. He was almost sure to make the Friday meeting on time. Not only that but also his thanks and praise of Jason gained Fielding's support and showed his executive skill.

As Darry stepped outside on the porch of the caretaker's cabin, John Peterson asked, "Are we going to get plowed out?"

"You sure are. The manager of the Wilson Creek Mine is sending three snowplows right now." Darry was in his element now, smiling, boastful, and cocky. "My father, Mike Baltz, has made plowing this road the top priority for his entire mine crew."

Peterson beamed and clapped Darry on the back.

"That's great, but it's not enough," said Pat Mahoney one of the three graduate students from Idaho State University. "We need to get back to Pocatello by tomorrow to register. Highway 93 leading southeast from Challis is our best route but it's probably blocked by snow drifts." Darry turned to the Idaho State backpackers. "Jeff Fielding, my father's mine superintendent, is going to drive me to Idaho Falls using Route 93. If it isn't plowed out. I'm sure he'll have a couple of snowplows clearing the road for us as far as needed."

Pat shook Darry's hand making Darry feel like a hero.

He turned to John Peterson and asked, "Where do you live?" "Boise," the man replied. "I need to be back in a couple of

days."

"Why don't you follow us to Idaho Falls ... then you'll be on the interstate with clear driving to Boise."

John Peterson sought out his wife to tell of their good fortune. Darry heard him suggesting to her that they stay in an Idaho Falls motel for the night.

The call from Fielding had come too quickly for Darry to think of what would happen to Pam, Ann and Jason. He walked down the snowy road to clear his mind. There would be room in Jeff Fielding's car and the corporate jet for Pam. She could go back to L.A with him. As he rounded the corner of one of the abandoned mill worker's cabin, Darry realized that Ann would be a problem. She needed to be at Ashland, Oregon, to register at Southern Oregon College on Monday. The solution hit Darry in the face. Jason was the answer. He needed to begin the fall semester at the University of Idaho next week. He would be driving home to Twin Falls to get what he needed at college. Jason, good old Jason, could take Ann to Twin Falls to his parents' house tonight and make sure she got a plane or bus to Ashland, Oregon, tomorrow.

The sun was shining momentarily as Darry walked back to the parking lot and explained the arrangements to Pam, Ann and Jason.

Blizzard in August   85

Pam said nothing but ran to Darry and threw her arms around him. "This works out well for me," admitted Ann. "But isn't it out of Jason's way?"

"Not at all." A smile creased Jason's face. "My parents would be pleased to have you stay tonight, Ann. I need to go back to Twin Falls to get my stuff for college. I'll just be going a few days earlier than I planned." He grinned at Ann. "Tomorrow I can put you on a plane for Medford, Oregon, where you could catch a bus or taxi to Ashland." "Yes, yes. Thank you," Ann appeared both pleased and flustered.

"Now that you have taken care of so much," Jason said smoothly, "I should phone the Forest Service about Kelli and Hank. They can't make it down by themselves."

"It's very important," Ann said. "We can't leave Idaho without knowing that Kelli is safe."

Darry thought quickly. Of course, he'd need to inform the Forest Service, but he wanted the credit for having made the phone call that saved Pam's aunt. Darry said, "I'll make that call right now."

Darry went back to the phone and dialed the number of the Clayton Ranger Station. The line was busy. A few minutes later, Jason went with him and tried. The line was still busy.

Turning to Jason, Darry said. "You worry about getting your car dug out. I'll get through to the Forest Service."

Jason left for the car lot and Darry tried the Clayton Ranger Station at two-thirty and twice more before three. Busy signal. There were other Forest Services offices listed such as the ones at Redfish Lake and Champion Creek, but these were miles away and Darry decided not to phone them.

Darry stood on the porch of the caretaker's cabin. He could see that Jason was working hard with a snow shovel. As Darry went back inside again, he had a chilling thought. Suppose Hank Barclay blamed him for Kelli's fall into the water. If he was rescued by helicopter and brought to Livingston Mill, wasn't it possible he might attack Darry? Darry shuddered at the thought of facing the fists of this giant of a man.

Although this was unlikely, Darry was now having some qualms about telling the Forest Service about Hank and Kelli.

Darry waited for a while and called three times more. Twice he received a busy signal and the third time he momentarily panicked when someone answered. "There are some people stranded in the White Clouds," he said in a high falsetto voice that he was sure no one could identify.

"Where?" asked the voice at the other end of the line.

"Frog Lake, among other places," he answered and then broke the connection.

By then it was three-thirty; the caretaker's house was bathed in sunshine. Darry went outside to see Jason and Ann packing Jason's car. Jason had put chains on his car and shoveled an area large enough to turn it around. Pam was waiting for him on the porch. "You did call the Forest Service about Aunt Kelli, didn't you?" Pam asked.

"I thought you thought of her as "Dragon Lady," Darry said with a smile.

Pam was not smiling. "I did, but I don't want her to freeze to death up there. My mother could get very angry at me." Pam paused and whispered to Darry. "And you promised to get help for that family we met coming down from Island Lake."

"I called the Forest Service at least four times, but there was a busy signal. I tried again and got some woman...told her there were some people stranded in the White Clouds...but we were cut off." Darry looked away, a little ashamed of his half-truth.

"Can we try," Pam said. "We've got to be sure someone knows where Kelli is."

Darry shrugged and led both Pam and Ann to the radiophone. They each phoned; the line was busy both times.

Finding himself sweating now, Darry realized that he could just tell the mill caretaker. But would that man try to organize a search party—a venture that might keep Darry from his all-important meeting tomorrow morning? Better wait until the snowplows arrived to call the Forest Service again. Darry left the caretaker's cabin with Pam and Ann, promising to call again in another fifteen minutes.

He led Pam on a walk in the snow to give him time to think. The pine cabins formerly used by the mill workers gleamed in the sunlight. They walked hand-in-hand between the cabins and down by Big Boulder Creek. He told Pam that he had to keep his mind on his father's orders and his promise to make tomorrow morning's meeting. They were just coming back from the creek when the mill caretaker came running out the door into the area where the cars were parked.

"I have a Senator Wagner on the line," he yelled. "Did any of you see a family of five camped on any of the lakes you were on? The Herman Wagner family is missing."

John and Edna Peterson and the three Idaho State students said they had not seen anyone else at Walter Lake or on the way down. Ann said she hadn't seen this family at Sapphire, Cove or Island Lakes.

Blizzard in August   87

The caretaker yelled at Darry, "Did you see a family of five?"

"No," Darry yelled back. It was the truth, but only a half-truth. Pam opened her mouth, but Darry put a hand on her arm and she remained quiet.

The caretaker looked closely at the assembled group. "I'll tell Senator Wagner that no one saw his brother's family. If someone had, the Senator wanted me to get all the able-bodied men together and lead a rescue mission." He paused. "I'd do it, but I wouldn't relish going out in these two-foot drifts. Course, he'll want me to look at the sign-in board."

Darry relaxed after the caretaker left. He seemed safe enough now. If only those road graders arrived in time.

Darry heard them a little after four. One low, welcome growl and then a second. He heard Jason yell, "The graders are here."

It seemed that everything happened at once. Jason went up to the first grader and greeted the driver by name. "He wants us to be ready to leave as quickly as possible," Jason said. "You and Pam are to be in the cab of the first grader and your gear in the bed of the truck. Jeff Fielding will meet you in his four-wheel-drive Suburban at the cutoff near Challis.

"What about you and Ann?"

"We're going to follow in my car." Jason explained. "We'll drive almost all the way to Challis and cutoff southeast on Highway 93 to Arco. From there we're out of the snow and on good roads to Twin Falls. I'll call my parents from Arco. They have a spare bedroom. We ought to reach their home tonight." Darry could see the excitement in Jason's voice and supposed his mind was on his trip.

"And the others, the Petersons and the Idaho State University students?"

"Their cars will follow mine," Jason said. "But the truck drivers want us to hurry."

Darry turned to pick up his pack which was leaning against Jason's car.

"Not so fast," Jason said. "I need to know. Did you tell the Forest Service where Kelli and Hank are camped?"

"I did," Darry lied.

"I could go into Challis and make sure," Jason said.

"Trust me," Darry said intending to call the Forest Service at a gas station near Challis.

Darry's watch showed six by the time the first road grader reached the junction with Highway 93 near Challis. He phoned the Clayton Ranger Station with Jason at his elbow.

No answer. Perhaps, everyone had gone home.

Jeff Fielding met him at the gas station. "The road isn't completely plowed," he said. "I'm going to have one of the road graders lead us. We've got to hurry. My men and I need to get back to the mine tonight."

With Jason helping, they quickly loaded Darry and Pam's gear in Fielding's Suburban. The convoy moved slowly out in the highway—first the truck with the snowplow and then Fielding's Suburban, Jason's Ford, the Peterson's Dodge, and the old Chevy with the Idaho State students.

Darry said little on the way to Idaho Falls. Worried that he had not told the Forest Service of the location of the Wagners or Pam's Aunt, he pondered what to do. An anonymous phone call was best. He could make that at the Idaho Falls airport from a pay phone. Should he call the sheriff's office if the Forest Service didn't answer? No, better not get the sheriff involved. He would ask too many questions.

At the airport at Idaho Falls, he had one more chance to reach the Clayton Ranger Station. It was after nine and no one answered the phone. "I tried again," Darry told Pam, as he emerged from the phone booth. "I'll try tomorrow from Los Angeles."

Big Mike's personal pilot soon joined them in the waiting room at the airport, leading them to the plane. It was only when the jet was in the air that Darry relaxed and became his gregarious, smiling self. He was safe now and he knew it. He was out of Idaho. In California tomorrow he would get the Central American job. He would be out of the country before the draft board met. He looked at Pam smiling beside him. What a beauty. Maybe, just maybe, he'd marry her in Mexico.

As he opened his briefcase to study the materials he brought on the Central American hotels owned by Big Mike's corporation, one nagging thought crossed his mind. Had he done anything illegal - something he might be prosecuted for? Kelli would not prosecute him. Pam would see to that. But the Wagners might—but of course the boy was too far away to identify either Pam or him, hidden as they were under the branches of a pine. Then Darry grinned as he considered the fact that within two days he would no longer be in the United States and subject to the puny law enforcement efforts of a hick Idaho sheriff. With this thought, Darry at last began to relax.

Chapter 21

White Clouds Mountains – Thursday evening

Wilma Anderson heard it first – the low drone of a small propeller plane northeast of where she was sitting. It hadn't been a good decision to go up to Frog Lake on Tuesday morning. There was no snow on the ground when they started up the trail, but more than two inches when they reached the lake. Wilma felt exhausted when she reached the top and her boots rubbed raw blisters on the back of her heels. She spent most of the next two days in the tent while her husband, George, fished. But this morning she had walked down by the shore, stepped in a soft spot, and twisted her ankle. Bored and increasingly worried about the blizzard, Wilma hoped the Forest Service would rescue them.

The plane came closer and Wilma scanned the horizon. It must be over Livingston Mill now, she thought. Clouds covered much of the sky, but there were open spaces where blue showed. Through one of the gaps the plane swooped down on Frog Lake. "Look! A plane." Wilma yelled to her husband and stood, waving her arms.

George ran from beneath the limbs of a pine and began waving his large, peaked cap in his hand as a greeting. The pilot made one pass over Frog Lake and came around for a second. Wilma waved her arms again in a frantic effort to get the pilot's attention. The pilot waggled his wings as if to make clear that he understood their plight and left, flying westward along the ridge.

George came up to Wilma, "What have you done? The pilot may think we're in trouble."

"We are," Wilma said, "My feet are still raw with blisters, my ankle is sprained, I'm catching a cold, and we may get another foot of snow tonight."

"But we have plenty of food."

"For a few days," Wilma responded. "If they send someone up tomorrow to help us get back to Livingston Mill, I for one am going to be grateful."

Tom Wagner was the next to hear it. Clouds nearly obscured the entire sky and he saw it only once flying along the ridgeline up from Frog Lake. He could see the plane dip down below his line of vision and hear it three miles to the south—possibly near Five Mile Meadows. Then the noise of the motor faded into the distance. Tom felt like jumping up and waving his hands but he knew it wouldn't do any good. Nothing had gone right for the Wagners that day. Emily's breathing was very labored, and her mother, Trudy, spent much of the morning forcing hot soup down her throat. By afternoon it was apparent that Emily had pneumonia and eight-year-old Lisa was coming down with a cold.

Tom spent the morning sitting in his hiding place under a large pine, protected from the wind, his eyes on the trail. He had found an extra ground cloth in his father's pack and tied it to some pine branches to provide additional protection from the snow. It was a long, lonely morning but he had two books to read and didn't complain. He didn't understand why no one came up or down the trail.

At noon his father called and Tom ran to the tent.

"The snow has almost stopped. I need to get out of the tent and get some air," his father said. "Help me."

Tom pulled on his father's back as his father muscled himself forward, wincing in pain. "Thanks," he said as Tom propped him against a log.

It was then Tom smelled it—a rotting odor. He wrinkled his nose. "What's that smell?""

"My wound has been very badly infected. I hope I'm not getting blood poisoning...or worse, gangrene." The lines around Herman Wagner's face were deep and taut.

Tom's father sat against the log all afternoon, directing Tom as he built a fire to dry wet clothes and cook the evening meal. Trudy and Lisa came out of the tent only long enough to eat and take soup in for Emily.

Tom's father's eyes widened when he heard the plane. He tried standing but fell back in pain. The light dimmed in Herman Wagner's eyes when he heard the plane fly away.

"We're in bad shape," he said. "We have food for only a little more than a day. Emily may be dying, your mother is very sick, and Lisa seems to be getting the bug. I can't walk with my right leg broken and badly infected. You're the only healthy one in the family. Try to stay that way and sleep as far from your mother and sisters as you can tonight."

"I could go to Livingston Mill tomorrow morning," Tom said. "I could make it."

"Maybe in a sunny day, if the snow was half what it is now," his father said. "We may have to risk it. But surely that red-haired man must have reached Livingston Mill today and told the Forest Service. We should be rescued tomorrow."

Blizzard in August   **91**

A long, piercing wail broke the stillness of the late afternoon. It rose, then fell, and broke into uncontrollable sobs.

"That's Mama," Tom said, "Something terrible must have happened." He ran to the tent and then, weeping, ran back to his father. "It's Emily. She's dead."

"Oh, Lord. No!" Herman began to sob and then scream, "It's my fault. I should have left her with my brother and his wife." He turned to Tom. "Help me back in the tent so I can comfort Mom."

Hank and Kelli were the last of the backpackers to hear the plane. Muffled by their tent, the plane's engines could be heard for only a few minutes. "Sounds like it's to the east of us down the valley," Hank said. "Maybe the plane turned back because of the snow."

"I'm sure they'll send help tomorrow," Kelli said. Hank said nothing, but the tight lines of his mouth showed he was not as optimistic. He still didn't trust Darry to call the Forest Service.

"It was eight that evening before Ray Winters reached Senator Wagner by phone. "Good news," he said.

"Did you locate my brother and his family?"

"Someone telephoned in that there were campers near Frog Lake," Ray said.

"And."

"I hired Wally Zondrine to fly his Cessna over the area around Frog Lake. He spotted a couple camped near the shore. The man was big like your brother Herman. The woman was more petite and waved her arms like she wanted us to rescue them."

"Did you fly over other areas?"

"Wally got as far west as Five Mile Meadows and saw no one there. Then he ran into a snow storm with poor visibility and flew back to Challis."

"Can you send in a rescue team?"

"I'll send in Ed Grant tomorrow morning. Davidson, the other wilderness ranger was hurt in a jeep accident coming out of the Yankee Fork Road." Ray paused. "Ed is my best man. He can get through."

"I hope so," the Senator said. "I appreciate what you've done for me very much. I'll be praying that it was my brother and his wife that Wally spotted. Herman likes to camp at Frog Lake ... what terrible luck he brought his whole family."

Chapter 22

Friday Morning, August 30,1969

Joe Brezinski felt like the general who had thrown his entire force into a crucial battle and won, not a lasting victory but just a momentary advantage in a continuing struggle. Galena Summit had been plowed from the south by the two graders promised by his supervisor, but the graders had returned to the Twin Falls District. For a six-hour period Highway 75 was almost free of snow from Twin Falls to its terminus at Challis.

The tide turned at seven in the evening. Light snow turned to heavy blinding snow, and by nine, Joe Brezinski had called in his snowplows and sent his weary drivers home. By six in the morning, there were ten new inches of snow on the streets of Stanley as Joe walked to work. The six-thirty weather forecast predicted the Pacific low and the ridge of Arctic air would mix and slowly revolve over central Idaho for another two or three days. Joe turned to his assistant, "All we can hope to do today is keep the Galena Summit and the route down the valley open during the daylight hours and hope that the stores at Smiley Creek, Obsidian, Redfish Lake, and Stanley can get restocked by wholesalers."

"How about the backpackers in the Sawtooth Mountains?" his deputy asked. "A ranger told me there were nearly two hundred backpackers stranded.

"We can't plow out to the trailheads just yet. I hope they have enough food," Joe replied.

Ray Winters was looking at a huge wall map of the Challis Ranger District. "My first priority is to get all my fire fighters except a mop-up crew back from the Panther Creek fire. Then I have to worry about the backpackers."

"I'm particularly worried about the situation in the White Clouds," said his assistant, Stan Oxley.

"The East Fork Road and the Livingston Mill Road were plowed out yesterday afternoon," Ray said. "Some big shot was trapped up there and they flew him back to LA. But we need to plow the rest of the East Fork Road."

"What about Senator Wagner's brother?" Stan asked.

"The pilot of a small plane I hired spotted him at Frog Lake. That confirms the telephone report we had this afternoon. If Ed Grant is the shop, please send him in." When the tall, square-shouldered blond man sat down beside him, Ray said, "We've got a problem. State Senator Herman Wagner is the biggest political power in these parts and he fears that his brother, his wife, and their three children are in serious trouble. We think they're at Frog Lake."

"What do you want me to do?" Ed asked.

"Load up your backpack and drive a jeep up to Livingston Mill right away. Then get up to Frog Lake as soon as you can and bring down the Wagners. Take a medical kit with you."

"Suppose they're not the Senator's brother's family?"

"Then bring down whoever's there unless they object. This blizzard may get worse."

Darry Baltz had only five hours sleep that night. The jet bearing Pam and him from Idaho Falls to Los Angeles arrived just after midnight. He took Pam to her home by taxi. Pam's mother and father threw their arms about their daughter telling her how worried they'd been. After recounting the events of the backpacking trip, Darry convinced Pam's parents that it was his cool head and executive leadership that saved their daughters. Pam supported Darry's account by saying it was he who led them down the mountain in a snowstorm after Kelli left them to sleep with a "Mountain Man."

Melissa Pettigrew was angry with her sister and told her husband that Kelli's action was a "betrayal of trust that she could never forgive."

"Is there any reason she couldn't have come down with you yesterday?" Richard asked.

"Well, she twisted her ankle," Pam said. "She could have walked out but it would have been painful."

Darry had gone to his father's house at nearly two in the morning and found Big Mike pacing the floor. "I have some financial briefs on the three hotels we own in Mexico," he said as he handed over a sheaf of papers. "Have them reviewed before the nine o'clock Board Meeting."

Although tired, Darry was thoroughly prepared and supremely confident at the meeting. His short presentation was flawless and he fielded the few questions with knowledge and skill. The board was impressed. "Chip off the old block," a senior board member remarked to Big Mike when Darry was excused from the room. The board not only approved Darry's appointment to Director of the Central American Resort Division, but also approved a $50 million budget increase to renovate the Guymas Hotel and buy land for a new resort. Darry was to fly to Mexico that day.

Remaining in the boardroom after everyone else left, Darry smiled as he picked up his papers. Everything was going his way. The problems he faced in

Idaho yesterday seemed light years in his past. Weariness from the backpack trip and lack of sleep overcame him.

In his back pocket of the pants he wore backpacking was the sign-up sheet from the box half a mile from Livingston Mill. He'd tear it up later today. He thought of making another phone call to the Clayton Ranger Station and picked up the phone. Weariness overcame him. He got the area code wrong. "What the hell," he muttered to himself. "Idaho is two thousand miles away and I'll be in Mexico by evening. The draft board and the backpacking trip are behind me. I've got to concentrate on my new job."

Chapter 23

Cove Lake – Friday Morning

Kelli Johnson woke at six with a slight pain in her right hip from sleeping so long on her side. She shifted her body in the tight confines of the sleeping bag she shared with Hank and her hands tightened on his chest. His body felt broad, strong and solid and the touch excited her. She moved her fingers to his stomach and felt its toughness and strength. She had a momentary urge to move her fingers further but resisted the temptation.

She had feared Hank the first night she shared a sleeping bag with him— feared that he would use his great strength to take advantage of her. But for three nights they had lain, side-by-side in the same sleeping bag and he'd made no advances. Was this because he didn't find her attractive or was this part of his strong, instinctive code of honor? She couldn't be sure.

Hank was a complex, perplexing man. He was an Associate Professor of History at a medium-sized state university, but he did not fit her stereotype of the erudite, intellectual professor. He took a great interest in innovative teaching techniques and getting to know students on a one-to-one basis. He would be at home in the Phi Delta Kappa meeting she attended once a month. He acknowledged that college professors had much to learn about teaching from public school teachers. Kelli found this open-mindedness very interesting and attractive.

Of course. Hank needed to publish to gain tenure and advancement. She needed to ask more about this side of his life since she had not, as an elementary school teacher and principal, faced pressure to publish. He evidently had published histories of pioneer life in Idaho. This would be fascinating to read and would have brought him into close contact with pioneers and their offspring.

But Hank was far from the typical college professor—certainly different from the two or three she had met in Southern California. He grew up in a logging family, had been a logger, and was proud of his logging heritage. Kelli found this aspect of Hank's life both puzzling and disturbing. A Los Angeles television station had attacked the cutting of giant redwoods and pictured a grinning logger felling a three hundred-year-old tree despite the protests of decent people like herself. Loggers were macho men—hard-living, hard-drinking, unfeeling and often unfaithful to their wives. Was Hank like this? He certainly would not get along with her environmentally-minded friends. He would just not fit in well with her Los Angeles, Sierra Club crowd, she thought. In fact, she could not see him happy in any large city.

But Hank did not fit her stereotype of a logger in several ways and this Kelli found disconcerting. He came from a strong family background led by his mother and uncle. He went to church regularly, but his Christianity seemed more judgmental than forgiving. She would need to learn more about this to better assess his character. The most amazing thing of all was, he didn't drink. How could he manage to be part of a logging crew and turn down invitations to go to local bars after work? She could see how his views on drinking had been influenced by the drunken logger who killed his father and, more recently by the drunken driver that had killed his wife.

Kelli tried to picture how Hank could ignore all the peer pressure he received from loggers to drink with them. Hank was certainly strong-willed, but didn't he face physical threats as well as social ostracism? What did he do on those occasions? Of course, he used his fists. He was six foot five with the physique of a heavyweight fighter. And, she imagined, he could have a strong temper when aroused. Kelli had read accounts of violent fist-fights in logging camps and could well imagine Hank a violent, effective fighter.

How did this image of Hank square with his role as a husband and father? He was obviously deeply in love with Susan and was still grieving over her death. Did he ever beat her? Or did he beat his daughters, on occasion, to keep them in line? There was so much she didn't know about Hank.

There was one thing she did know about him. He had some sort of instinctive moral code and to this she owed her life. He had not hesitated about leaving her freezing on the edge of the lake even though taking her in might endanger his own life. It seemed to make no difference about her, age, sex, color—or anything about her. Leaving her, or anyone else to freeze, was morally wrong. There was a great strength to this implicit moral code. She wondered how he had built up this instinctive core of values, what it encompassed, and how inflexible it was. In a way it was like the values she had seen in the ranchers and lawmen in movies of the old west.

Kelli considered herself a good student of human psychology, but she decided that Hank was one of the most bewildering men she had ever met. His blue-collar, logger background conflicted with his role as a university professor. His instinctive kindness alternated with a strong, judgmental streak and, she suspected, a violent temper. She would find this bundle of contradictions a challenge to unravel.

Kelli's reveries were broken at seven when Hank stirred and looked at his watch. "I need to go out and take a look at the snow conditions and weather," he said. "If it's clear it would be nice to dry some clothes and, perhaps, with enough time, your sleeping bag."

"And you need to catch more fish." Kelli said. "How many do you have in the freezer?"

"There are three in the snow bank but we could use six or seven more for insurance. We've used up most of our other food."

"Don't you think we'll be rescued today? Darry must have reached Livingston Mill and called the Forest Service. There was a plane which flew up the valley yesterday."

"But the plane did not fly beyond Five Mile Meadows," Hank pointed out. "The pilot could have flown up to the lake basin but didn't. Perhaps he was looking for someone else farther down the valley. In any case, I need to get outside and see how much visibility there is today."

Hank pulled on his clothes, unzipped the tent fly, and was back in ten minutes. "We had another ten inches of snow last night and it's snowing lightly. The problem is that there's a dense fog. Until that lifts a plane couldn't spot us."

"What shall we do?" Kelli asked. "Do you think I should sit outside?"

"Oh, yes, with your poncho on you won't get very wet and it will do you good to get the fresh air. How's your ankle?"

Kelli sat up and put on her boots gingerly. "The swelling's down, but it still hurts when I put on my boot. I'll be all right if I don't stand up too much." Kelli put on her poncho and crawled out of the tent where Hank picked her up in his arms and carried her to a log that faced away from the wind.

"I want to fish the other end of Sapphire Lake for an hour or so," he said. "There are some big trout where the stream from Cirque Lake flows into Sapphire."

"I hope you're successful. Please get me my novel so I can read while you're gone." Kelli paused. "If I hear a plane flying over. I'll wave my arms."

Kelli quickly tired of reading and looking out across the lake. She began to assess her life. What was it she really wanted? The answer came immediately. She wanted to marry a man she loved and trusted and she wanted a baby. Was Hank a man she could love enough to marry? She had known him only three days and knew so little about him. Was he attracted to her? Was he still grieving too much over the death of his wife to think of marriage? Would he want children with a second wife or just a stepmother for his three girls? Was he sufficiently flexible to allow her to continue her beloved teaching career? Were their likes, dislikes, hopes, and dreams just too far apart? Kelli's mind whirled with contradictory ideas. Befuddled she picked up her novel again and was soon immersed in the steamy romance.

Hank came back two hours later with a string of six large trout. "We're not going to starve for a few days," he said cheerfully.

"What else is for dinner?" Kelli asked.

"Just a bowl of freeze-dried soup. We need to save the graham crackers and a few apricots for the evening meal. But we can have two of these big fifteen inch trout for dinner."

Hank seemed cheerful as he ate. He discussed other times he had fished the lakes and thought he could continue to catch fish as long as the nightcrawlers held out.

"How many nightcrawlers do you have left?" she asked.

"About a dozen. And they each better catch a fish," he said.

Twenty minutes later it began to snow hard and they went inside the tent. Kelli peeled off her loose-fitting outer ski sweater revealing a tight-fitting yellow cashmere that seemed molded around her full breasts. She sat down beside him on the sleeping bag and smiled.

Hank stared at her, grinned, and moved closer.

Kelli couldn't control her emotions. She wanted Hank to kiss her so she moved her head towards him, staring at him passionately. Hank's eyes shone and his lips seem to purse. He put a hand gently on her shoulder.

Was he going to kiss her? Or would he again show restraint? A minute passed without either speaking. Then, Kelli could stand it no longer. She threw her arms around Hank and kissed him.

Chapter 24

Twin Falls, Idaho – Friday noon

Jason Green had worn a brown tweed sports coat, white shirt, green tie, and brown slacks to take Ann Pettigrew to the Twin Falls airport. "Hope you didn't mind sleeping in the spare bedroom last night," he said carrying her backpack and suitcase to the check-in counter.

"The bed was comfortable," Ann said. "And your mother is a wonderful cook. It was very nice of your family to take me in."

"I don't bring girls home for them to see very often. I hope they didn't ask too many nosy questions." The older couple ahead of them checked their bags through and Jason put Ann's backpack and suitcase on the baggage slot.

"I hope I passed the test," Ann said lightly as she paid for her ticket and received the stubs for her backpack and bag. Then she inquired once more about when the plane reached Boise and the route it would take to Medford.

Jason looked at Ann with approval. She wore red plaid slacks and a white cashmere sweater. She was not beautiful but had a wholesome, well-scrubbed look. "Sorry, I can't take you by car to Ashland, but I need to help my father paint the house before I head back to the University of Idaho."

"I understand," Ann said as they walked towards benches in the waiting room. "Do you suppose Darry and Pam made it to LA all right?"

"Sure, Darry travels in style. They were on the corporate jet from Idaho Falls to LA." There was a little bite to Jason's voice.

"You don't like Darry, do you?" Ann asked suddenly.

Jason sat down beside Ann on a bench in the airport waiting room. "I have mixed feelings about Darry. He can be very generous. He paid me $500 for being the guide for the trip, and he took me out to dinner the night before we met you at the best restaurant in Challis."

"He was just insuring you would do what he wanted," Ann's voice showed her disapproval.

"It was more than that," Jason said. "He really wants to be liked and he can have some good impulses. There was this poor Hispanic family that couldn't pay the entire bill at the restaurant. It looked like things would get a little ugly until Darry approached them, speaking Spanish. He ended up paying the tab for their dinner."

"Well, I didn't like the way he ordered you around all the time and the way you had to carry all the packs across the log crossings." She paused. "Is Darry lazy or what?"

Jason smiled, "He's just playing the role of the big executive, just aping his father. He'll grow out of it eventually."

"It was wrong to leave Kelli at Cove Lake with that man she didn't know," Ann persisted. "I was just too timid to buck Pam on that.

I feel badly. I'm just not assertive enough."

Jason looked down at his lap. "I failed, too. The big man was right. We should have all camped together at Cove Lake. I just … I just buckled under when Darry threatened my uncle's job. That came close to blackmail and I was angry." He paused. "But it was my fault for not standing up to Darry when I knew he was wrong."

Ann smiled wryly. "You and I are alike, Jason. We just don't like to make waves. I just hope Kelli is all right."

"I'm sure the Forest Service has rescued her by this time," Jason said. "Darry called them several times. He told me he reached them." "Are you sure Darry can be trusted?" Ann asked.

"Positive," Jason responded. "He wouldn't lie on something so important." Then he changed the subject. "What are you going to major in at Southern Oregon College?"

"Elementary education," she said. She went on to describe her love of younger children and her hope of being an inspiring teacher. Jason had always been shy around girls but he found Ann easy to talk with. Before she boarded the plane they exchanged addresses and promised to keep in touch. There was so much Jason wanted to say about his hopes and plans for the future. But this could wait. He would write her tomorrow and ask her to send the number of the phone in her dorm.

Chapter 25

Cove Lake – Friday Afternoon

Hank was taken completely by surprise. One minute he was sitting there with Kelli on his sleeping bag, admiring the way she filled out the beautiful, yellow cashmere sweater. The next minute she had her arms around him and was kissing him. He opened his mouth, their tongues sought out each other briefly, and then she pulled back, smiling. "Sorry. It was a sudden impulse."

There were too many thoughts racing around for Hank to speak. What struck him now was that Kelli had an absolutely beautiful figure—long legs, strong hips, slim waist, and large, well-rounded breasts. Her face was very pretty but it was her figure that excited him. As she brought her face close to his again, he knew she was expecting a reaction but it was difficult for him to say anything. "It was not a good impulse," he said. "You're stirring me up."

"So you do find me attractive," Kelli said. "I wasn't sure." "Yes." Hank said. "But I've no right to take advantage of you. We've known each other only a few days." He looked at her with lust—how he would like to seduce her—but it would be wrong, morally wrong, to do so.

"And you're still loyal to Susan."

Kelli seemed to say this on impulse but Hank pondered what she was leading into. He studied her face carefully. "I still miss Susan terribly, but this doesn't mean that I won't fall in love and even marry some day. Susan and I talked about what would happen if one of us died first. I was taking a lot of plane trips at the time."

"And."

"We felt the one of us who lived should remarry. We shouldn't try to live a monastic life, and marriage was a better alternative than just living with someone."

Kelli changed the subject to Hank's relief "I was wondering, as I was sitting outside looking across the lake, how you managed to avoid going to a bar after work with your logging buddies."

"Most of the time I told my friends that I needed to get home to my wife. I got kidded, but seldom challenged about that. Sometimes my friends would get me off the hook. But there were a few times some new guy would call me a wimp who couldn't hold his liquor."

Kelli turned so she could watch Hank's face. "What would you do then?"

Hank smiled. "I'd reason with him first. Say I didn't drink—or had some urgent business at home." He paused, his face growing more serious. "If the man still challenged me...called me a coward...I'd have to fight him."

"Would you win?"

Hank was wondering why she persisted. "Oh, yes. Uncle Ted trained me and I was good."

"Did you ever lose your temper when you fought?" Kelli asked and Hank could sense that Kelli was afraid he had a violent temper. "Good fighters seldom lose their tempers if their opponents fight fairly. And my opponents generally fought fairly as I did. Once I had a guy pull a knife on me."

Hank regretted mentioning this and was uncomfortable when Kelli asked the next question.

"What happened?"

"He cut my arm a bit. Then I hit him hard in the stomach, and when his head jerked up, I gave him two hard uppercuts. He was out cold." Memories flooded back. He had lost his temper badly. There were more than two uppercuts and he had climbed on top of the fallen man and pummeled him. He remembered being pulled off by his friends, the call for the ambulance and the man being carted off. The memories were too painful now. He lapsed into silence unwilling to speak of his anger and the aftermath. He told Susan but none of his university friends knew the full story. He certainly wasn't going to tell Kelli.

Kelli had moved away from Hank now and was eying him cautiously. "Did you ever lose your temper with Susan?"

"No." Hank said vehemently. "I loved Susan. I never beat her."

He paused. "Sure, we had a few arguments. What couple doesn't. But neither of us ever really lost our temper or went to bed angry. We had our differences of opinion, but we had a very good marriage." The lines of Hank's mouth tightened. He asked, "Why all these questions?"

"I've never met a logger or former logger before," Kelli said. "One of my teacher friends told me that loggers are violent men. One of them beat her sister so badly she was hospitalized and later went into a home for battered women. I guess I..."

"Were you worried I might beat you?"

"No," Kelli said. "You're just different from anyone I've met before. You're a logger and man who can use his fists, but you're also a college professor and were a loving husband to Susan. A bundle of contradictions, that's what you are."

Hank was indignant. "I'm just being me. What's confusing about me?"

"Well, you're a professor but you're definitely not some ivory- tower intellectual. You get involved in issues like the closing of mines and mills. And you like teaching and you're interested in learning. I just don't know any professors that are like that."

"Is that bad?" Hank asked not sure whether he was being praised or criticized by Kelli.

"It's very good. Terrific. But 1 don't see where your university career is leading."

Hank couldn't understand the point of all this. He'd never laid out a ten-year plan for himself; he lived from one semester to the next. "You're really making me think," he said. "Maybe that's good. I guess...I guess I want to become a full professor at the University of Idaho. And some day when our department head retires. I'd like to have a turn at being Chairman of the History Department. And I'd like to have two or three books on Idaho history published. And more than anything else, I want my students to remember me as a really good teacher."

Kelli smiled warmly. "I understand what you're saying now. Teaching comes first. You want to stay put and do the best job you can." She paused and added, "I admire you. I admire you a lot."

Kelli lapsed into silence. Perhaps she understood him better now. Hank began to ask her questions about her work as a principal and about her own future professional goals. "I'm like you," Kelli said. "I want to do the best job I can in my present job. I'm not looking for advancement." She paused. "I'm due to start work next Tuesday. They may have to start without me."

"Will you be fired if you're late?"

"No. I'm under contract. They might deduct a few days' pay. That's all."

"And you'd never move from your school district?" Hank's flat tone of voice made this more of a statement than a question.

Kelli's cheeks became red and she couldn't speak for a moment. "If I met the right man and he really wanted me to continue my professional career in his community, I would marry him and move." "Even to Idaho?" Hank asked with a sudden rush of emotion. Kelli thought a minute and her cheeks colored again. "Even to Idaho."

Neither spoke for a minute. Hank said, "It's time for our supper. A square of graham crackers and some dried apricots."

Chapter 26

Goat Lake Trail and Frog Lake – Friday Afternoon

"What's wrong with Mama?" Lisa Wagner asked, her eight year-old mind wrestling with Trudy Wagner's strange behavior during the day. Her mother's cough was deeper and more labored now than yesterday and she refused to come out of the tent to sit around the campfire with the others. Lisa, herself, felt better; her cough and sniffles were gone.

"Ma's heart-broken that Emily died last night," Tom said gently.

"I feel bad about that too. But Ma hasn't been out of the tent all day except to go to the bathroom," Lisa pointed out.

"She's in deep depression," Herman said. "A man can't really understand what it's like for a woman to go through nine months of child-bearing, give birth to a child, and have that child die."

"But it's not fair that you and Tom have to do the work. Mama should come out of the tent and help some." Lisa said. "It's hard for you to help with your broken leg," she told her father.

"Your mother has pneumonia. She needs her rest," Herman said putting a gentle arm on Lisa's shoulder. Deep inside, Lisa was worried that her father would die as Emily did.

"But why should you have to do most of the work? You have a broken leg. You can't stand up," Lisa said.

"It's Tom who's doing most of the work," Herman said. "Tom, you've become a man. You're essential to us here … you need to stay with us. That's why I don't want you to leave for Livingston Mill." Tom turned to look his father squarely in the face, "How much food do we have left?"

"Enough for two more meals, but we'll ration and stretch it over an entire day," his father said. "Tomorrow we're going to be rescued. I know we are."

"How so. Dad?" Tom asked.

"The red-haired man you saw should have gotten to Livingston Mill yesterday. You'll see. They'll send three or four men up from Five Mile Meadows this afternoon or tomorrow to take us back to the Mill with stretchers."

Blizzard in August

"And what if the red-haired man didn't tell anyone we were here?" Tom asked.

"My brother will find us. He'll know by now that we should have been back. He'll call our house and get no answer. Then he'll get the Forest Seiwice to search for us."

"But suppose he doesn't know where to look?"

"We've got to believe he will," his father said. "If we give up hope, we'll die. We need to pray together." Herman Wagner, Tom and Lisa formed a small circle and prayed for the recovery of his Trudy and the safety of their family.

By two-thirty the lazy flakes of snow that had drifted down from the pines most of the morning were replaced by thick white flakes. "Take me in," ordered Herman, and his two children pushed and pulled until they finally got him back into the tent.

"What are you going to do now?" Lisa asked her eleven-year- old brother.

"Stay out here and watch the trail."

"But won't you freeze in all that snow?"

"I built a shelter with a ground cloth under the pines. It keeps most of the snow off me."

"Could I stand watch with you? It's hard to sleep with Dad moaning and Ma crying and breathing so hard." Lisa said

"I know," Tom said. "Bring a book out. We can each read for a while."

Lisa brought her book, but found talking to Tom more interesting than she ever had before. At home, he seemed a world apart, absorbed in his books, friends, and work on the ranch. He never seemed to have much time for her. But here under his makeshift ground cloth shelter, Tom was much more patient and understanding. They talked about Emily—how much they would miss her—how sudden her death had been. "I'm worried about Mother and Dad too." Lisa said, her head downcast. "Why does Dad smell so bad? Why doesn't Mom have any energy?"

Tom explained as best he could.

Lisa began to cry. "Are Dad and Mom going to die?"

Tom put a comforting arm around her. "We'll be rescued," he said, but his voice didn't have much conviction. "We need to be down from the campsite near the trail so we can holler if we hear anyone." They sat side-by-side reading their books until almost four. The snow was slanting down in big, thick flakes. Tom appeared to fall asleep, for his head went down on his chest. He shook his head and asked, "Could you watch for a while? I'm so awfully tired."

Tom slept half an hour, then an hour. Suddenly, Lisa saw a large pair of green-yellow eyes in the shadows beyond the fire pit. The trees rustled and the head and chest of a large brown bear emerged from the brush. Lisa screamed in terror.

Tom woke up and saw the bear. He slowly bent down to retrieve two empty tin cans by his feet. The bear didn't move. Lisa's face turned green and she froze in her place. Tom turned to face the bear and beat the cans loudly with a stout stick.

Lisa screamed again, sure that the bear would attack. After a long pause, the beast turned his head and slowly ambled off to the left. "He was looking for food," Tom said. "Lucky, we hung our packs up high."

Lisa moved closer to her brother. "You were terribly brave," she said.

"It's just something Dad taught me to do." he said. "I'm glad we were so far from the tent that we didn't seem to wake Ma or Dad."

"They were probably both sleeping," Lisa said, wondering with fear whether either one could be dead.

"Let them sleep. They need it. It's getting dark now. We should go into the tent."

Lisa moved closer to her older brother. "It's up to us, isn't it?" she said.

"Yes, it's up to us," he replied.

It had been a tough climb for Wilderness Ranger Ed Grant, even with snowshoes. Still tired from his work extending a fire line around the Panther Creek fire, he had little rest before beginning this rescue mission.

It was nearly eleven before he could drive his jeep up to the Livingston Mill. He checked in with the mine caretaker and started crunching through more than eighteen inches of snow up the first steep slope. Reaching the sign-in board, he found it strange that the last page had been torn off.

The trail was tramped down some so he made fairly good time until the junction where the Frog Lake trail branched off to the south and the Walter Lake trail headed west.

The way was steep and Ed frequently tired. About two, the snow began slanting down hard between the pines and visibility grew worse. It took all of Ed's skill not to lose the trail. He worried that he wouldn't reach Frog Lake before dark and would have to set up camp on a hillside.

Just at five, when he was almost exhausted, the trail leveled. A hundred yards ahead was a tent and a couple sitting around the campfire. "Hi there. I'm the Wilderness Ranger," he shouted.

Blizzard in August 107

"You looked like a ghost with all that snow on your coat," the man answered. "I'm George ... George Anderson and this is my wife, Wilma. We were about to have some hot chocolate. Would you like some?"

"I sure would." Ed paused and looked around for another tent. "Is there another family camped up here? The Wagners?"

"Not that I know of," George said. "And I fished most of the lake."

"The Wagners are lost. I better call Livingston Mill." Ed brought out his four pound, handheld radio and made the call.

"Are you planning to spend the night here?" George asked.

"Yes, it's too dangerous to make it back in the dark in this snow when I'm so tired. Can I set up my tent near yours?"

"It would be our pleasure."

"And will you be going back to Livingston Mill tomorrow morning?" Wilma wanted to know.

"Yes, and I'd like to try to persuade you both to go with me." "That's what I want." Wilma said. "I turned my ankle and it feels like a bad sprain."

"I towed a lightweight ski stretcher up with me. You can get a ride back on it."

Wilma smiled. "Let's go tomorrow while we still have a chance."

George nodded. "Snow camping in a blizzard isn't much fun and the fishing is lousy."

Chapter 27

Clayton and Livingston Mill – Saturday morning – August 31st

Ray Winters walked through freezing rain from his house to the Clayton Ranger Station at six-thirty Saturday morning, August 31st. He wondered if this was going to be the beginning of a Chinook? Would streams now overflow with the melting snow?

Ray hung up his coat and phoned his friend Joe Brezinski. Joe would be up at this time and have contacted his special weather sources in Boise. "Joe, what's the weather report?" he began. "We have a freezing rain in Clayton."

"It's snowing here in Stanley," Joe replied. "So far we've had seven inches of new snow overnight and it's still snowing. However, the temperatures are going up and my weather sources predict some clearing by tomorrow."

"How was your night?" Ray Winters asked. "Could you keep any roads open in last night's storm?"

"Not a one. Didn't even try after ten last night. My last two graders have aged five years in a week. My men are ready to drop dead from exhaustion. I may not even send the plows out until it lets up a little this morning." Joe paused. "What was your night like?"

"Hectic. I had Senator Wagner in my guest bedroom and he was itching to lead an expedition at ten last night to Livingston Mill." "Still looking for his brother and his family?" Joe asked.

"Yes. We had a sighting of a couple by air and sent Ed Grant, our best wilderness ranger, to Frog Lake to check it out. He found a couple that needed to come out but they weren't the Wagners."

"I've just been on the phone with Jim Watkins of the Redfish Lake Ranger Station," Joe said. "He said he's got more than a hundred backpackers still out in the snow. It's not my responsibility, but I'm worried about the backpackers."

Ray reached over his desk and plugged in the coffee pot. "I'm worried too. Many backpacking groups must be running out of food. Their families are worried too. I get a dozen calls a day."

"How about Senator Wagner?" Joe asked. "I bet he's making plenty of noise."

Blizzard in August   109

Ray grimaced. "He's bedded down at my house. He phoned the Governor twice trying to get him to call out the National Guard."

Joe's voice raised a notch. "Is the Governor going to do it? I could use them right now on Galena Summit."

"No." Ray looked at the rain outside. "It's raining in Boise and other lower elevations. The Guard is stretched thin because of the War and the Governor doesn't think this is enough of an emergency." Ray paused and said, "The Senator isn't beaten yet. He wants me to call a news conference to see if anyone can help him locate his brother."

"You're in luck, if you want a news conference." Joe said. "The Twin Falls station has a man who wants to do a special TV show on the blizzard. He's coming from Challis. I suggested he stop off at your ranger station."

"Thanks. That's all I need," Ray said as he hung up.

At eight. Senator Wagner walked in the door of the Ranger Station. He had been well fed by Mrs. Winters and was full of energy. He welcomed the news of the television special. He wanted Ed Grant to hike down to Livingston Mill as quickly as possible and then start packing up towards Walter Lake.

Wagner suggested an interesting way of discovering his brother's true destination. "Why don't you have Ed take a graphite stick or soft lead pencil and rub it on the sign-in-sheet below the sheet that was torn off. This may show what was on the top sheet."

"Good idea," Ray said enthusiastically. "I'll leave a message for Ed with the mill caretaker to do that first. That may save Ed from another trip to the wrong lake."

The television crew arrived at ten and Senator Wagner reveled in the publicity. He depicted his county as paralyzed with snow, with brave men in the Forest Service trying to get all the campers and backpackers safely out. He zeroed in on the plight of his brother and his family and said they might be sick or injured. "If anyone knows what lake my brother is camped at, please call this Ranger Station immediately," the Senator said and provided his viewers with the phone number.

Ed Grant fought his way through driving snow that morning on his way down from Frog Lake. Wilma Anderson was bundled up in a blanket on the ski stretcher with Ed pulling on the front rope and George Anderson holding on to the back rope when the stretcher was going downhill.

The wind howled as they came down the steep slope into the valley, and the snow that slanted in on them was so thick that visibility was less than twenty feet. Time and time again Ed lost the trail and had to leave the stretcher with George while he back-tracked. It was three-thirty before the weary party reached Livingston Mill.

Ray Winters had left a message for Grant with the mill caretaker. It was too late for Ed to start up the trail to Walter Lake that night, but he could hike a half a mile back to the sign-in box taking with him some graphite and a soft lead pencil. The first page that had not been tom off recorded the names of only three parties. Ed was able to rub the page with soft lead and find the line on which Herman Wagner signed his name and listed his destination as Frog Lake or maybe Goat or Island Lakes on August 25th.

Ed tried to decipher the other lines. Darry Baltz and party went in on August 26th and out on August 29th. Darry listed Walter Lake as his destination. The Peterson party went in on the 24th to Walter Lake and out on the 28th. A man named Patrick listed himself and two others signed on August 24th to Walter Lake and out on the 28th. The earliest entry was blurred. He could read only that Cove Lake was the destination of some unknown backpacker.

Ed called Ray Watkins when he returned to the Mill. He was instructed to hike up towards Goat and Island Lakes on Sunday and try to find the Wagners.

Chapter 28

Cove Lake – Saturday morning

Kelli lay in her sleeping bag thinking about Hank. Her questions last night were sharp and persistent, but she had learned much about him. She knew he had a strong degree of self-control. She could count on him.

As the first rays of light filtered through the tent, Hank slipped out of the sleeping bag. A minute later. Hank yelled with dismay. "Something, or somebody, knocked our frying pan off the stone and pushed the stones of the fire pit around."

Kelli listened as she heard Hank walk towards the hill and then heard him saying, "Oh, no, I thought I had them well buried." "What's wrong?" Kelli asked as Hank returned.

"I think there was a bear in camp last night while we were asleep. He found the three fish buried up the hill. And he tried to get at the backpack that held the food. But I had it tied too far off the ground and too far from each tree."

"Thank goodness. Then we're all right." Kelli said through the tent.

"We're not okay. All we have left in the backpack is one package of graham crackers, a handful of apricots, and a package of freeze-dried onion soup. That won't feed us properly today."

"But can't you catch any more fish?" Kelli asked.

She heard him pull out the worm box from under the tarp. "Good news. The bear didn't discover my worm box," he said. A minute later he added, "I have just eight nightcrawlers left. I'll have to make every one count. We'll need to pray that I catch fish today."

Hank came back in the tent. "We had a special talk last night. It has been wonderful knowing you. No matter what happens to us, we'll have some pleasant times to remember."

Kelli was touched by his remarks. Hank was special—so different from Sterling, her ex-husband. Her mind drifted off. Hank would probably have made a much better husband than Sterling, she thought. And I'd have babies by now.

Hank sat on a corner of the sleeping bag and said nothing for a moment. "I hate to bring it up," he said quietly, "but I'm worried about whether the Forest Service knows where we are."

Kelli became shocked and concerned now. "What do you mean. Hank? Darry must have told them. Or one of the others. They must have reached Livingston Mill by now."

"I'm not sure," Hank said. "This is Saturday. Darry and his party must have reached Livingston Mill on Thursday. There was a plane on Thursday but it sounded like it flew over Frog Lake and Five Mile Meadows. It got nowhere near us. There were no planes flying over us Friday and no search party." He paused, his eyes downcast. "I just wonder whether anyone told the Forest Service where we were." "Why wouldn't Darry tell them? Or have Jason call them? Maybe the phone was out at Livingston Mill." Kelli tried to keep her voice reassuring but she was having doubts too.

"If they reached Livingston Mill Thursday, they would have two days to get to Clayton or Challis and report our position," Hank said. "I'm sorry to say this, but I just don't trust Darry. I'm not sure he made that call." Hank's faced flushed. "Darry's a bastard."

"That's the second time you've called him 'a bastard.' What do you mean...he's illegitimate?"

Hank's voice had an edge. "No. By 'bastard' I mean someone who is completely self-centered and selfish … will do anything to reach his goals … doesn't give a damn about others. His father is like that you know … some day I'll tell you about him."

Kelli was disturbed and taken aback by this flash of Hank's temper. She waited a minute. "But one of the others would have called," Kelli said reassuringly.

"Maybe not, if Darry had told them he had phoned the Forest Service." There was a hard, bitter line to Hank's mouth. "I've come to hate him. Maybe I should go outside and pray about this."

"What's it like outside?" Kelli said. "I'd like to go outside with you. Please, Hank. It isn't good for you to be knotted inside with hate. Let me help."

"Well, it's snowing lightly and it's foggy. There's another eight inches of snow on the ground and it's tough walking." He paused. "With your poncho on, you won't get too wet." He smiled. "I'd love to have you with me, Kelli."

They pushed the snow off a log and sat side-by-side watching snow descend through the fog and hearing the stream rushing over the rocks into the lake. The wind was light and only slightly rippled the water. The bobber was in a perfect place—just where the current entered the deeper water. But there were no bites. Hank's mouth turned down at the ends. Kelli put an arm around

Blizzard in August 113

his shoulder to comfort him. Kelli broke the silence. "You know I thought Darry rolled a rock down on me. I'm not sure I'm right."

"How come?"

Kelli thought a minute. "When I got to the top of the slope I saw someone watching me with binoculars. He was about two hundred yards to the east down the ridgeline. That couldn't have been you, could it?"

"No, I was fishing Cove Lake all afternoon. And I didn't bring binoculars. He stroked his chin. "I wasn't where I could see the ridgeline. Could it have been Darry?"

"I'm almost positive that Darry didn't bring binoculars. Or did any other person in my party. Besides, Jason and Ann went to Cirque Lake while Darry and Pam continued on to Sapphire." Kelli looked north towards the ridgeline. "You don't suppose there's someone up there in that line of scrub pine spying on us right now?"

"And stealing our food and fish?" Hank frowned. "It's possible, but not likely."

They sat on the bank for three hours that morning and heard not a sound other than their own talking. They talked about their families, their jobs, the music they liked, their friends, and about Hank's daughters. Kelli came to trust him enough to say that she would like to have children of her own some day. It began to snow a little but she felt warm inside.

Finally, at about one. Hank's bobber went under. He set the hook and brought in an eleven-inch trout. It was the smallest fish he had caught thus far but they were grateful. Hank went upstream to gut the trout, washed the blood and entrails out of it, and brought the head and tail back to the lake to toss as far out in the water as he could.

As the snow began to fall faster, he made a fire, cooked the package of soup and cooked the fish. "We'll save the graham crackers and apricots for tonight's meal," he said. "Tomorrow, I'll try to catch more fish."

"Tomorrow, we'll be rescued," Kelli said.

Hank didn't respond. He looked out at the damp snow falling rapidly from a leaden, foggy sky and then looked up at the ridgeline. Kelli shivered. Somewhere out in the lake basin was one or more hungry bears or, perhaps, a hungry, desperate man with a pair of binoculars.

Chapter 29

Goat Lake Trail – Saturday

Tom Wagner slid out of his sleeping bag a little before seven. He had not slept much that night. His mother had difficulty breathing and her labored breaths, her coughing, and her wheezing made sleep difficult. When he did manage to sleep, his father would cry out in pain. Dressing quickly and quietly, Tom hoped for warmth and quiet under his shelter. It would be nice if we got some sun today, he thought, as he unzipped the tent flap.

A damp fog had settled in the narrow valley and Tom could see it had snowed about eight inches overnight. Snowflakes were drifting through the trees, so at first Tom didn't see the two brown bears a hundred feet away. Somehow, they had knocked down the backpacks he had hung up on a rope last night. One had his nose in Tom's father's pack, pushing it slowly over the wet snow, searching for something to eat.

The other had his mouth in a tin-foil-wrapped, freeze-dried dinner. Probably the hot chili dinner that the family decided to leave for today. Tom and Lisa's packs were also on the ground and both appeared to be open. Tom was appalled. They didn't have much food remaining, and the bears had probably gotten it all.

Advancing to the fire pit, Tom rapped his tin can and a stick. The bears stood their ground. He walked fifteen feet more towards them, banging the tin can. The nearest bear stood up and made a noise that almost sounded like a growl. Tom retreated, but the bear didn't follow. He watched in silence, helpless to keep the bears from finishing the last of their food.

When they finally moved into the woods, Tom inspected the packs. All four had been opened—either by being clawed open or having their sides bitten through. All food remaining in the four packs had been consumed. Tom kicked at the snow angrily; he should have kept watch from his shelter last night.

Tom was beginning to feel hunger in the pit of his stomach when Lisa unzipped the tent and came out.

"Ma is sure loud when she breathes," she complained. "I'd like some hot chocolate for breakfast."

Blizzard in August

"There's none," Tom said, his voice edgy. "The bears got all our food last night."

"I had some in the bottom of my pack," Lisa said. "It wasn't with the rest of the food."

"Go look." Tom pointed to where the packs lay.

Lisa went to where the packs lay and inspected her own backpack. "You're right, a bear got everything in my pack too ... the hot chocolate, part of a Hershey bar, and even my soap. What are we going to do now?" she wailed.

Tom put a brotherly arm around her, but he had no consoling words. They sat under the tarp in Tom's shelter until their father woke up and called for them. "What's it like outside?" he yelled.

"Cold, damp, foggy, and snowing—but not snowing hard," Tom responded. "We need to know what to do. The bears got the rest of our food."

"Damn. Help me out of here," his father demanded. Together, they pulled and tugged and helped their father crawl to the fire pit. They brought the packs over for inspection and he expressed anger and dismay as he opened each one.

"What do we do? We've got to have something to eat. Shall I try to make it to Livingston Mill?" Tom asked.

"You can't do it in one day with more than two feet of snow on the ground. You'd freeze to death." Herman pondered a minute. "Are there any worms left?"

Tom went over to his shelter and opened the worm box. "A dozen, maybe a few more," he said.

"Goat Lake has some ten-inch brook trout. Wait an hour or two until it's warmer. Then go down the trail and try to catch as many as you can. Use the worms sparingly ... just a third or half a worm at a time on the hook."

"Who will watch the trail?" Tom asked.

"Lisa and I will," his father replied.

After an hour Tom took his rod, put some hooks, bobbers, sinkers, and a pair of thin-nosed pliers in his pocket, and carried the worm box in his other hand. Goat Lake wasn't that far away but it took three quarters of an hour to reach it through the more rapidly falling snow.

Tom had a sense of peace and serenity fishing Goat Lake. The water was almost calm as he cast his bobber out. The mist was so dense that he couldn't see the other side of the lake and he imagined it to be an immense Arctic lake filled with huge, fighting rainbows. His bobber went under, he set the hook and pulled in a fish. It was about nine and a half inches, he thought, as he brought a stringer out of his pocket and hooked the fish through the gills.

Fishing was good that morning. Three hours later he had six fish, though he had used up most of the worms. The way back was steep and several times he feared he had lost the trail. It was about one when he finally reached his shelter. His father was lying on his side in pain and Lisa had an arm around him.

"Six trout," Tom said proudly.

"Great. I knew you'd come through," his father said through gritted teeth. "Now you need to cut off their heads and tails and gut them." He paused. "Better go downstream so as not to attract the bears."

When Tom returned from cleaning the fish, his father had him build a big fire. There was some dry wood under the tarp to use for a start, and once that was burning Tom and Lisa could add the underbranches from a thicket of pines nearby. There was a lot of smoke next to the dry burning branches at first, then the wetter twigs caught fire and finally the branches. The iron fry pan was close to one of the packs the bears had ripped open. At his father's request, Tom washed it in the stream and set it on three flat rocks near the fire. Then he filled the pan with four of the fish and put it on to cook.

When the fish were done, Tom brought them to show to his father and put three on plates. Tom's father wolfed down his fish as Tom and Lisa ate theirs more slowly. The fourth fish went back in the pan to be warmed, and then Herman Wagner asked his son and daughter to help him back into the tent with a plate of fish. "Trudy will love this," he said. "She loves fresh-caught fish."

There was no heavy breathing when they got inside the tent, and Tom was glad at first. His mother was resting more easily. Her mouth was wide open, he saw, and her eyes staring ahead. His father pushed the plate of fish under her nose so she could smell it but she didn't react. His father put down the plate, touched her brow and then put his fingers on her wrist.

Suddenly his father was howling, then crying, then wailing like a mortally wounded animal. It was terrible, eerie, a wail that Tom would remember all his life. Lisa burst into tears. Tom put his hand on his mother's pulse and started to cry too. His mother was dead.

Chapter 30

Cove Lake – Saturday night

Hank had difficulty falling asleep after he climbed into the sleeping bag with Kelli that night. It was partly his concern about the lack of food, and the bears (or possibly a man) out there that was stealing their food. He wasn't sure how long they could exist without food—possibly two days—perhaps as long as a week if they didn't expend much energy. He kept thinking it was partly his fault—that he shouldn't have lost his temper at Darry when the man had stood at the top of the snow bank, refusing to come to their help. He also blamed himself for not hiding the fish better.

Earlier in the evening he had mentioned his concerns to Kelli just as they got into the sleeping bag. She had given his chest a squeeze with her arms and told Hank that he shouldn't blame himself—that he had saved her life and had done more to help her than any man she knew would have done. She cried a little and gently kissed the back of his neck.

Kelli went to sleep but Hank could not. He kept thinking of how close he and Kelli had become in just a few days. She was a self-confident, professional woman whom he admired. But she also had a very feminine, nurturing way of lifting his spirits when he felt depressed. And he couldn't forget her kisses. They burned into his mind. They were signs that she had a very passionate nature.

By eleven Hank still couldn't sleep and he had worked himself up to the point that he ached to hold Kelli in his arms and make love to her. But he knew he shouldn't. All he could do was lie there, as still as he could, and imagine making love to her.

Close to midnight, Hank heard a noise outside the tent. Kelli heard it too and woke up. "What's that?" she whispered to Hank.

"Don't know," Hank whispered back. He slipped out of the sleeping bag, dressed, and got a flashlight and his hunting knife.

"Be careful," Kelli said. "I don't know what I'd do if I lost you."

Once under the fly of the tent, Hank banged two cans together. He looked out to see two large brown bears ambling away. He shone his powerful flashlight on them and they disappeared up the slope beyond his beam. He waited for a few minutes and then re-entered the tent.

"Just two bears. I scared them away," Hank said nonchalantly so as not to alarm Kelli.

"I'm frightened," she said. "I haven't had this experience in my California backpacking. Or the heavy snow either."

Hank looked sympathetically at her. There was not much he could say to reassure her. He put an arm around her and said, "We'll make it through."

She said nothing but her arms went up around his neck and she kissed him passionately. Hank returned the kisses and his mouth sought her earlobes and neck. Suddenly they found themselves lying full-length on their sides on the sleeping bag with their arms entwined around each other.

"I care for you very much," Kelli said between kisses. "I don't know how it's possible to fall in love in just four days, but I have."

"Oh, Kelli, I have strong feelings, too." He paused kissing her full on the mouth. "I didn't come on this backpack trip to meet someone. I was grieving for Susan … I still am. But you're such a wonderful woman. I'm losing my heart."

"I've lost mine," Kelli said. "I'm a passionate woman and I want you … I ache for you." She took Hank's hand and placed it on her breast.

Hank tried to sit up but her arms held him down and her breast felt so soft. "Kelli, I'm losing my self-control and I'm not prepared," he said. "We need to cool it."

Kelli smiled. "I don't want to stop." She began to pull off her sweater.

Hank could not fully remember everything that happened in the next hour. They both undressed and climbed in the partly unzipped sleeping bag. Lovemaking was slow and sensuous at first. He explored Kelli's breasts and legs while she explored his entire body. Then, they came together and Hank found his heart pounding and his passion reaching new heights. When it was over, they lay together for more than half an hour—kissing and touching and expressing their love. Kelli said, "I have never in my life been this excited before."

Hank replied, "I was very excited, too." Inwardly, he began to feel a little ashamed at his burst of passion. Was he disloyal to Susan? He pondered this as they both climbed out of the sleeping bag to put on their clothes. Before they returned to the sleeping bag, Hank brought his hunting knife and flashlight within easy reach.

Kelli seemed to have forgotten about the bears and was soon sound asleep. Hank had not forgotten and lay awake for a few minutes listening for them.

Chapter 31

Cove Lake – Sunday Morning, September 1st

Kelli woke Sunday morning at 4 a.m. with hunger pains in her stomach but a glow in her heart. She was in love. Hank was such a patient and skillful lover—and so passionate when fully aroused. Suddenly, Kelli heard a noise. A log had moved near the fire pit. She raised her head to hear better. Silence. Then the frying pan clanged against a rock. "Hank, wake up," she called.

"Huh," he said. "It's still dark."

"I heard the pot banging against a rock. It may be a bear," Kelli warned.

They both listened. The frying pan was banging again. "The bear's probably licking it," Hank whispered. "Let's be quiet. Maybe he'll go away."

Kelli saw Hank slip out of his sleeping bag and pull a hunting knife from its sheath. She shivered and wriggled further into the sleeping bag.

A scraping noise came from the front of the tent near the fly. Kelli tried to remember what had been left there besides firewood— the wet ponchos were there and the box of nightcrawlers. Fortunately, they had brought their boots inside the tent last night. There was silence and then the sound of the poncho and worm box being mauled. Then suddenly the tent fly collapsed.

Kelli was terrified. Was the bear trying to get into the tent? She started to get out of the sleeping bag and her shoulder hit the edge of the tent. Almost instantly she felt a sharp pain in her shoulder as a bear claw pierced the side of the tent where it had bulged and ripped into her shoulder. Kelli cried out in pain and fell back.

Hank motioned Kelli to move more to the center of the tent and he waited, knife in hand. The bear widened the hole in the tent with his mouth, stuck his head through, his jaw huge. Kelli wanted to scream but the sound was stifled in her throat.

Hank dropped his knife and picked up the two sides of his large sweater and his flashlight. The bear pushed his head farther and farther into the tent. Suddenly Hank's powerful flashlight shone directly into the bear's eyes. His hands moved quickly, pulling his sweater over the bear's head and then just as quickly reaching for his knife.

The bear seemed bewildered and tried to rub the sweater off on the tent. Hank's hand moved with amazing speed slicing into the bear's throat, cutting the jugular vein and windpipe. The bear moved backwards and brought his head out of the tent. Kelli heard him take a dozen heavy steps, then a thump as if he had fallen. Was the bear dead? Kelli hoped so, for there is no more dangerous an animal than a badly wounded bear.

Hank waited silently. She wondered if he was worried about the danger of more bears? She heard nothing except the wind coming through the tear in the tent and shook in fright.

Kneeling with his knife upraised. Hank appeared stunned for the moment. "How badly were you clawed?" he asked.

The pain was sweeping over Kelli, "It hurts awful," she managed to say.

"I have to patch the tent before everything gets wet," Hank said. "Then we'll bandage your shoulder."

Slowly, carefully, Hank unzipped the tent and pushed himself out, flashlight in hand. Kelli couldn't breathe. Was another bear waiting silently outside ready to claw Hank to death? Then Hank called, "All clear. Just one bear, and he's dead down by the lake."

Kelli relaxed and then the pain hit her again. "My shoulder hurts bad; hurry fixing he tent."

It took Hank just a few minutes to put Duct tape first on the outside of the tent where the bear had bitten a hole, and then on the outside of the tent flap. "They're just temporary repairs," Hank said. "But they should hold for a few days." Hank removed Kelli's heavy sweater, her sweatshirt, and even her bra. In the light of his flashlight. Hank disinfected the wound with hydrogen peroxide, applied some antiseptic salve, and then expertly bandaged it. Kelli cried out in pain as the hydrogen peroxide stung her wound, but she felt a little better after it was bandaged.

After that they lay in silence in the sleeping bag listening intently for the sound of another bear. None came. At dawn Hank cautiously crept out of the tent and reported, "No bears around. I don't want this carcass around either, but a few bear steaks would give us extra food." He cut a dozen large chunks of bear meat from the shoulder and buried them in the snow. Then, using a log as a lever, he rolled the rest of the carcass into the lake.

Kelli came out of the tent about ten o'clock and sat on a log while Hank fished. She could not see across the lake because of the snow and a dense fog. Kelli's cheeks were drawn; she was still in pain.

It took an hour for Hank to catch his first fish. He tried flies to no avail. Then, after losing his bait to a fish that pulled his bobber under, he caught a fourteen-inch rainbow on the other half of the nightcrawler. Thirty minutes later, with the loss of another nightcrawler, he had his second fish. After

Blizzard in August 121

cleaning both fish, he started a fire and cooked them. Hank said he would save the bear meat for tomorrow to eat and try to use as fish bait.

Kelli went into the tent at 2 p.m., but Hank stayed outside to signal a plane or helicopter if one should fly over. None came. At five, he entered the tent, saying that the dense fog never lifted.

"What are our chances of survival?" Kelli asked.

He hesitated. "Less than fifty-fifty even if we aren't attacked by bears again. All we have left is some tough bear meat, and you need to see a doctor. We've got to pray the fog lifts and someone flies over our campsite soon."

"It's been wonderful knowing you," Kelli said. "If I die, I'll die remembering the love we shared. I'll never regret that."

Hank kissed Kelli lightly on the mouth. She crawled into the sleeping bag and he followed. She tried to go to sleep but couldn't. Each little sound outside was magnified a hundred times in her mind. Would another bear come tonight? she wondered.

Chapter 32

Goat Lake Trail - Sunday

The pain in the pit of Tom Wagner's stomach played a persistent bass tune on his nerves. Tom looked out from his makeshift shelter at the gently falling wet snow and the clinging white fog. "We're in bad trouble," he said. "Dad is hurt bad, and no one can find us by air in this fog."

He thought of his mother and Emily lying dead in the tent and became deeply depressed.

Lisa, sitting by Tom's side, began to cry softly, and Tom put an arm around her shoulders.

"I'm hungry," Lisa whined.

"I'm starving," Tom complained. "There's nothing to eat in this camp. But maybe that was a good thing last night."

"Why?" Lisa asked.

"We had bears last night. At least two of them."

"I didn't hear them," Lisa said.

"I did. They were nosing around the fire pit and pushing our packs around. But they didn't find a thing. They finally went away." Tom remembered his relief when the bear noises stopped outside the tent. He was afraid the bears would attack and wondered if it was the smell that kept them away. It was the smell of death, Tom thought. It was the putrid smell of his mother who died yesterday, Emily who died two days ago, and his father whose leg was festering. He had fallen asleep finally and dreamed of a black scarecrow-like figure flying through the air—picking up Emily first—then his mother—then his father—then Lisa—and finally flying back for him.

Tom dared not share his dream with Lisa. He read for a while and then said, "We've got to eat to keep up our strength. I need to go fishing again at Goat Lake."

"Don't leave me alone," Lisa wailed. "Don't let the bears get me."

"I'll have Dad come out and stay with you," Tom said. He went to the tent but no amount of talking and persuading could get his father to leave the tent. He kept saying that his leg hurt too much and that Trudy needed him to be right there.

Blizzard in August   123

In the end, Tom took Lisa with him to Goat Lake. The trip down was not all that difficult. The snow was getting wet as they reached the lower elevation near the lake; they found they could slide down the slope on their boots.

Once at the lake, Lisa sat beside Tom as he fished. It was amazing how she clung to him now. It was if he had become the father in the family.

The worms looked sluggish in the worm box he had strapped to his waist. He counted them; just six left. He better use them up; they wouldn't last another day. But luck was with Tom, or was it because Tom had done some praying before he made his first cast? Looking out on the dense gray fog hanging over the lake, he saw his bobber go under. He set the hook and soon had a ten and a half inch rainbow on shore. In the next two hours, Tom caught six more fish and used the last of his nightcrawlers. The trip back up the trail was much harder than the descent. Lisa kept slipping and sliding backwards and Tom needed to climb behind her to keep her from a dangerous fall.

Tom was exhausted when he reached the campsite, but he started to build a fire immediately. Fortunately, there were a lot of dead branches and twigs on the undersides of the pines.

With Lisa feeding the fire, Tom cleaned the fish in the stream and crammed four into a pan. He shoved the pan as close to the fire as he could without smothering it, expecting any minute to see a bear come into sight. None came.

Fifteen minutes later the fish were done. Tom and Lisa each took one on their plate. Tom wolfed his down, took another, and gave one to Lisa.

Between bites, Lisa said, "Are you going to give any to Daddy?"

"I'm saving the last three for Dad," he said. When he finished his second fish, he gave another to Lisa and went to the tent, skillet in hand.

"Dad," Tom shouted. "You need to come out of the tent. I have three fish for you. I'll help you outside so you can eat them. We don't want food in the tent. Bears will smell it."

"I don't want to come out," his father said.

"But don't you want to eat?" Tom used his most persuasive voice.

"No, leave me alone. Trudy needs me."

"But Ma is dead," Tom said, puzzled and alarmed that his father did not realize this.

His father's eyes were glassy as he mumbled, "I don't want to eat. I just want to be with Trudy. Leave me here to die."

"You can't die. You can't. You can't. You've got to eat," Tom's voice rose in agony. His father zipped up the tent fly. In deep despair, Tom and Lisa ate the last three fish.

Chapter 33

Twin Falls, Idaho - Sunday evening

Jason Green, listened to war news on television at six this Sunday evening, and then heard a report on the continuing blizzard in central Idaho. The camera showed three foot drifts where a snowplow had cleared the summit on Highway 93 between Arco and Challis. This was followed by interviews with Ray Winters and Senator Rudolph Wagner at the Clayton Ranger Station.

Jason listened closely when Senator Wagner told about his brother and his family lost in the White Clouds. Winters had first thought the Wagner family had gone to Frog Lake but a wilderness ranger had not found them there. The search now focused on Goat and Island lakes.

The Senator begged anyone who knew his brother's whereabouts to call the ranger station. Jason took down the number that flashed on the screen. He suddenly remembered a sound he had heard, a sound he thought on Wednesday might be a cry for help, a sound that Darry investigated and said was two trees rubbing together.

Then Jason wondered. Did Darry really inform the Forest Service where Hank and Kelli were camped? He went to the phone and called the number. It was six-thirty and the voice that answered identified himself as Ray Winters.

"I think I have some information on the whereabouts of Herman Wagner and his family," he said.

"Where are they?"

"I'll tell you in a minute," Jason said. "But first did you receive any notification of another couple camped at Cove Lake? The man was Hank Barclay and the woman was Kelli Johnson. She had a broken ankle and could not come down with the rest of Darry Baltz's party." "No, but let me check the records. When should we have been notified?"

"Thursday, the 29th," Jason said. "Darry told me that he phoned you," Jason said.

"Then he lied," the ranger replied. "Anyone who took the call would have logged it in." He paused. "Now tell me what you know about the location of the Wagners."

"When the news broadcast mentioned Goat Lake, something clicked in my mind. On the afternoon of Wednesday the 28th, I was leading Darry Baltz's

Blizzard in August   125

party down from Island Lake towards Five Mile Meadows. Ann Pettigrew was following me closely and Pamela Pettigrew and Darry Baltz were in the rear. When I got close to where the Goat Lake trail intersects the main trail, I heard a strange noise. It sounded a little like a wail or a cry but might have been two trees rubbing together. I wanted to go back to investigate but Darry told me and Ann to keep going and that he and Pam would go back and find out."

"What was it?" the ranger asked.

"When Darry caught up with us later, he said it was two trees rubbing together."

"And you think he might have lied?"

"Yes." Jason said. "But please don't tell Darry I said that. He might try to get my uncle fired."

"Who are you?" the ranger asked. "It's important we know. We may need to contact you later."

"My name is Jason Green. My uncle is superintendent of the Wilson Creek Mine, and I work for him during the summer. I'm studying mining engineering at the University of Idaho.

"What's your connection to Darry Baltz and the Pettigrews?" the ranger asked.

"The mine is owned by the conglomerate run by Big Mike Baltz, Darry's father. Darry was invited on the backpack trip by Pam Pettigrew, his girlfriend. Darry had never backpacked into the White Clouds and hired me to lead the party."

"Who was in the party again?" the ranger asked. "The sign-out sheet was tom off but we made a carbon impression of the backup sheet. The sheet just listed Darry Baltz and party."

"Darry...that's Darrington Baltz, Pamela and Ann Pettigrew and me. The four of us packed out to Livingston Mill on Thursday the 29th. Then there was Kelli Johnson, the girls' aunt. She was supposed to be their chaperone. She fell into Cove Lake from a snow slide and broke an ankle. I went into the lake after her and brought her to shore. Hank Barclay came running up soon afterwards and helped pull her out. We took off her boots and her ankle was badly swollen."

"Who is this Hank Barclay?" the ranger asked.

"1 don't know. He's huge. Unshaven as he was, he looked like a mountain man. He urged us all to camp with him where the stream empties into Cove Lake. I agreed. It was a good idea to camp together and all go out together the next day. But Darry wanted to leave Kelli there and get down to Island Lake that night."

"So he left Kelli with this mysterious mountain man, with a broken ankle and probably wet clothes. And the mountain man took her in." The ranger paused. "Do you think this Hank is a Good Samaritan or interested in something else?"

"He was a nice guy, I think." Jason said. "He certainly tried to argue us out of leaving Kelli with him. You'll send a plane up there to see if they're still camped at Cove Lake, won't you?"

"Tomorrow morning. I'll try to get a helicopter to overfly Cove Lake. But we'll need better visibility than we had today. The helicopter can also try to find the Wagner campsite but that valley is covered with tall pines and we may not be able to spot them."

"Will you be sending some wilderness rangers there on foot?" Jason asked.

"I have one of my best on his way up to Five Mile Meadows," the ranger assured him. "There's three feet of snow on the ground, so I'm not sure he will get farther than that tomorrow. Say, Mr. Green, will you be at this number for a few days?"

"Yes," Jason said. "I don't drive back to the university until the fifth of September."

"Good," the ranger said. "I'd like to talk longer now but I need to make preparations for a helicopter to fly over tomorrow. And I need to call Senator Wagner. He will be very anxious to hear the news."

"He will be pleased we have a better fix on his brother's location and will want to thank you. But he won't be pleased about this Darry who passed his brother's party by without helping. Say ... who was it that signed out your party on Thursday the 29th."

"I was going to. But Darry told me to go on with the girls; he said he would sign out. Didn't he sign out?"

"The top sheet was torn off," Winters said. "And it looks as though your Darry was the last person to see the sheet. I think the Senator will be very interested in that bit of information."

The ranger hung up, leaving Jason feeling pleased that he had relayed the information that might save both Kelli and the Wagners. But Winter's final comment about the Senator left Jason uneasy. Jason had heard that the Senator had opposed Big Mike Baltz and his conglomerate takeover of the locally owned mine. But Jason was also getting uneasy about the ethics of his backpacking companion, Darrington Baltz.

Chapter 34

Three Mile Meadows – Sunday Evening

Vomit welled up within Ed Grant's throat. Dizzy, sweating, he tried to keep from falling. Suddenly it all came out, like molten lava exploding out of a volcano—a green, smelly liquid that spewed on his boots and the ground in front of him. Unable to stand, he sat down heavily and took off his pack.

A second wave of nausea hit Ed three minutes later and he was able to direct it away from where he was sitting. What was it? Ed wondered. Food poisoning? A twenty-four hour stomach flu? His stomach had felt queasy since one o'clock. Now, three hours later, he had gotten so sick that it would be hard to stand up, let alone carry a pack.

A third wave of nausea racked his body and he moved afterward so he did not have to smell his own puke. He passed his hand over his forehead trying to keep the sweat out of his eyes. He had to think. He was a few hundred yards from a level place he called Three Mile Meadows; there was no way he could get to Five Mile Meadows before dark. In his condition, he doubted he could get to Island Lake tomorrow.

A fourth wave of nausea engulfed Ed. Damn, he thought. I shouldn't have promised Ray Winters I would be camped at Five Mile Meadows tonight and be able to explore Goat Lake and Island lakes tomorrow. Wearily, he thought of the past week—twenty-hour days on the fire line—a tedious rescue mission to Frog Lake—poor food and little sleep. And now I'm sick.

Ed threw up five more times in the next half hour and felt himself getting weaker. There was only one thing to do to: survive the night. He had to get to a level spot as quickly as he could before it became dark. Ten minutes later he shouldered his pack and trudged slowly up hill.

Half an hour later, Ed found a level space among the trees at Three Mile Meadows. He unpacked, set up his tent, and put his sleeping mat, sleeping bag, and clothes inside. He hung his pack between two trees as a protection against bears. Then he tried to call Ray Winters on his radio. It was seven before he reached the Clayton Ranger Station. He was standing in the dark holding the hand-held radio, hoping he didn't attract the attention of any bears.

"Ray," he said. "I'm at Three Mile meadows. I have food poisoning or a twenty-four hour stomach flu. I can't get to Five Mile Meadows tonight."

Ray's voice crackled over the line. "Look, I've gotten a tip that the Senator's brother and his family are camped close to where the Goat Lake trail intersects the Island Lake trail. Can you get there tomorrow?"

"I doubt it."

"I'll send another wilderness ranger up from Livingston Mill tomorrow morning. If neither of you can get to the Goat Lake trail by tomorrow at dusk, camp at Five Mile Meadows and clear a place for a helicopter landing." Ray Winter's voice crackled and then was gone. Ed put down the antenna on the radio and went inside the tent. His stomach was not churning but he felt very weak. He muttered, "Ray expects too much from me"

Ray Winters could hear the snow dripping off the roof of the Clayton Ranger Station. It was eight p.m. and he had one more phone call to make before he walked home. "Senator," he said when Rudolph Wagner was on the line. "I have good news and bad news."

"Give me the good news first, I need it," the Senator replied. "I received a tip that your brother and his family are camped close to where the Goat Lake trail intersects the trail between Five Mile Meadows and Island Lake."

"Can your ranger get to him tomorrow?"

"I don't know, Senator. Ed called in. He's camped for the night two miles short of Five Mile Meadows. He has the stomach flu or food poisoning; he can't go on for a while. I'm sending Vito Morelli up from Livingston Mill tomorrow morning, but he and Ed may only get to Five Mile Meadows by tomorrow evening."

"Can you get a helicopter?"

"I've set one up for a couple of flights tomorrow morning," Ray said. "But I have to warn you. The helicopter can spot people on relatively open ground like some areas around Goat and Island lakes. If my memory is correct, the Wagners are camped in an area of dense forests; the helicopter pilot may not be able to spot them there."

"You've got to get someone there tomorrow," the Senator's voice betrayed his sense of urgency. "They must be out of food. In two more days, someone in that family might be dead."

"I have another plan to get someone there tomorrow." "What?"

"I'll let you know later." Ray changed the subject. "Do you have any late news on the weather?"

"It's supposed to be sunny tomorrow with a freezing level of eight thousand feet in central Idaho." The Senator paused. "I'll be at my law office in Challis tomorrow. Call me when you have any more news."

Ray hung up the phone, put on his coat, and trudged home. Small streams had formed on the sides of the highway and the snow on the side of the road was wet. Perhaps, on September first, the August blizzard was finally over.

Chapter 35

Cove Lake, Goat Lake Trail – Monday Morning September 2nd

Hank woke at five to the unmistakable scraping of the pan near the fire pit. This time he was ready for them. He pulled himself out of the sleeping bag and clanged the back of his hunting knife on a large empty can.

Kelli woke with a start. "What's happening?" she asked. "There are bears in the campsite. Two, I think. Get closer to the center of the tent."

With effort Kelli crawled to the middle of the sleeping bag. "Do you hear anything?"

Hank banged away at the can with his knife. The footsteps retreated and then drew closer again.

"We need to do something now before the bear attacks," Kelli said, bringing her arms up to cover her head. "I dislike guns, but I wish you had one now."

"There's one more thing I can try," Hank said grimly. He pulled a round firecracker with a fuse from the side of the tent. "It's a cherry bomb. I keep one in my pack for emergencies." He unzipped the tent fly and lit the fuse. With a swift motion he threw it out in the direction of the noise.

Whaaam. The firecracker made even more noise in the still night air than Hank had remembered it would. Scampering footsteps followed. "I hope I've scared them off for good," Hank said.

He dared not sleep, but Kelli volunteered to stay up listening for an hour while Hank slept. Kelli promised to wake him at five-thirty but she stayed on watch until the dawn light showed through the tent. Then she woke Hank. Getting dressed quickly, he went outside cautiously. "No bears," he announced. "There's only about three inches of new snow … and the old snow is settling." Hank looked to the west beyond the dark outlines of the trees and rocks in deep shadow to the brilliant orange and buff of the Emperor and the ridge leading down to Cirque Lake. And beyond that was the brilliant light-cream-orange-tan of the Triangle rearing its head up to 11,500 feet. "Get dressed and come out," he said. "The sunrise is breathtaking. The bears have gone."

Blizzard in August 131

Kelli hobbled out two minutes later on a crutch Hank had made for her. She leaned on him and said, "This is one of the most beautiful sunrises I've ever seen. I wish I could paint it. Can you get my camera from my pack?"

She sat down and Hank brought the camera. Kelli took three pictures and had Hank take others. As it became lighter, the early morning sunlight hit other mountains. The Sorcerer to the south was brilliant orange-tan on the east side and burnt umber on the west. The ridge that led down to the snowfield was a cream-orange-tan and the snowfield itself, in shadow, had a bluish tinge. "It's a good omen," Kelli said. "I feel we're going to be rescued today."

"If they send a plane over, we should be spotted," Hank said. He tried fishing. The nightcrawlers were all gone, so he tried flies. The fish weren't biting on flies, so he tried one of his two spinners. It hung up on the bottom.

Hank looked at Kelli with concern. "How do you feel this morning?" he asked.

"My shoulder hurts me a lot more this morning," she said. "It may be infected. And my ankle is more painful now if I put any weight on it."

"We need to sit outside where a plane can get a good view of us." Hank paused. "We're completely out of food except for some chunks of bear meat that I'll need to skin before I cook. We need to drink a lot of water and conserve our energy, and I'll skin and cook the bear meat at noon, saving a little as fish bait." He paused. "I'm very worried about your shoulder and ankle. I'd like to pray now."

"You believe in prayer don't you," Kelli said.

"Yes, but prayer should begin by thanking God for all our many blessings and confessing our faults. Then I usually say some Bible verses that seem appropriate at the moment. It's afterwards that I pray to God for what I need."

"And what are your many blessings today?" Kelli asked.

"The beautiful sunrise and the colors of the mountains, for one," Hank said. "The sunshine today, the lack of any large amount of new snow, and most importantly that when I was deeply depressed by Susan's death, I met you. You've given me hope, a sense of purpose."

"I love you," Kelli said and put an arm around Hank's shoulders. "I suppose you have a Bible verse for the occasion," she kidded.

"Psalms 118:24," he said. "'This is the day which the Lord has made; let us rejoice and be glad in it.'"

"And you have faith in our future?"

Hank looked at the orange in the Emperor becoming lighter by the minute. "I think God has a plan for our lives. I don't think he'll let us die. But if we do, our spirit lives on if we have faith. Let's pray now."

They did pray then with arms around each other. Hank felt uplifted and prayed silently that Susan, in Heaven, would approve. Then he filled his canteen and gave it to Kelli.

They were sitting side by side on the log when at a little after nine, Hank heard the thump-thump-thump of a helicopter. It sounded like it was over Island Lake and then the sound grew louder. Suddenly over the low ridge on the west shore of Cove Lake it came, the most beautiful sight Hank had ever seen. He took off his sweater, stood up, and waved it. Kelli stood up on her crutch.

The chopper flew over Cove Lake, took a quick turn over Sapphire Lake, and came back. The chopper came down to about thirty feet, a door opened, and a bundle flew out. It came down in deep snow about fifty feet up the slope from his tent. Hank ran to get it.

"Food," the pilot yelled over the whir of the motors. "And a hand-held radio wrapped in blankets."

Then the chopper lowered a rope with a piece of paper attached. The rope dragged slowly across the ground and Hank caught up with it. Opening the note, he read. "Is this the lady with a broken ankle? Are you the man who cared for her?" Hank wrote "yes" to both questions and sent the note back up.

The rope was raised into the helicopter and lowered once more. Hank caught the rope, took off the note and read it to Kelli. "We can't land. It's too rocky. But we can lower a sling on this rope and lift the lady into our helicopter. It's quite safe. We'd like to take you, but we don't have room for four with the food we have."

Kelli read the note. "I won't leave without you," she protested.

"Please, Kelli," Hank begged. "The snow is settling. With a sunny day like this I can get down to Island Lake … maybe even to Five Mile Meadows and I'll have plenty of food from this pack and a radio to use if I need it. If you're safe, I'm free to pack my way out. And you need to see a doctor."

Kelli finally agreed. Hank motioned for the rope to be lowered and was surprised when a toboggan and snowshoes were tied on to the sling. "What's the note say?" Kelli asked.

"It has instructions about using the sling." Hank said. "And then it says there's a family camped where the Goat Lake trail intersects the Island Lake trail. They want me to find them and take the toboggan with me, in case I need to transport any injured. I can also put my tent and the food on it if I want to lighten my pack." Hank saw the worried look on Kelli's face. Was she going to refuse to leave again because of this new mission for him? He quickly smiled and said, "It won't be hard. I'll see you in Challis in a day or two. The hospital is there."

Blizzard in August

Hank gave her a hug and said, "I love you." They clung together and kissed; then he reached for the sling.

Kelli looked frightened as Hank placed her in the sling and tightened the straps and ropes. The helicopter pulled up the slack and she was whisked up into the air and reeled in. Hank saw a man in green pull her inside and wave his hand. Then the helicopter gained altitude as it flew over the high ridge to the south, probably to drop food to another family in the next lake basin.

It took an hour for Hank to take down the tent, pack up and tie their packs, the food, and airdropped supplies to the toboggan. The stream at the outlet of Sapphire Lake proved to be his first obstacle. He leapt across without his pack, bringing with him twenty feet of rope attached to the toboggan. Then he began to inch the toboggan across on the flat rocks.

The snow slide proved the most difficult. Hank chose a route well away from the overhang above the water. The snow had softened, giving him a good foothold. But it was very difficult pulling sixty pounds of food and packs up the two-hundred foot bank.

With all this effort, it was nearly one by the time he reached the divide separating the Cove and Island Lake basins. He looked back for a final view of Cove Lake. He put on the snow shoes and angled the toboggan upward towards the ridge route and, for the first time, worried whether he would run out of daylight before he reached the campers on the Goat Lake trail.

It had been a terrible night for Tom Wagner. The stench in the tent was almost unbearable and his father's cries of pain seemed unending.

When the roof of the tent received its first pale fingers of light, Tom left his sleeping bag, put on his boots, unzipped the tent flap and went outside. The first full breath of clean air was invigorating. He went to his shelter with his book, leaned his back and head against a tree, and promptly went back to sleep.

An hour later he heard his eight-year-old sister calling, "Where are you, Tom?"

"At the shelter," he yelled back.

"Any bears?" Lisa called.

Tom looked around. "No, I think they were into our packs again last night and knocked them around. But they're not here now."

Lisa joined Tom a few minutes later. "Anything to eat?" she asked anxiously.

"Nothing." There was an ache in the pit of his stomach that would not go away. He went to the creek, filled his canteen, and took a long drink. He offered his canteen to Lisa saying, "We need to drink a lot today."

Close to eight, his father called out for water. Tom filled his canteen and handed it to him. His father appeared wild-eyed and haggard as if he was a bit crazy. "Why don't you crawl outside? I can build a fire." Tom said.

"Gotta stay close to Trudy, son. She'll need me," his father's voice sounded weak and dazed.

"Ma's dead," Tom said. He was suddenly filled with a much stronger sense of loss than he felt yesterday.

"No, she's just sleeping," his father said. "I'm staying here."

Tom left the tent, ashamed he hadn't tried harder to get his father out. The stench had driven him off. It was the smell of death and his father was seeped in it. He wondered whether there was really an angel of death robed in black that came to get dying people. Tom knew his father would go to Heaven when he died and he would meet his mother. There were tears in Tom's eyes when he went back to his shelter.

"Would Dad come out of the tent?" Lisa asked.

"No," Tom said. "I think he's waiting there to die."

"Are we waiting here to die?" Lisa wailed.

"No. We're going to live," Tom yelled with all his strength. "We're going to drink lots of water. We're going to build a fire to keep warm … and we're going to live. We'll be here within sight of the Island Lake trail and yell like crazy when someone comes along."

About an hour later Tom heard the helicopter. It came up from the east, like it had flown over Five Mile Meadows. It flew up the valley well beyond the treetops, took a turn towards Goat Lake and came back to the valley west of their campsite. Tom and Lisa yelled and waved but the helicopter flew on and the spark went out of Tom's eyes. He had been hoping against hope that the red-haired man had finally told the Forest Service where he and his family were. Now he finally realized that it wasn't true. He considered for a moment whether Lisa and he should start down the trail to Five Mile Meadows.

He couldn't leave his dad, he realized. If his father died today, they might have the strength to pack the tent and try to leave tomorrow.

But would they have the strength tomorrow? Tom doubted it.

Chapter 36

Goat Lake Trail – Mo]nday Afternoon

Hank stood on the top of the steep slope above Island Lake and looked down. He had come in much too high on the ridge; he should have begun his descent earlier. Before starting down, he picked up the hand-held radio, which had been dropped with the supplies from the helicopter and called the Clayton ranger station. Ray Winters answered.

"I'm Hank Barclay, the man who was camped at Cove Lake."

"Yeah," the voice crackled back. "Where are you? I can barely hear your voice."

"At the top of the slope going down towards Island Lake," Hank reported.

"Can you get to the Goat Lake trail by dark?" Ray asked

"I'll give it a good try," Hank said. "I'm starting down the slope now. Over and out."

Hank pushed in the antenna, put the radiophone in his pack, and looked down the slope. His greatest danger was twisting his ankle.

Tom checked on his father three times during the day and brought him water. The stench in the tent was growing worse. He begged his father to come out into the fresh air but he refused.

Tom and Lisa had dozed off and on against the tree under the shelter as the sun flickered through the trees. The air felt warmer. The fire Tom built earlier that day had died out; there was no purpose for a fire now. He fished the stream briefly with flies and not gotten a bite so there were no fish to fry on the fire. Tom might have tried flies at Goat Lake but he didn't have the strength.

Tom and Lisa talked a little about school in the fall, but school seemed light-ages away to Tom. It was going to be different for them both. He would need to take on more responsibility at home now that Ma was dead.

Tom dozed in the relative warmth of the noon hour. He woke at three to see Lisa reading her book. "Have you heard from Dad since I went to sleep?" he asked Lisa.

"No. I thought of waking him, but I was scared," she said.

Tom went to the tent and heard no loud breathing or wheezing and no pained cries. He unzipped the flap and called, "You want me to fill up your canteen. Dad?"

No answer.

Tom looked inside. His father's mouth was open wide, his face was drawn, and his eyes staring as if he could see a long way off. Tom felt his father's wrist. No pulse. No breathing. His father was dead. Suddenly, Tom felt like crying, or howling like a wolf as his father had done at his mother's death. Instead, he put his head down on his chest crying softly in the tent until the stench drove him out.

"How's Papa?" Lisa called.

Tom checked his tears. "He's dead," he called with a wavering voice. He tried to compose himself, tried to appear strong for Lisa, but he broke down and cried in front of her. And so did she.

It was too late to pack up and start down the trail now. Tom sat for a long while, crying off and on with an arm about Lisa. He went back to the tent and tried to pull his father out. He couldn't budge him. And he couldn't budge his mother. They would have to spend the night in the tent with two dead parents. Would he and Lisa both be dead by morning?

Tom heard it way off about dusk. It was a voice up the trail towards Island Lake. It seemed too faint to be real at first. Maybe you hear things you want to hear when you are desperate—like the traveler in a desert sees a mirage—a water hole that's not real.

Then the voice became louder. "Haloo," it sounded like.

Tom jumped up and yelled. The voice kept getting a little louder.

Suddenly Tom realized he couldn't let anyone go by on the Island Lake trail like he let the red-haired man go by. He ran upstream a hundred feet where the log crossed the stream and pushed himself across the log on the seat of his pants.

The voice was louder now. Tom wasn't where he could be seen from the trail. He ran towards the trail, crashing through the underbrush and deep snow, yelling as hard as he could, hoping he wasn't going to be too late.

"Haloo," the voice called again. "I can hear you. Where are you?"

"I'm coming towards the trail," Tom yelled. "Stand still. Don't pass me by."

"I'm standing still," the man yelled. "I'll keep yelling so you can find me."

Two minutes later Tom burst through the underbrush, reached the Island Lake trail, and saw the man less than sixty feet away. "Don't leave me," he yelled in desperation.

Blizzard in August

"Why would 1 leave you?" the man asked. "I came down this trail to find you. Aren't you camped near the Goat Lake trail? Where are your parents?"

Tom looked up into the unshaven face of this giant of a man. He hoped to God the man was friendly. "They're both dead," he said simply. "And so is Emily. It's just me and Lisa left. My name is Tom." The man remained silent, glancing down at Tom.

"Why didn't the helicopter pick us up?" Tom asked.

"This is a narrow, brushy valley. I imagine the pilot couldn't see where you were and couldn't land to find out." Hank pulled a granola bar out of a side pocket in his pack and gave it to Tom.

Tom tore of the wrapping and devoured the granola bar. Hank gave him a second bar, which he ate more slowly. He smiled as he realized that he and Lisa wouldn't starve. Tom began to lead Hank back to his campsite. When they got to the log bridge, the tall man asked, "Is Lisa too sick to walk?"

"No," Tom replied.

"Then I'll carry my pack and the food bag across on the log and leave the toboggan on this side," the man said. Five minutes later they had reached Lisa. She screamed for joy when Tom explained that this man had come to rescue them.

Hank introduced himself He got out a granola bar for Lisa and she ate it quickly. Hank gave her another bar and she smiled. "We're saved, aren't we?" she asked.

"Yes," Hank smiled back and then went into the tent to examine the bodies of Emily and their parents.

"Are you going to pull them out of the tent so it won't smell so bad?" Tom asked.

"No," the man said. "The tent would smell bad even if I did pull them out. Better to leave them there and I'll set up my own tent. There's room enough in it for both of you. After I do it, we'll have dinner."

With daylight fading fast, Hank pulled out a flashlight from his pack and had Tom hold it. He cleared a place under a tree on high ground and then spread a ground cloth. He unrolled the tent and asked Tom to help him. After the tent was set up, he put a huge fly on it and fastened it down. There was a big flap in front and Hank set his pack down there. Then he took his radio out of his pack and tried calling the. ranger station. The radio squawked, but there was no answer. He must have damaged the radio when he fell once coming down from Island Lake, or they might be too deep in a valley for good transmission.

Bone tired, Hank just wanted to rest but he knew that they all needed to eat a good supper. It was almost dark when Hank and Tom gathered firewood and started a fire. Hank set up a small grill, put a pot of water on it, and asked. "Do you want chicken almondine, turkey with peas, or spaghetti and meat balls?"

"What?" Tom asked in amazement. "Do I have a choice?"

Tom chose the turkey, Lisa chose the spaghetti, leaving Hank with the chicken. While they were waiting for the water to boil, Tom said in great relief, "I was so afraid you'd pass us by like the red-haired man did."

"When was this?" Hank asked.

Tom thought back. "About five days ago," he said.

"What did he look like?" Hank asked.

Tom thought again. "He was across the stream so I didn't see him real good. He had bright red hair. That I'm sure of I'm certain he had green goggles like the ski racers wear. He wasn't tall or wasn't short. That's about all I remember."

"Was he called Darry?"

"I didn't hear his name. There was a blonde lady beside him, but she didn't say his name." Tom replied.

"Was the blonde tall and slim or short and pudgy?"

"Tall and slim," Tom was taken aback. "Do you know them?" "Unfortunately, I do," said Hank and he told Tom and Lisa all about Darry's role in making Kelli fall into Cove Lake and leaving her there.

"Just like Darry left us," Tom said. The water was boiling now and Hank poured it into the freeze-dry dinners.

"Did he promise to get help for you?"

"Yes." said Tom, anger boiling inside. "He said he would get help at Five Mile Meadows or Livingston Mill. I don't think he did." "I'm sure he didn't," Hank replied. "Your mother and father would be alive now if he had."

"But why didn't he help us?" Tom asked.

"Because he is a thoughtless, self-centered, spoiled man," Hank replied harshly.

Tom's anger boiled over. "I'm going to see he pays for this. He's going to jail for murdering my father and mother ... maybe he'll hang ... I wish he would."

"I want the same thing," Hank replied strongly.

The freeze dry meals were ready to eat and the conversation shifted to the ordeal Tom and Lisa had faced in the past few days. Tom told about the bears,

Blizzard in August

the snow, fishing Goat Lake to get food, and how he felt when Emily and his parents died.

Hank listened without interruption and then shifted the conversation by asking, "Do you like your Uncle Rudolph, the State Senator."

"He's all right. He's stern but he's fair. It's Aunt Marjorie that I really like. She's about five years older than Mama was, but she hugs you a lot and makes real nice cookies and pies," Tom replied.

"You and your sister will need to live with someone for a few years," Hank said.

"Why can't I live on the ranch and run it? I'm old enough. I'll be twelve next month."

"You're a strong, tough young man," Hank observed, "but I don't think Child Welfare would let you live alone with your sister on the ranch. I'll call your uncle when I get back. He's a lawyer and he'll know what's best for you both."

"You know my uncle?" Tom asked.

"Sure," Hank said and he went on to explain how the Senator had helped him on his project that recorded the stories of Custer County pioneers.

After dinner, Tom had five squares of graham crackers, a candy bar, and three cups of hot chocolate. He was getting full and sleepy when Hank brought their sleeping bags and mats from their parents' tent and put them in his own. Tom and Lisa packed their clothes. Before he crawled into Hank's tent, Tom said, "You better hang a good bear pack. The bears got into our packs and ate all our food."

"I will," Hank promised and got out two pulleys and about forty feet of rope. He selected two trees about thirty feet apart. With the pulleys he soon had the large food bag hanging about fifteen feet between the trees and more than ten feet off the ground. The trees selected were a hundred feet from Hank's tent, Tom noticed with approval.

Tom trusted this bearded man. He was like his father in many ways. Two minutes after he slipped into his sleeping bag, Tom fell asleep.

Chapter 37

The Trail to Five Mile Meadows – September 3rd

Hank heard bears twice during the night but they evidently contented themselves with nosing around Tom and Lisa's packs and trying, unsuccessfully, to reach the food bag. Leaving the tent before seven, Hank scanned the snow and sky. There had been no new snow overnight and the sun was shining on the higher branches of the pines. He roused Tom and Lisa and built a fire.

Tom rushed out of the tent, made a bathroom stop, and then gathered firewood. "What's for breakfast?" he asked.

"Tang, hot cereal, and hot chocolate," Hank replied. "There are a dozen individual packets of hot cereal so you can have your choice." Lisa emerged from the tent just as Tom and Hank began to eat. She selected oatmeal with maple sugar as her cereal and drank two cups of hot chocolate.

As soon as they finished breakfast, Hank put his clothes in his pack and Tom and Lisa did likewise. They packed all of their clothes, sleeping bags, and mats but left the belongings of the three dead Wagners in the Wagners' tent. "We'll leave your folk's stuff for the Forest Service to pick up," Hank said in justification.

They started down the trail at nine-thirty with the packs and the food bag tied on the toboggan. On relatively level areas, Hank pulled the toboggan from the front and Tom took the rear rope to keep the toboggan from sliding. On downhill stretches, Hank took the rear rope to prevent the toboggan from going too fast and Tom steered with the front rope. They made good time when they reached the first log bridge at eleven.

They couldn't safely wade Big Boulder Creek; the water ran too high and swift. Hank asked Tom if he could cross on the log bridge on the seat of his pants. "I crossed it on the way up to Goat Lake," Tom said proudly.

After Tom crossed without mishap. Hank got Lisa to sit on the log and slide across just in front of him. "I can catch you if you start to slip," he assured her. The problem was the toboggan. There were no stones to slide the toboggan on as there were at the inlet of Cove Lake. Finally, Hank untied the packs and carried them across on his back in two trips across the log and then he came back for the empty toboggan, which he pulled through the water with a rope. It took ten minutes to tie the packs on the toboggan and they were off to the next log bridge. Hank looked at his watch when they approached the next stream crossing. It had taken nearly fifty minutes to cross the first bridge and reach the second stream. At this rate it would be nearly five when they crossed the last of the bridges—barely enough time to set up their tents at Five Mile Meadows before dusk closed in. He began to worry.

Tom had crossed the second log bridge and Hank was crossing with Lisa in front of him, when he saw a tall, darkhaired man in green coveralls approaching. "I'm Vito Morelli," the man said. "I'm a wilderness ranger. Did you see the Wagner family on the trail to Goat Lake?"

Tom stood up straight and tall. "I'm Tom Wagner," he said. "My sister, Lisa, is crossing the log ahead of my friend, Hank Barclay." Hank saw the dark-haired man pass his hand over his mustache and turn his attention to Tom. "Where is the rest of your family?"

"They're all dead." Tom choked with emotion. "We left their bodies ... back there." Tom couldn't say more and Vito asked no more questions until Hank was across.

"And you're the mountain man I've heard a lot about," Vito said.

"I suppose so," Hank said. "But I'll look a lot less like a mountain man when I can get a shave. I've been in the White Clouds eight days. Who's been calling me a mountain man?"

"A woman who we lifted out of Cove Lake by helicopter. She's been telling everyone about the bear you killed with a knife when it bit a hole in your tent," Vito replied.

Tom's eyes widened. "You didn't tell me about that, Hank." Turning to Vito he added, "Hank came along when we had just about given up hope late yesterday afternoon and gave us food and a good place to spend the night."

"My buddy, Ed Grant, was supposed to reach you yesterday afternoon but he got the stomach flu. He's down at Five Mile Meadows recovering, but he expects to be better tomorrow." Vito paused, looked at his watch, and said, "We'd better start back to our camp. We hope to get a helicopter to fly in late this afternoon."

With Vito helping, the river crossings took much less time. In between river crossings, Vito questioned both Tom and Hank and received a complete account of the deaths of Tom's parents and Emily. He also learned about the red-haired man who had left both Kelli and the Wagners. "The Senator is going to want to know about him," Vito said. "He's going to take the death of his brother real hard."

By the fourth log bridge, Vito had taken over supervising the crossings, and Hank relaxed. The helicopter needed to take the kids first. But it would be nice if the chopper had room for him. Hank longed to see Kelli again. He smiled when he thought of the story she told about him killing the bear. It probably weighed over a thousand pounds and stood eight feet tall, the way she told it. Well, he wouldn't mind being a hero to her. He just hoped that her bear claw wounds in her shoulder were not very serious. At four they crossed the last log bridge and were on the level ground of Five Mile Meadows. When they reached the three trees in the center, Hank saw two tents set up and a space cleared for a helicopter landing area.

A blond wilderness ranger introduced himself as Ed Grant, warning that he was still recovering from stomach flu. He pulled out a radiophone and talked to someone at the Clayton Ranger Station. Then he handed it to Vito who told about the death of the two Wagner parents and the little girl.

"The chopper will be here in twenty minutes," he reported. "They can take one load—you, Hank, and the two kids."

"What about you, Ed?" Hank protested. "You should take my place. You have the stomach flu."

"Thanks, but I'll be better by tomorrow. I'll need to help Vito recover the bodies."

"And the Senator specifically asked that you be brought out this afternoon," added Vito.

Hank shrugged and took off his pack. It was nice to be flown out this afternoon. He would see Kelli sooner. But why did the Senator specifically want him flown out today?

The helicopter landed in about twenty minutes and everything happened fast. Tom and Lisa were put in the back seat with the packs and Hank sat beside the pilot. There was just enough time for seat belts to be fastened before the pilot took off. As they flew down the Big Boulder Creek valley over miles of white landscape, Hank wondered whether the Senator would be meeting them when they landed at the Challis airport.

Chapter 38

Challis – Tuesday

Kelli put down the phone beside her hospital bed with a worried expression. She had called the Clayton Ranger Station three times since noon and gotten a busy signal each time.

She looked anxiously at the wall clock. Surely Hank must have found the campers they were looking for by now. Why didn't he call the ranger station? She thought of Hank breaking his leg on the hill above Island Lake and lying in the freezing cold all night.

For the third time that day she wondered about Hank. He was brave; it took tremendous courage to kill the bear poking his head into the tent. He had great strength of character. He showed strong will power to go from being a logger to a professor of history, to avoid smoking and drinking when your friends were doing it, and to bring an injured person into your tent while realizing you were greatly endangering your own life. Yes, his bravery, dependability and his moral code made him attractive. But there were many things she still didn't know about him.

Fifteen minutes later, a tall, stoop-shouldered, gray-haired man with a pronounced limp entered her hospital room with two children. "I'm Rudolph Wagner," the man said, "And these are two of my late brother's children, Thomas and Lisa."

Kelli shook the hands of the thin, brown-haired boy and an even slimmer blonde girl. "Why are you here?" Kelli asked, puzzled.

"You don't know then," Senator Wagner said.

"Know what?" Her face tightened in fear. "Is Hank dead?"

The senator smiled reassuringly. "No, I brought him from the airport to the hospital. He's trying to phone his uncle and find a razor to get shaved. He'll be here soon."

"Thank God." Kelli burst into tears, all her pent-up fears and emotions spilling over.

The senator waited for a minute or so and said, "I wanted to tell you that your Hank probably saved the lives of Thomas and Lisa. They hadn't eaten for a day, their parents were dead, and there were bears around. He brought them food, hope, and a dry tent. He reached them yesterday afternoon when the wilderness rangers could not reach them until today. Your boyfriend is a hero."

"It smelled awful in the tent with Dad, Ma, and little Emily dead in there," Tom said. "And I couldn't budge Dad, couldn't get him out of the tent. We couldn't have slept in the tent last night. We might have frozen to death outside." Tom paused in his excitement. "When I grow up, I want to be a rancher," he said. "I can ride good already. And Hank said I could study agriculture at the University of Idaho and take a history class from him."

The senator looked fondly at Tom. "This is a brave young man. He took over leadership in the family after his mother died and his father was delirious with infection in his leg. He's no longer a child." "And me?" Lisa asked.

"You're a brave young lady," the senator said.

Kelli's mind whirled. Obviously, Hank had found the missing Wagner family and saved its two remaining members. But what happened to the father, mother and little girl? Why did they die? Kelli was about to ask about that when Hank walked in clean shaven with both his and Kelli's packs." "It's so wonderful to see you," he said and gave Kelli a big kiss right in front of her other visitors.

The senator smiled, "It's time for us to go and get these two youngsters to a doctor. Course they look as fit as a fiddle, but it's a good precaution." He nodded towards Hank. "I want to thank you again."

"Before you go," Hank said. "Do you know how I can get a ride to Livingston Mill? My car is in the parking lot at the trail-head."

"And mine too," Kelli said.

The senator's face wrinkled in concentration. "Yes, I think I can do it. Be at my law office at nine tomorrow morning and bring your car keys and Kelli's." He paused. "Do you need a ride tonight?"

"Yes. I need a motel. Could you make a reservation for me and give me a ride?"

"Be happy to," the senator said. "Phone me at this number when you're ready to go." He handed Hank a card with his phone number on it. "I expect you folks have a lot of ... catching up to do," the Senator said as he left the room with Tom and Lisa.

Kelli and Hank did have a lot of catching up to do. Kelli wanted to know in detail what happened to Hank after she was whisked up into the helicopter two days ago.

Kelli asked about how the father and mother of the two Wagner children died. Hank told her and added, "It all could have been prevented, you know."

"How?" Kelli asked.

Blizzard in August

"Darry saw Tom Wagner on Wednesday the 28th ... that's six days ago ... and he promised Tom to get help. He didn't." Hank's voice was harsh and Kelli was uncomfortable.

"How did Tom know it was Darry?" Kelli asked.

"He had red hair and green ski goggles."

"Oh, God," Kelli was almost sick to her stomach. "Did he recognize anyone else?" she asked.

"He saw a thin, blonde girl ... probably Pam," Hank said. "This redhead could have been the man with the binoculars I saw Tuesday, a week ago, on the ridgeline." Kelli replied. "Maybe he has a wife and they went down to Island Lake."

Hank didn't comment. Instead he asked, "How are you?" "My shoulder was badly infected but the wounds are not too deep. They put a cast on my ankle and reset it. I'll be able to walk with crutches." "When will you be able to leave the hospital?" Hank asked. "Tomorrow evening or Thursday morning," she said. "And then?" She looked up smiling, tentatively, wondering what Hank's plans were.

"And then I drive you home to Los Angeles," Hank said. "You won't be able to drive yourself and you need to get your car back."

"But when does your fall semester begin?"

"Not until the third week of September," Hank said. "Plenty of time to visit with your folks and for you and me to make some plans.

What kind of plans? Kelli wondered. Was Hank thinking about marriage? Kelli pondered the wisdom of asking Hank this while they chatted about her hospital stay and Hank's trip with the Wagner children. No, she decided. We'll have plenty of time to explore our feelings on the trip to Los Angeles. Kelli was not sure what she would say if Hank decided to propose.

The first thing Hank did after he checked into the motel in Challis was to phone his Uncle Ted. He had tried just after he reached the hospital but no one answered his phone.

"Sorry, I didn't call sooner. I was caught in the blizzard...I'm all right ... but ... but I need you and Marjorie to keep my girls another week. I can't make it back by the sixth," Hank said apologetically.

"What happened?"

"Well ... I met this woman ... she's an elementary school principal ... she's really nice," Hank found himself unsure of what to say.

"And you want to spend a few days with her," Ted Barclay said. "It's more than that. She broke an ankle. I told her that I'd drive her back to the Los

Angeles area in her car so she wouldn't be late for work." He paused. "I think I'm in love with her."

Ted Barclay chuckled. "You sound like a tongue-tied high school kid. What's her name?"

"Kelli Johnson."

"I hope things work out for you and Kelli … oh, you know what I mean." It was Ted's turn to be embarrassed. "We'll be happy to keep the girls another week or ten days. Now, you better talk to each of them."

Sara, Julie, and Jo each came on the phone and Hank shared some of his adventures in the White Clouds and learned some of the things that were going on in their lives. Before the phone call ended he told each of his daughters that he loved her.

Chapter 39

Challis, Idaho – Wednesday morning – September 4th

Hank thought of his daughters as the senator finished some paper work. He missed them, but he had made a commitment to Kelli to drive her back to Los Angeles. Admit it, he thought. You're falling in love with her. You want to have this time alone with Kelli to know her better, to decide whether you want to propose marriage.

The senator looked up from his cluttered desk and rang for his secretary. A stout woman with a ruddy face entered. He handed her some letters he had signed and told her they were not to be interrupted. "Except for the sheriff," he added.

The senator could be gruff or he could be cordial. This morning he was depressed but still hospitable. He took Hank on a brief tour of his plainly furnished, pine-paneled office, explaining why he received the plaque of appreciation from the Association of Idaho Cities and the framed letter of commendation from former Republican Governor Robert Smylie. Hank looked at the heads of a bear and mountain goat on the wall and asked about how they were shot. The senator inquired about how Hank's oral history project on Idaho pioneers was going. Hank had expected that they would be on the road to Livingston Mill by then but he didn't wish to raise a question. It was too important that he stay in the good graces of Senator Wagner.

The door opened presently and a large, muscular man with a handle bar mustache entered. "This is Sheriff Robinson," the senator said. "One of his deputies will go with us to retrieve your car and Kelli's. But he wanted a chance to talk to you first."

The sheriff held out a hand. Hank shook it noting that his handshake was firm and hard and his expression was shrewd and serious.

"How can I help you. Sheriff?" Hank asked.

"First of all I want to thank you for rescuing young Tom and Lisa Wagner. You saved their lives."

"I was pleased to be able to do it," Hank responded smoothly. "Tom is mature for an eleven-year-old and deserves a lot of credit, too."

"Quite a remarkable young man," the sheriff commented. "I talked to him this morning, just half an hour ago. He tells me that a red- haired man and a blond girl saw him on Wednesday the 28th. He asked them to stay and help but they left saying they would get aid. Apparently they never phoned the Forest Service. At least the Forest Service never got a phone call until Sunday, September first."

Hank studied the pictures of the senator hunting and fishing and said, "I suppose you want me to identify this man."

"Him and the other members of his back-packing party," the sheriff said smoothly.

"I think the red-haired man was Darrington Baltz, son of Big Mike Baltz." Hank replied, in no mood to try to shield Darry.

The sheriff whistled and leaned forward. "What makes you think so?"

"He was passing by the Goat Lake trail Wednesday morning. And he has red hair and green ski goggles." Hank paused. "Tom told me the man was wearing green ski goggles."

"And this Darrington Baltz, is he a friend of yours?" the sheriff asked evenly and added, "His father has not made many friends in this county."

"He's hardly a friend of mine," Hank added hotly. "Let me tell you about what he did to Kelli Johnson." Hank found his voice rising in anger as he told every detail of what he overheard Darry say, how Darry snapped the whip with Kelli on the rope, and how he got his backpacking party to leave Kelli cold and freezing by the side of Cove Lake.

"No morals; just like his father," the senator observed.

"Would you be interested in pressing charges on this incident?" the sheriff asked.

"I'd have to talk to Kelli Johnson first. She's in the hospital recovering from an ankle that was broken as a result of the fall from the rope. She was supposed to be a sort of chaperone for her nieces, but Darry ..." Hank paused, realizing that he was giving information that Kelli might not want him to provide. And what could he say if the sheriff asked about Pam and Ann, Kelli's nieces? "I should call Ms. Johnson," he said.

"No need," the sheriff said. "You're a hero. You're not under investigation for anything. We just need some information." The sheriff turned his aquiline face towards the senator. "Rudy," he said. "I find I can drive you both to Livingston Mill. I'll let your secretary know that I will be taking you both, not Deputy Pingelli. Shall we get started?" Hank recognized the ploy. The sheriff wanted to keep him from conferring with Kelli, keep him from tempering his testimony. As Hank watched the senator nod in agreement, he realized that he could not antagonize the sheriff without causing a rift in the excellent relationship he had over the years with Senator Wagner—a relationship which

Blizzard in August 149

one top university official called, "invaluable to the University of Idaho." But why should he temper his criticism of Darry Baltz? What had Darry ever done for him? So Hank merely said, "Let's go."

Once in the patrol car, heading north from the center of Challis, the sheriff pulled out a tape recorder and turned it on. He said, "This is Sheriff William Robinson. It is 9:35 a.m. Wednesday, September 4th. I am driving to Livingston Mill with Hank—no make that Henry—Barclay and Senator Rudolph Wagner. I am helping to retrieve Mr. Barclay's car and hoping to obtain some important information from him. Mr. Barclay is not, I repeat not, under investigation or accused of any crimes. In contrast, Mr. Barclay deserves a commendation for his bravery and … and for the way he saved two of the children of Mr. Herman Wagner."

Hank relaxed a little. The sheriff was making it abundantly clear that Hank was not his target.

"Mr. Barclay told me a few minutes ago of the actions of Mr. Darrington Baltz in causing Kelli Johnson to break her ankle." The sheriff was speaking to the tape recorder and paused a minute. "I would like him to repeat what he said for the record." The sheriff passed the tape recorder back to the back seat and the senator placed it between Hank and himself.

Would his recorded voice be played in court? Probably. This was a more serious situation than he realized. He wished he could get out of the car and phone Kelli or a lawyer. But he couldn't without antagonizing the sheriff and the senator. And Hank would not jeopardize these relationships to protect Darry. But he would be very careful. Hank decided, and make every sentence he uttered the exact and complete truth. With this in mind, he recounted the incident at the Cove Lake snow slide Tuesday in full detail. When he was through, he handed the tape recorder back to the sheriff.

With tape recorder in hand, the sheriff said, "Now I am going to ask Mr. Barclay to provide a full description of four members of the backpacking party that left Kelli Johnson at Cove Lake. You might start by identifying the date and time this occurred. I would like Mr. Barclay to provide not only a physical description but describe their age, their occupation, and their relationships to each other."

As he received the tape recorder from the sheriff. Hank realized that Darry was not the only one in danger from the sheriff's investigation. He could see the direction of the sheriff's inquiry now and knew that the others in the backpacking party, particularly Pam, were also in danger. He could refuse to answer further questions, but would it accomplish anything besides antagonizing his friend, the senator? And by this time Hank realized, that Senator Wagner had a legitimate concern as well. Perhaps, Hank thought, if I cooperate with the sheriff and the senator, I can strike a deal or at least point the finger of guilt more towards Darry and less toward Kelli's nieces.

With this in mind Hank gave a full description of Darry, giving emphasis to his red hair and green ski goggles. His description of Pam, Ann and Jason was also complete but he de-emphasized the blond hair of Kelli's nieces. Hank provided what he knew of the job and educational background of the four backpackers, ending with the comment that "Darry Baltz was the son of Big Mike Baltz, renowned in Custer County for closing the Panther Creek Mine." He was rewarded with a big grin from Senator Wagner who had fought the closure.

With the tape recorder back beside him, Sheriff Robinson asked, "Would you describe where the party of four backpackers intended to spend Tuesday night, August 27th, and where they were going the next day?"

"They intended to stay at Island Lake the night of the 27th and go on the next day as far as they could towards Livingston Mill." Hank said.

"And if they left early the next morning for Livingston Mill, when would they be passing the Goat Lake trail where it intersects the Island Lake trail?"

Hank felt as if he was on the witness stand, but shook off his queasy feeling. "About ten, I would say," he said. "I spent a night at the Wagner campsite. It would be very difficult for anyone on the trail to see the campsite because of the brush, but someone at the campsite who yelled could be heard on the trail."

"Ah," the sheriff said. "And would you say that Tom Wagner has a loud voice? And that Tom Wagner saw two people come from the trail within sight of him."

"Tom has an excellent voice," Hank said. "He is a courageous and trustworthy young man. He told me that he saw a red-haired man with green goggles come to within a hundred feet of him on the other side of the stream. I believe him."

"And would you say that the red-haired young man was Darrington Baltz?"

With a chill. Hank realized that the sheriff might be preparing him to be a star witness in a murder trial against Darry Baltz. He paused a minute, but remembering what Darry had done to Kelli, anger boiled again inside him. "I can't be sure because I wasn't there," he said. "But the odds were overwhelming it was Darry that Tom Wagner saw. The physical description fits, the time fits, and Darry was the type of self-centered, callous person who would do a thing like that."

"And who do you think the blond girl was?" the sheriff asked.

Blizzard in August

This was the question that Hank was dreading. The sheriff knew it had to be either Pam or Ann and they were both Kelli's nieces. Hank thought of Pam standing at the top of the snow slope keeping Ann from going down to help. "I'm less sure of this," he said. "From the physical description Tom gave me, I'd say it was Pamela Pettigrew."

"And so you would identify Pamela Pettigrew as cooperating with Mr. Baltz in leaving the Wagners without providing assistance?" Hank objected. He certainly wouldn't say that on the stand. Not if he wanted to marry Kelli. Yet, in a way the sheriff was correct. Pam was too in love with Darry to object to what he did that day on the Goat Lake trail. What was Hank going to do?

The car slowed and the sheriff turned left off Highway 75 onto the paved road up the East Fork of the Salmon River. Suddenly, Hank had it. "Turn off the tape recorder," he said. "I think I know what you want. And there's something I want in return."

"What do you think I want?" the sheriffs voice was guarded. "You don't have an air-tight case against Darry," Hank said. "Tom Wagner can testify that he saw a red-haired man with green ski goggles. I can testify that Darry had red hair, green ski-goggles and would have been there about the time that Tom saw a red-haired man. It isn't enough. You need someone in Darry's party to testify that Darry was there."

The sheriff grinned. "Smart man. With your brains and build you'd make a good deputy." He paused and studied Hank closely. "Will you help? You certainly don't like Darry, do you?"

"No, I don't like Darry or his father," Hank said. "But I'm not going to do anything illegal to help you."

"No. I certainly don't want you to do anything illegal," the sheriff said emphatically. "I want you to do what I am doing now. Go to the two persons in Darry's party who did nothing wrong and ask them to describe what happened, both at the snow slide and on the Goat Lake Trail. And put it on the tape recorder."

"Not secretly. I don't want to be wired," Hank said with alarm. "Not secretly. Tell them you're doing it first and get their permission. Make clear that they are not suspects, but that we need their cooperation. Tell them I just want the facts on what happened."

"Why don't you do it yourself?" Hank asked.

"It's partly because I have only two deputies and I'd lose one for almost a week if I sent him to Twin Falls and Ashland. And it's partly that Jason Green and Ann Pettigrew know you and trust you."

"What's in this for them?"

"Well, you will be stating on tape that Jason pulled Kelli out of the water and Ann wanted to help at the snow slide. And that you believe they would never have left the Wagners if they had seen them," he paused.

"Will you agree not to bring criminal charges against them?" Hank asked.

"Yes, if they cooperate," the sheriff said. "They do not seem to be at fault in either the snow slide incident or the abandonment of the Wagners."

"And Pamela Pettigrew?" This was the big question and Hank wished he could study the Sheriff's face as he answered. "I can make no promises about Pamela," the sheriff responded. "I think, and I take it you think, she was standing beside Darry as he talked to Tom Wagner. I can't make a deal that overlooks this. But Senator Wagner can."

"What do you mean?" Hank's mind was whirling. What did Senator Wagner have to do with this?

"Well, Hank," the senator said almost apologetically, "I am filing a civil suit against Darry and the three other members of his backpacking party. Because of them, two fine children lost their parents. I am convinced that Herman and Trudy Wagner, and perhaps their daughter Emily, died because Darry and his party did not come to their help and did not inform the Forest Service of their plight."

"How much are you suing for?" Hank turned to try to read the senator's face.

"Forty million dollars. You know, Herman's earning power, loss of parents, pain and suffering."

"Surely, you're not going to sue Jason Green and his family?"

"Not if he cooperates. And I expect he'll cooperate with you in giving a factual statement."

Hank clapped his hand to his head. "And Ann surely was not responsible. She didn't even see Tom Wagner."

"I expect that Ann will give you a factual statement of what happened when you explain the importance of it. I agree that Ann does not appear to be responsible." The senator spoke in measured, friendly tones but there was no mistaking the pressure he was putting on Hank, Jason and Ann.

"And Pam. Do you expect me to put a tape recorder in her lap and have her admit she was with Darry when Tom Wagner saw him?" Hank's voice had an edge now. "Pam is in love with Darry ... so deeply in love, she might want to throw the tape recorder out the window. What motive would there be strong enough to implicate Darry on tape?"

Blizzard in August

They had reached a solitary outhouse on the bank above the East Fork of the Salmon. The sheriff turned off onto the pullout. "I need to go," he said and left the senator and Hank sitting in the car.

"Now, Hank," the Senator said in a conciliatory tone. "Don't get your back up. We've been good friends over the years...and I've been a big help to the University of Idaho as a member of the Senate Finance Committee." He paused and saw Hank's face soften. "You know who we're really after, Darrington Baltz and his father. Big Mike closed the Panther Creek Mine to strip it of its assets. I hate Big Mike and so does the sheriff. His brother lost his job when the mine closed. And, if I remember correctly, you were quoted in a magazine article as saying that Big Mike Baltz is the kind of rapacious, unscrupulous corporate raider we don't need in Idaho."

"You're correct about my quote, and I still stand by it," Hank said. "But are you punishing the son for the sins of the father?"

"But I am punishing the father." The senator's mouth tightened and his voice had a harsh, angry tone. "Who has the deep pockets here? Who's going to pay most of the freight? Do you object?"

Hank boiled inside. He was angry at Darry, angry with Big Mike, and angry at the situation he found himself in. He was more than annoyed at the senator and the sheriff but he realized it was not politic to vent this wrath at either of them. "I don't give a damn about Darry and his father. I wouldn't mind if the father went bankrupt and the son was convicted of murder. It's the Pettigrews I care about. I'm thinking of marrying Kelli Johnson and she's going to be mighty upset if I help convict one of her nieces or help bring financial ruin on her sister's family. Look at this from my point of view. Senator."

Senator Wagner scratched his weather-beaten cheek. "Now, Hank, I understand your problem and I sympathize. Would it help if I eliminated Jason Green and Ann Pettigrew from the suit before I file it tomorrow, assuming of course, they will help?"

"Yes," Hank said. "But what about eliminating Pam from the suit?"

"I could," the Senator said. "But I won't. This is a trump card that I can't discard until the case against Darry is solid. We need ironclad evidence that it was Darry who heard Tom Wagner's pleas, Darry who ignored them, and Darry who did not contact the Forest Service. You can best protect Pamela Pettigrew from jail and her family from a multi-million dollar debt by helping us get the evidence we need."

Hank marveled at the intricate way the senator was forcing him to enlist in their cause. Was the sheriff in this too? He asked, "By we, you mean the sheriff and yourself?"

"Of course. This is a small county. We've been friends since grade school. I worked closely with the sheriff during the ten years I served as county prosecuting attorney." The senator smiled again. "I have the highest regard for you, Hank...always have, and I've sent more than one commendation letter about you to the president of the university. You agree, in general, that Darry Baltz and his father are scum. Help us. All we want are the facts, just the facts, on tape."

There it was, Hank thought. He was being put under great pressure—a sort of sophisticated, indirect blackmail to bring down Darry Baltz and his father. And much as he hated to admit it, he was just as much in favor of doing it as were the senator and the sheriff. If he went along, and he decided at that moment he would, then he might have leverage to get what he wanted. "I agree. I dislike Darry and his father as much as you. And I realize you are asking me to do nothing illegal, just get the facts. But if I do this and I help get an air-tight criminal action and civil suit against Darry, would you and the sheriff drop the suits against Pam?" Hank grinned, realizing that he was applying his own brand of pressure.

"You'd make a damn good defense attorney," the senator said. "Look, Big Mike is filthy rich. We both know that. If my nephew and niece get what they need to give them care, a good education through graduate school, and a good start in life afterwards...if they get this from Big Mike, then I'll overlook what Pam did." He paused. "I don't know about the sheriff He doesn't know you as well as I do. He may plea bargain in Pam's case if Darry is headed for murder one or two."

"There's something else I need. Senator," Hank said. "Pam may say some mighty disparaging things about Kelli and me when we confront her in Los Angeles. I need some favorable publicity. I need a newspaper article to bring to Los Angeles that gives the truth of why Kelli remained at Cove lake...that portrays me as a hero."

"That's easy," the senator smiled. "You are a hero. Hank. The Challis newspaper owner is a friend of mine. I'll see that you're interviewed this afternoon. The paper is published on Thursday morning. Don't leave town without a copy." The senator paused, his face becoming serious again. "Don't tell Kelli or anyone else about the civil suit until after it is filed tomorrow morning. I can't afford a leak on this."

"I won't leak it," Hank promised.

Then he realized that he couldn't tell Kelli about the suit or anything else about the meeting until they had left Challis tomorrow. Was he going to be entangled in his web of promises—entangled so badly that he might be telling half- truths to Kelli? But wasn't he protecting Kelli's sister's family in doing this? Surely, Kelli would forgive him when she realized this.

The sheriff saw that Hank and the senator had stopped talking so he got back in the car and started to drive. He stopped a minute at a pull off where the Livingston Mill Road turns right off the road that follows the East Branch of the Salmon River. "I assume you are with us on this taping, Mr. Barclay," he said.

"I'm with you," Hank said and his mind flashed back to a scene in the Korean War when he said this to an army captain and took his platoon out of its protected trenches to charge the enemy. For better or worse he had thrown in his lot with the senator and the sheriff.

"Good," the sheriff said and he started up the winding, one-lane dirt road that hung like a ribbon of brownish-red spaghetti on the side of the cliff. The snow had nearly melted in the valley of the East Fork but there were increasingly large drifts lining the side of the road as they ascended.

In the trailhead parking lot near the caretaker's cabin, they separated. The sheriff wanted to interview the mine caretaker about Darry Baltz before he drove his patrol car back to Challis. Hank drove his own car and gave Kelli's keys to Senator Wagner so he could drive to the hospital parking lot.

Hank met the senator at the parking lot and picked up Kelli's car keys. The senator said he would phone Kelli's room when he had the newspaper interview with Hank arranged. They shook hands, old but causal friends, now tied together in a common cause—or was it a vendetta? They wished each other a good afternoon and went their separate ways.

Chapter 40

Twin Falls, Idaho – Thursday, September 5

Kelli smiled Thursday morning as a nurse gave her a wheelchair ride to her car. She had Hank; his strength and love helped her through the past week.

"I wasn't sure which car you wanted me to drive to LA." Hank said as the hospital attendant loaded Kelli in the passenger seat of her cherry-red Ford sedan. "If you'd rather have me drive my car, it's in the parking lot and it's easy to switch."

"This is fine," Kelli said. "It's a bigger car with fewer miles on it." Then she thought, if we take my car, it would be easier if I decide to stay in Los Angeles. I wonder if Hank considered that?

Hank made a brief stop at the newspaper office to get a copy of the Challis weekly paper. Kelli saw him scan it carefully before getting back in the car and then give it to her. "The newspaper editor wanted to do a story on me before I left town," he said.

Kelli opened the paper and found the half-page article with Hank's picture on page three. The headline read, "U. of I. Prof Saves Three in Snow." The story provided a brief biography of Hank and recounted the incident of the snow slide in which Hank took care of Kelli after she broke her ankle. It gave even greater space to his rescue of Tom and Lisa Wagner. The article described the death of the parents of the Wagner children and commented that the prominent rancher and his wife from the north end of the county would not have died if other backpackers had not passed them by.

Hank turned on Route 93 just south of Challis while Kelli reread the article. "Very nice. It calls you a hero. You are to me." She paused. "There's one puzzling part. The bit about backpackers passing them by. The article said that the man had a broken leg and his wife had pneumonia."

"What puzzles you?" Hank asked.

"You don't believe it was Darry and Pam who passed them by, do you?" Kelli asked. "Yesterday, you sounded as if you did."

"Tom Wagner caught sight of two backpackers. One had red hair and green ski goggles. The other was slim and blond. I believe he's telling the truth."

Kelli was devastated. Her stomach churned and her throat went dry. "Oh, God," she said. "You believe they left the Wagners like they left me."

Blizzard in August 157

"Yes, I do," Hank said quietly. "And Herman Wagner, his wife, and, perhaps, their three-year-old girl died because they didn't get medical attention and food. Tom and Lisa were getting weaker when I got there. In another day or two they might have died as well."

Kelli was silent for a long time, trying to think of the consequences of Darry's action and whether it was really Pam with him. Surely the authorities would take some action. But what and how would Pam be affected?

They were approaching the 7,160 foot Willow Creek Summit and there were two-foot snowdrifts on both sides of the road. The road was a little slick and Hank slowed the car carefully as he went into each turn.

It was on the other side of the Summit that Kelli's curiosity overcame her fear of opening a can of worms. "Do you think the authorities will take action against Darry?"

"Yes," Hank said. "I expect the county sheriff will issue a warrant for Darry's arrest."

"For what?" Kelli felt fear rise in her throat.

"Maybe unpremeditated murder. More likely, manslaughter. I don't know for sure," Hank said.

Kelli looked at Hank's face. It seemed hard and implacable. "Will Pam face criminal charges?" Kelli said anxiously.

"Depends on what she said and did. She may have tried to talk Darry into staying and helping."

"And what about Ann and Jason?" Kelli said, wondering if they would be brought up on criminal charges.

"I don't think they will be charged with anything," Hank said evenly. He paused as if he might continue but he kept quiet.

Kelli had an uneasy feeling as she looked at the road between snow-covered sagebrush fields. Why was Hank so reticent to talk? He seemed even more reticent in the hospital last night. She had to smoke him out with direct questions. "How are you so sure Ann and Jason won't be charged with some terrible crime?"

"Well, yesterday morning I went to Senator Wagner's office. You remember he promised to drive to Livingston Mill with someone else so we would have three people to bring back your car, my car, and the car we drove up in."

"Yeah."

"Well, the sheriff decided to drive the senator and me in his patrol car. He has studded tires."

"And." Kelli had to know everything that Hank knew.

"The sheriff pumped me about what I knew about Darry, Pam, Ann and Jason and about what Tom Wagner told me. And he recorded my answers on a tape recorder."

"And you let him do it?" Kelli's voice had an edge now.

"I saw no harm in it. He just wanted the facts and I was certainly going to tell the truth whether it was taped or not." Hank paused. "Besides, if I cooperated, I might get some concessions from the sheriff."

"Like what?" Kelli's lips were drawn in a tight line.

"Well, I told the sheriff about the snow slide incident at Cove Lake, and I told him that Jason jumped into the lake to pull you out. I explained that it was Darry who really wanted to leave you and that Ann and Jason objected. And I surmised that Jason and Ann were nowhere near Darry when he spoke to Tom Wagner. When I did this, the sheriff agreed not to bring up charges against Jason or Ann."

Hank had meant to win her approval and Kelli was pleased that Jason and Ann were free of criminal charges. However, Kelli did not express her approval.

"Did you discuss Pam?" Kelli wanted to know.

"Yes," Hank drawled. "I told the sheriff that she was led around by Darry, that she wanted to marry him. But the sheriff said he couldn't drop some criminal charges against her if she was with Darry at the time he spoke to Tom Wagner and did nothing to stop Darry from leaving the scene."

Kelli was furious. "You did too much talking to the sheriff without me and a lawyer present. This is my niece you were talking about."

Hank's voice was apologetic. "We were in the car. I wanted to phone you but I couldn't. Besides if I cooperated I hoped to gain concessions...and I did for Jason and Ann."

"But you gave the sheriff more fuel to arrest Pam! You should have said nothing at all." Kelli was deeply suspicious of the sheriff now. She had seen too many movies and television shows in which the police used unethical methods to trap their victims.

"Well, I did strike a bargain with the senator on his civil suit, which may very well get Pam and your family out of it." Hank's voice had a defensive tone.

"What civil suit?" Her voice raised an octave.

"The forty million dollar civil suit he was bringing today against all the four backpackers for the wrongful deaths of Herman, Trudy and Emily Wagner. I..."

Blizzard in August

"You what?" Kelli screamed. "This so-called friend of yours was going to file it today. Why didn't you tell me about it last night in the hospital so I could warn my sister?"

"I didn't want to upset you. That's one reason," Hank's voice was smooth and placating. "And I thought I could talk Senator Wagner into taking Pam, Ann and Jason out of the civil suit."

"And did it work?" Kelli suspended judgment on Hank for a minute.

"Partly," Hank said. "The senator agreed to change his suit before he filed it to take Ann and Jason out of it. He kept Pam in but he wanted me to help him and the sheriff get evidence against Darry ... find out for sure whether it was Darry who talked to Tom Wagner and whether Pam, if she was with Darry, tried to talk him out of leaving. He said he just wanted me to get the facts. And if the case against Darry was strong enough, he would drop Pam from the civil suit."

"And you did this without consulting me!" Kelli was livid. Hank turned into a pullout and faced Pam. "Look," he said. "I know I should have phoned you. But I figured I could do more good for your nieces and sister by cooperating with the sheriff and senator than I could by getting them angry at us."

Kelli understood what Hank was saying and cooled a little. "How did you promise to cooperate?"

"By getting the facts from Jason and Ann about what really happened at the snow slide and when they got near the Goat Lake trail. I was to assure them they were not involved in the criminal case or civil suit and get them to give the facts on tape."

"Tape record them? No way." Kelli's temper flared again. "With their knowledge and permission of course," Hank said in a conciliatory tone.

"It's still wrong," she said with finality.

"Don't you see, Kelli, that we have little to lose and everything to gain by cooperating? That's the way I got Ann and Jason out of the criminal and civil suits. I could get Pam out of the civil suit and maybe out of the criminal suit if I cooperate." Hank's voice was pleading but there was a growing undercurrent of annoyance.

"And get Darry hung," Kelli said. "Let the senator and the sheriff do their own dirty work."

"I don't give a damn about Darry," Hank exploded. "He deserves to hang. He tried to kill you by rolling a stone down at you. He put rocks in your pack. He snapped the whip so you would fall down the snow slide into the water. He left you by the side of Cove Lake freezing cold with a broken ankle. He didn't help the Wagners when he could have saved the lives of three people. He killed three of the Wagners by his selfish inaction and he could have killed you too. Why do you care what happens to Darry?" Hank slammed his fist on the dashboard in anger.

"Because," Kelli began. She stopped, her mind racing.

She really did dislike Darry and he probably did all the things Hank accused him of. Did she really want to get in a terrible fight with Hank over what happened to Darry? It was just that Hank should not have bargained with the sheriff and senator without taking her into his confidence. All her pent-up feelings about Darry, about her nieces, and most of all about Hank boiled over. She began to cry.

Hank put an arm around her. Kelli didn't push his arm away and she sat there crying softly for a few minutes. "I don't care much for Darry," she said finally. "And I really love you. It's just that you should have consulted me on this. You shouldn't have bargained with the senator and sheriff without me being present."

"I'm sorry," Hank said contritely. "We were all in the car together and I thought I had an opportunity to get both Ann and Pam out of both the criminal and civil suits. I know now you should have been in on the conference. I will consult you first and bring you in on anything that vitally affects your family in the future, but I couldn't this time."

Kelli was partially mollified but asked, "But the audiotaping?"

"I promised to do that and I always keep my promises," Hank said.

Kelli considered a strong objection but could see from Hank's face that it would do no good. "Well, all right," she said. "But I won't be in the room while you're doing it."

They said nothing for a while. Then Hank called Kelli's attention to snow-covered Mount Borah on the left. "It's the highest mountain in Idaho," he said.

"It's beautiful," she said but it was her last word until they had driven the forty miles to Arco.

Hank had called ahead from Arco, and Jason's father and an attorney were at the Green's house in Twin Falls to meet them. Hank explained that Jason was a hero for jumping in the water to save Kelli's life and for supporting Kelli and Hank in urging Darry to camp at Cove Lake rather than leaving Kelli. After heaping praise on Jason, Hank told the Greens and their lawyer that he had been assured by the sheriff that Jason would not be included in the criminal suit against Darry and assured by the senator that he would not be part of the civil suit.

Blizzard in August 161

"I'd like to put this on tape, Mr. Barclay," the Green's lawyer said. "Any objection?"

"None. It's a good idea." Hank said. "I'd like to get it on tape myself."

With the two tape recorders going. Hank recounted Jason's good deeds at the Cove Lake snow slides and repeated his assurances from the sheriff and senator that Jason would not be included in the civil and criminal suits. Then Hank asked Jason to describe in more detail what he saw and heard at the snow slide and near the entrance to the Goat Lake trail.

Jason obliged but could not add much to what Hank already knew about Darry's actions at the snow slide. He had the impression, as did Hank, that Darry snapped the whip on Kelli but he was not much closer than Hank when it happened. Jason did provide three significant facts about the next day. He confirmed that he heard a noise like a voice when they were close to the intersection with the Goat Lake trail. "It was Darry and Pam who went back to investigate," he said. "Darry reported it was two branches rubbing in the wind."

"Was Darry wearing green ski goggles at the time?"

"Yes," Jason said.

"What time was it?"

"About ten-fifteen."

"Did Darry make any attempt to call the Forest Service about Kelli or the Wagner's when you got to Livingston Mill?"

"We both went to the radio phone and tried calling the Clayton Ranger Station. The line was busy," Jason said. "Then, I went out to dig my car out of the snow and Darry stayed in to phone. Darry said he phoned the Clayton Ranger Station at least four more times and finally got through. He assured me that he did tell the Forest Service where Kelli and Hank were camped." Jason paused. "Say, is Darry going to get into any trouble on this?"

"He's already in a lot of trouble," Hank said. "Did you call the Forest Service from Challis later that day?"

"No." Jason said sheepishly. "I wanted to but when I told Darry, he talked me out of it. He said he had reached them. 'Trust me,' he said."

"And you trusted him?"

"Yes," said Jason. "But when I heard Senator Wagner's plea on television for help in finding his brother and he mentioned Goat Lake, I called the Forest Service."

"And you told them that Kelli and I were at Cove Lake?"

"Yes."

Hank smiled. "That phone call saved our lives. I thank you with all my heart."

The taped interview was soon over. Kelli came back in the room with Jason's mother. Dessert was served and they all sat around amiably in idle chitchat until it was time for Hank and Kelli to go to their motel in Twin Falls.

Chapter 41

Ashland, Oregon – Friday Evening – September 6th

Surprised at receiving a phone call an hour earlier, Ann met them in the common room of her dorm at Southern Oregon College. When Hank Barclay strode in with Kelli, Ann didn't recognize him at first without his "mountain man" beard and sideburns. Kelli looked different, too. She used crutches and her shoulder seemed padded under her blouse. Ann thought that she herself might be difficult to recognize. She proudly wore a long black skirt and a tie-died orange and purple blouse that she borrowed from her roommate who had bought them at the Oregon Country Fair. In one week at college she had changed a lot. "We need to meet somewhere privately," Kelli said. "My room is the place," Ann said. "My roommate is out for the evening. She has a peace rally to go to."

When they entered her dorm room, Ann wheeled and confronted Kelli. "What do you want to see me for? It wasn't my idea to leave you on the shore of Cove Lake. I started to help but Pam restrained me."

"I know," Kelli said reassuringly. "I'm not blaming you for anything. I just want to tell you what happened to us, and Hank wants to ask you some questions."

Ann listened with mounting interest as Kelli described her life each day at the Cove Lake campsite. Ann's concern mounted as Hank and Kelli's food grew short and Kelli described how the bear attacked her in the tent. After Kelli told her about her rescue by helicopter, Ann said. "I should have called the Forest Service to tell them you had broken your ankle at Cove Lake and needed help. I thought about it but Darry said he would notify them."

"Darry didn't," Hank broke in. "It was Jason who finally called the Forest Service after a TV appeal for information. And Kelli was rescued the next day."

Ann's faced beamed at the mention of Jason's name. "How is he?" she asked.

"Jason's fine, if that's who you mean?" Kelli said. "We saw him in Twin Falls last night. He sends you his best regards. ... I think he has more than a little interest in you. He'll be going to Moscow next week to start his junior year at the University of Idaho."

"I like Jason," Ann said. "He's real. He's not a phony social climber like my sister and not a phony executive like Darry."

Kelli looked shocked. "I thought you and your sister were good friends."

"Hardly," Ann replied. "She's always lorded it over me...told me what to do as if I didn't have a mind of my own. We know how it is, Aunt Kelli. Ma has always pushed you around and gotten you to do things you didn't want to do. I know how she almost forced you to baby-sit with us when we were little. And how she twisted your arm to be a chaperone on this backpacking trip. 'Chaperone,' the word almost makes me sick. I bet Ma screwed around when she was Pam's age and yet she expects Pam or me to remain virgins. That's a laugh. I shock you, don't I?"

"I am a little shocked about what you say about your mother and Pam," Kelli said. "But I'm not surprised about what you think about Darry."

"It's just that coming to college has changed me. Well, I was changing my senior year in high school. I think the Vietnam War is immoral and I've gone to one peace rally already. I think we spend far too much money as a nation on war, new cars and new fashions and far too little cleaning up our environment. I think social climbing women are dinosaurs held over from the 19th century and have no legitimate role in today's society. My roommate agrees with me. Her family comes from Scarsdale, a plush New York suburb.

"What do you think about me?" Hank asked. "You're a holdover from the 19th century too. You'd be at home among the fur traders at Jackson Hole … a real mountain man, strong, brave, and hard drinking. But you're in the 20th century now and probably a logger. You're real. Not many men could have killed a bear with a knife."

Hank chuckled. "I thank you for the flattering description of me. I grew up in a logging family and I logged off and on during high school and college but I'm now an Associate Professor of History at the University of Idaho."

"Golly, who'd have thought it," Ann remarked. "Of course I saw you only once with your beard and hiking clothes." She paused. "What do you want to talk to me about?"

Hank explained his mission and Kelli made no effort to leave the room. Ann said, "I don't mind being taped. I'm real. I have nothing to hide."

With Hank asking questions, Ann described her view of the scene at the snow slide. She said, "Darry shook you off the rope, Kelli, so he could sleep with Pam. And I'm almost sure Pam knew about the plan and approved."

With respect to the Goat Lake trail incident, Ann said she was told to stay with the packs while Darry and Pam went back to investigate. They came back and reported that the noise they had heard was some tree branches.

Blizzard in August
165

"Jason was not part of this," she said. "He went on ahead for a ways to scout the trail."

"Why do you think Darry was so insistent about not staying to help the Wagners?" Hank asked.

"Because he had an important meeting in Los Angeles his father wanted him to attend," Ann said. "I told you he was a phony executive. Here's this guy right out of college and his father wants to make him head of his Central American Resort Division ... that is if he makes the meeting and gets Board approval. Darry busted his gut trying to get there."

"And did he get to the meeting on time?" Hank asked.

"I think so," Ann thought a minute. "He called his father's mine superintendent, that's Jason's uncle, and got him to plow out the road to Challis. There Darry and Pam were driven to Idaho Falls where they boarded a corporate jet for LA. I bet all of that cost a bundle."

"Do you know who tore off the top sheet at the sign-in box a half mile up the trail?" Hank asked. "The newspaper editor asked me that and I said I didn't know."

"I bet Darry did it," Ann said. "It was there when Jason and I looked at it. Darry said he would sign us out and Jason and I let him. Pam had gone on ahead."

"What do you think of Darry?" Hank asked suddenly.

"He's a real sleaze," Ann said.

"Darry may be indicted for the murder of the Wagner parents and their youngest girl," Kelli broke in. "You may be asked to testify at his trial. Would you mind seeing Darry convicted?"

Ann looked Kelli straight in the eye. "Two weeks ago I might have. Now, I wouldn't mind testifying. I'd see Jason there. And if that sleaze is really guilty, he should pay." Ann paused and eyed Kelli. "I shock you," she said.

"Are you trying to?" Kelli asked.

"Sure. I'm trying to show the new me. I'm not a pushover." Ann said.

"I think you should know that Senator Wagner is suing Darry and Pam for forty million dollars in damages to the Wagner kids for the loss of their parents," Kelli said. Ann was shocked. "Pam couldn't pay her share. It would have to be Dad. He's always the one who gets dumped on. It would bankrupt us."

Hank turned off the tape recorder and broke in. "You are exempt from the civil suit as well as the criminal suit. I got Senator Wagner and the sheriff to agree to that. I think that the senator would take Pam out of the civil suit if she would testify that she urged Darry to stop and help the Wagners and that Darry refused." Hank paused. "Do you think Pam would do that?"

"No way." Ann said. "Not unless Darry throws her over. Pam is crazy about him. He must be some stud. And she wants to be the wife of a conglomerate executive with a condominium in Aspen and a summer home on the Maine coast."

They talked on for another hour about poetry, the War, the environment, and about the courses Ann was taking. Ann appreciated the way Kelli and Hank listened to her without knocking her ideas. When they left for their motel she decided they were all right. They were real people. And she'd shown them the new Ann, and they'd understood.

Chapter 42

Los Angeles – Saturday, September 7th

Kelli watched the Northern California scenery as she rode in her own Ford with Hank at the wheel. She preferred driving herself but it was not safe for her to do so with an ankle in a cast and bandages restricting the mobility of her shoulder. They had gotten up at 5:30 a.m. and were on the road by six, intending to stop at a drive-in at Weed for a quick breakfast. She had worked out the times and mileages and felt they could get to her sister's house by seven in the evening.

Hank was a very competent driver and Kelli added this to his many good qualities. His use of a tape recorder, to which she had so strongly objected, had not been opposed by either Jason or Ann. Jason's father's lawyer surprisingly welcomed the use of a tape recorder as a means of putting on record Hank's statements that Jason was not to blame for the problems of Kelli or the Wagners. Ann was far more interested in parading her "new self" before Kelli than in the tape recording process. What would the tapes accomplish? They would add to the evidence clearing both Ann and Jason. And they would add to the facts implicating both Dairy and Pam.

Would Pam allow her own view of the snow slide and Goat Lake trail incidents to be tape recorded? Would she subtly place the blame on Darry? If she stated that she strongly opposed leaving the Wagners without giving them food or aid, she might avoid prosecution. Ann had doubted that Pam would do that and Kelli agreed. If Hank suggested tape recording, both Pam and her mother would strongly object and there would be a terrible scene. Kelli was afraid she would be caught in the middle between her strong-willed lover and her even stronger-willed sister and niece.

With a sick feeling in the pit of her stomach, Kelli realized that the backpack trip had been a huge mistake. Darry had not only slept with Pam but had gotten both of them into trouble. Ann and Pam were no longer best friends. Kelli had met an attractive man, but there had been a gulf between them since they had argued on the way to Twin Falls. Kelli needed to be the peacemaker in the family. She wanted to show off Hank and show off her family and make the meeting harmonious.

The weather became warmer as the day wore on and Hank drove farther and farther south. By the time they had reached Sacramento, the temperature rose to the low nineties. The September warmth was invigorating to Kelli, reminding her of her childhood, but by late afternoon the heat was oppressive.

They stopped at a drive-in for hamburgers and reached Granada Hills, a suburb north of Los Angeles, at a few minutes after 7:00 p.m. Kelli had always been impressed with the tree-lined streets and spacious houses of the area where the Pettigrews lived. Now it seemed even more desirable. Following Kelli's directions, Hank stopped in front of a two-story white colonial house with dark green trim. The colonial style, Kelli knew, reflected Richard Pettigrew's own New England upbringing.

Kelli ran a comb quickly through her hair while Hank walked around to open the door on the passenger side and got her crutches. After a full day in the car, she was stiff and her ankle hurt when she accidentally put weight on it. Kelli felt the thrill of anticipation as she used her crutches in walking to the front door. Melissa must have been worried about her; this was to be a wonderful surprise for Kelli to show up on her doorstep alive and well. With Hank beside her, she rang the doorbell.

Melissa came to the door on the fourth ring. Her first words were, "Well, you have the nerve."

"Can I come in?" Kelli answered in a weak voice. Gone were her self-confidence and the quick comebacks she had often used in debates and arguments with Hank.

"Who's at the door?" came a male voice from inside the house. "My sister and some huge man in a poorly fitting sports shirt," was Melissa's reply.

"Have them come in. I've been worried about Kelli." This was Richard, Kelli knew. Unlike Melissa, Richard was always hospitable and always tried to make her feel at home.

Melissa led Kelli into a short hall with a coat closet and then into a spacious pine-paneled living room. Richard rose to greet them, gave Kelli a brief hug, and shook hands with Hank. Kelli led Hank to a cream-colored couch and they both sat down.

"You have lots of nerve coming here after what you did," Melissa said to Kelli.

"What do you mean?" Kelli asked, her voice reflecting not anger, but bewilderment. Why, she wondered, was Melissa so antagonistic?

"You left my girls unchaperoned so you could sleep with some fisherman," Melissa responded.

"I couldn't go on. My ankle was broken." Kelli was on the defensive now and her voice showed it.

Blizzard in August

"Humph." Melissa turned down the comers of her mouth. "Pam told me you just had a sprain."

"It was a break, not a sprain. "I was in a hospital for three days in Challis, Idaho, and the doctor who set my ankle said it was broken. Didn't you notice I was using crutches?" Kelli asked.

"Oh, that's just a way of getting my sympathy," Melissa's voice had a bite. "I sent you to Idaho backpacking with instructions to keep Darry from sleeping with Pam and you failed. I won't forgive you."

"But I couldn't walk two miles to Island Lake after I broke my ankle. And I was freezing cold from sliding into the lake. I wanted Pam, Ann, Darry, and his friend Jason Green to camp at Cove Lake for the night, but Darry took them off to Island Lake with him. Darry abandoned me."

Kelli saw Melissa scowl. Why couldn't she understand?

"That's not what Pam told me." Melissa stood up as if indicating that Kelli and Hank should leave.

Kelli remained seated and she found her temper rising. "Pam didn't tell the truth," she said.

"How dare you call my daughter a liar." Melissa turned to her husband. "Richard, will you sit there and let my sister call your daughter a liar?"

Richard Pettigrew sat back comfortably in a maroon easy chair. He had on blue slacks and a white sports shirt with a small blue emblem on the chest. "Now, Melissa," he said. "Kelli has a right to present her side and she has a guest to introduce."

"I suppose this is your lover," Melissa said before Kelli could say a word.

"This is Henry Barclay," Kelli said lamely. Hank stood up, walked to Richard's chair and shook his hand. He ignored Melissa and sat back down beside Kelli without saying a word.

"Pam said she looked down from the rim of the lake and saw this guy carrying you off to his tent. How could you have allowed this? I thought you had more morals than that," Melissa said.

"But he had to carry me. My ankle was broken and the others had left me dripping in freezing water. I needed to go to his tent to get my wet clothes off before I got hypothermia." Kelli was back on the defensive now. She looked to Hank but he said nothing. Perhaps, Melissa had him cowed too.

"I suppose this mountain man took off all your wet clothes, dried you, and then asked you to get in his sleeping bag." Melissa was pressing her advantage.

Kelli was aghast. "No. It wasn't that way at all. I took off my wet clothes under the tent fly. I crawled in the tent, dried myself with a towel, and put on a spare set of Hank's clothes. Then, I crawled in the sleeping bag alone."

"Tell me that you both didn't sleep in the same sleeping bag that night," Melissa said triumphantly.

Kelli defended herself weakly. "We had to keep from freezing to death."

"Tell me you didn't have sex with him at all," Melissa was like a sword fighter who had her opponent backed against a stone wall and was preparing to give a final thrust.

Kelli exploded in anger. "That's none of your damn business, Melissa. We were there eight days until I was rescued by helicopter."

"Why didn't your boyfriend carry you down to the car in his arms?" Melissa gave a disdainful look at Hank. "He looks big enough."

"It was nine miles to my car and there were three feet of snow on the ground," Kelli said.

"In August. That's ridiculous," Melissa thrust home her saber. Richard intervened in a placid tone. "We've been experiencing a heat wave in Southern California," he explained. "But I did read of a blizzard in the Idaho mountains with several feet of snow. It was in the paper about four or five days ago." He paused, looked at Kelli, and asked, "Tell me how you happened to fall into the lake."

"It was Darry's fault," Kelli said indignantly. "He was pulling me up a snowfield with a rope. He snapped the whip on me. I mean he lowered his hands and the rope slacked and I slipped to the snow. Then he pulled up hard, jerking the rope out of my hands."

"Nonsense," Melissa interrupted. "You fell and let the rope slip. Pam said you were inexperienced with a rope."

Hank spoke for the first time. "I saw the incident. Kelli has described it correctly."

Melissa turned her biting tongue on Hank. "So your stud speaks. What does he do for a living? Is he a trapper or a logger?"

A broad smile spread over Hank's face. "I used to be a logger, ma'am," he said.

"An ignorant logger." Melissa turned triumphantly to her husband. "Richard, I think they should leave. I've had enough lies from both of them."

"Now, wait a second, darling." Richard's voice was smooth and placating but Kelli sensed he would not let her and Hank be thrown out of his house. "I would be interested to hear how Kelli and Hank survived the blizzard. They must have nearly run out of food."

Blizzard in August
171

Emboldened by Richard's invitation, Kelli described each of her days in the blizzard, including the attack by the bear and having no food to eat the last day. She ended by saying, "Darry was supposed to call the Forest Service when he got to Livingston Mill but he never did tell them where Hank and I were. So no one who could help knew we were stranded at Cove Lake until Jason Green, who joined Darry on the backpack trip, called on Sunday, September first. The next day I was airlifted to safety."

"Darry did phone. Pam told me that," Melissa said, sitting back in her blue recliner and smoothing back her blond hair.

Sensing that Melissa was now on the defensive, Kelli pressed. "Darry did something much worse." She turned to Hank and said, "Tell them about Darry and the Wagners at the Goat Lake trail."

Hank broke in before Melissa could give another thrust. He related the story of the Wagner family and described the two people who stopped briefly to talk to Tom Wagner. He described how desperately eleven-year-old Tom asked them to assist and how the red- haired man refused.

"Darry promised Tom he would telephone the Forest Service about the family but he never did," Hank said.

"And what happened?" Richard asked, watching Hank intently. "Herman and Trudy Wagner and their three-year-old girl Emily died. The two other children, Tom and Lisa, were alive but starving when I rescued them and brought them to Five Mile Meadows where the Forest Service brought in a helicopter."

"That's not true," Melissa interrupted, her voice shrill and belligerent. "Pam said nothing about a family at the Goat Lake trail." Hank turned to face Richard, noticing the way he sat back in his brown upholstered chair. Ignoring Melissa, he said, "Unfortunately, it is true. Darry is in a lot of trouble and Pam may be as well."

"Richard leaned forward, his placid smile gone. "What trouble?" he asked.

"Herman Wagner's brother is Rudolph Wagner, an attorney and a powerful Idaho state senator. Rudolph Wagner has filed a forty million dollar wrongful death suit on behalf of Tom and Lisa Wagner." "Against whom?" Richard shot back, lines in his forehead and cheeks etching his concern.

Hank looked up at a picture of Richard and his family on the mantel above the fireplace. He wanted to break the news gently. He said, "Senator Wagner initially had Ann and Jason Green in the suit but I talked him out of that. I tried to get him to drop Pam from the suit, but he refused. The suit he filed shows Darrington Baltz and Pamela Pettigrew as defendants."

Richard looked grim. "Describe again what Tom Wagner told you he saw and heard."

Hank repeated Tom's report of his conversation with Darry and how he described the red-haired man with the green ski goggles and the slim blonde girl that accompanied him. Then Hank added, "Both Jason and Ann said that Pam was with Darry when he went back to investigate a noise they had heard near the Goat Lake trail. I have talked to both and neither knows what happened, but it is clear that both Ann and Jason were not involved in the incident."

"And what did Pam say?" Richard asked.

"I haven't talked to Pam since that incident," Hank said. "But Ann and Jason reported that Pam said nothing about seeing an eleven-year-old boy." Hank turned to Richard. "To clear Pamela from the brunt of the blame, and I hope involvement in the Wagner suit, it is essential that she give her own account of the Goat Lake trail incident. If she could give her version of the incident and it was Darry's fault...." "Ridiculous," Melissa interrupted. Pam would never do that. She would never sell Darry down the river. She means to marry him." Melissa was near tears and Richard's voice was soothing but firm. "But darling," he said. "We talked about Darry's problems three weeks ago. I thought you were going to discourage the romance. That's why you had Kelli take the girls backpacking in Idaho."

"Kelli ruined it. She wasn't a good chaperone. Pam's pregnant thanks to Kelli, and her fling with this.....this moron."

Kelli broke in now, her voice rising in anger. "Don't blame Pam's pregnancy on me. It's only ten or eleven days since I was abandoned at Cove Lake by Darry and Pam. She couldn't know she's pregnant in these few days. If she's pregnant, she became that way before she went backpacking. I think she and Darry have been sleeping together for weeks."

"Lies. All lies." Melissa was crying now. "Kelli and this man haven't spoken a word of truth since they came into this house. I want them out, now."

Hank had planned to sit back, observe the interaction between Kelli and Melissa, and let Kelli do most of the talking with her own family. Surprisingly, Kelli, not usually at a loss for words, seemed to be on the defensive with Melissa. Kelli must find old habits hard to break. Hank decided, as he watched Kelli losing ground. Most interesting to Hank was the attitude of Richard. He called Melissa "darling", yet he clearly wanted Kelli to give her side of the story, and he certainly did not speak highly of Darry. With Melissa's attention focused entirely on Kelli, Hank pulled a newspaper article out of his pocket and handed it to Richard. Hank stood by Richard's chair as he skimmed the article.

Blizzard in August 173

Then he said quietly to Richard. "Where can we talk privately? Pam is in real trouble. I want to help."

Richard motioned for Hank to follow him. Seated in his maroon office chair in his study, Richard said, "So you're an associate professor of history. I'm impressed. My apologies for my wife's comments." "I'm not ashamed of growing up in a logging family." "There's no reason you should be ashamed. You've gotten where you are through your own abilities." Richard paused. "Senator Wagner gives you high praise for saving his brother's two children. What kind of a man is the senator? Why is the amount of his suit so high? Half of forty million, as you must know, will bankrupt me and certainly Pam could not pay it." Richard's voice was quiet, but a twitch in his mouth betrayed his concern.

"The senator is honest, an excellent lawyer, chairman of the Senate Finance Committee, and the most powerful man in Custer County. I doubt if you or Pam are the real targets of his suit."

"Who is?"

"Big Mike Baltz and his son Dairy."

"Wherever he goes. Big Mike leaves a trail of wounded behind, doesn't he?" Richard commented, with a trace of bitterness in his voice.

"He was the most unpopular man in Custer County when he closed the Panther Creek Mine six years ago," Hank said. "One of the men who lost his job was Rudolph's oldest brother. He got drunk a week later, ran off the road, and died. Rudolph had another friend who shot himself after losing his job. I don't want to be quoted on it," Hank said, "but I'd say that the senator wants enough to feed and educate his brother's two children, and to give them a lifetime nest egg. But more importantly, he wants revenge."

"Who can blame him?" Richard said. "I have friends hurt by Big Mike who wouldn't mind a little revenge also."

"You said something in the living room which indicated a little inside knowledge about Darry. What is it?"

Richard paused and color rose in his cheeks. "This is off the record too. Darry seems to have this love-hate relationship with his father. In high school it was mainly a hate relationship and Darry was busted twice for using drugs and once for selling marijuana. His father used his influence to get him community service and a stiff fine, not jail time.

"There's something else I learned from a man who was cheated by Big Mike." Richard leaned forward with a grim glint in his eyes. "Darry was supposed to show up for a Draft Board hearing a couple of days ago. He didn't show." Richard paused, spied a picture of Darry on the bookcase, and turned it faced down. Turning again to Hank, he said, "I'd say what Darry did in Idaho is perfectly in character. I believe your and Kelli's account of what happened, not my Pam. She seems to have picked up some bad habits from Darry."

Hank smiled appreciatively. This was a man he could work with. "We need to get Pam and your family taken out of the lawsuit." "I'm with you. What influence do you have with the senator?" "I've worked with him in the past on the oral histories of Custer County pioneers. Our relationship has been cordial. I also got Ann and Jason out of the suit by getting tapes describing the facts of what happened from their vantage point. The senator asked me to tape record them and I did so without objection from Ann and Jason. I have a duplicate copy of Ann's tape in the car, which I will give you, and a duplicate I will send to the senator. This is a big help, but it isn't enough."

Richard asked, "What does the senator really want?"

"The senator wants Pam to put on tape that she saw Darry talking to Tom Wagner. And it wouldn't hurt if Pam said she tried to persuade Darry to help the Wagners and Darry refused."

"It will be hard to persuade Pam to do that," Richard said. "Unless, of course, Darry jilts her. Then I imagine she will remember some terrible things Darry said on that occasion."

Hank smiled. "We think alike. But we have one more problem and this is very confidential until you see it in the newspapers." Hank paused, studied Richard's face, and pressed on. "I am quite sure the sheriff will get a grand jury indictment against Darry, perhaps for homicide. Pam may also be indicted on a lesser charge."

"Ouch," Richard said. "Will Pam's cooperation with the senator affect how the prosecuting attorney accepts a plea bargain?"

"It might even affect whether Pam is dropped from the criminal suit," Hank said. "The prosecuting attorney was once in the senator's law firm. The senator was his predecessor and worked closely with the sheriff. They're all buddies. Custer is a small county and Big Mike has very few friends."

"Now I know what I need to do," Richard said. "You know, I never liked Darry. I don't believe he will marry my daughter and I certainly won't encourage him. Darry runs out of every tough situation and I think he left the country to evade the draft. So I may have an angry, jilted elder daughter on my hands who might be very glad to cut a tape placing the finger on Darry."

Hank smiled. Richard was not the pushover that Ann thought he was. "Enough said. You have your work cut out for you," Hank said. "And please … please do not breathe a word of what we said to Kelli or your wife. Kelli is leery of my ties to the senator."

'Not a word," Richard said. "I take it you're serious about Kelli.'

"Yes.'

"A fine woman. Good luck." Richard paused. "I'd like to have you call my lawyer tomorrow and set up a meeting. You can give him a copy of the tape Ann made and discuss our situation with him. He'll keep everything confidential. Now, I expect we should go back. My wife will be wondering what we're doing in the study."

They both had broad smiles when they walked into the living room. For Hank the smile reflected the discovery of a new friend and a possible solution for a serious problem for Kelli's family.

Hank found Melissa and Kelli still in angry argument, but Kelli was battling back now on nearly even terms. Melissa appeared tired, unable to cope with the enormity of Darry's deeds and Pamela's lies. Her mouth drooped and there were crow's feet now under her eyes.

"I think it is about time we leave and find a motel," Hank said to Kelli. Richard shook Hank's hand warmly and gave Kelli a hug. "It was very nice seeing you both. I fully approve of your Hank. He's a good man." Melissa was speechless as Richard led both Kelli and Hank to the door. All Kelli could say to Richard was, "You've always been a good friend," and, ignoring Melissa, she and Hank walked outside to her car.

Chapter 43

Los Angeles Area – Sunday, September 8

Kelli had slept until nine that Sunday morning after spending much of the night awake. Her shoulder hurt and she didn't feel like making love to Hank after they had driven to her apartment in Garden Grove. She slept in her bedroom and Hank slept on the spacious living room couch. Kelli had a terrible dream. She and Hank were floating on air mattresses on the ocean; the tide was drawing them out and the fog was rolling in. They began to separate and drifted farther and farther apart until Kelli could no longer see Hank. She kept thinking that this was Hank's fault. And then she lost him, and try as she could, she couldn't find him in the fog.

After breakfast Hank wanted to go to church, but Kelli preferred to visit the beach she so often went to as a child. They drove to Pacific Palisades, parked, and Kelli used her crutches to walk out to where the waves were breaking on the sandy shore. She stood looking out over the ocean, remembering the time she was a five-year-old and her parents took her and Melissa to the beach with a picnic lunch. Melissa was thirteen at that time. She was skinny and blond, but not yet developed and attractive to boys. Melissa was there to romp with on the beach, run out into the waves, to build sand castles with, and to laugh together. It was a joyous time, but unaccountably, the memory made her sad.

They argued like sisters do while she was growing up, but she never remembered an argument as heated as last night. Melissa would never admit she was wrong about Pam. She still considered Kelli as a younger sister, eight years her junior, who had to be set straight. The wonderful reunion in which Melissa welcomed Kelli with open arms and expressed approval of Hank, the reunion that Kelli had envisioned on the drive south from Ashland, the reunion Kelli had expected, never came about. Melissa was at fault and, with more emotion than logic, Kelli blamed Darry, Pamela, Senator Wagner, Hank, and even the White Clouds Mountains. And Kelli realized that she was partly to blame for the scene that drove a deep rift between her and her sister. Kelli and Hank walked to where they could sit on a bench. She asked him about his meeting in Richard's study but he seemed evasive. He told her that Richard had wanted a full description of what he knew about Barry's actions at the snow slide at Cove Lake and at the junction of the Goat Lake trail. She asked

Blizzard in August 177

whether Richard would try to get Pam to record her memories of both incidents. Hank said Richard would but gave no details.

Then they visited the elementary school where Kelli was principal. It was closed on Sunday, of course, and all they could do was walk around the outside. But the brief visit made Hank realize how much of her life revolved around her school and her teachers. They would begin classes in two days, the day after Labor Day. They would be counting on her. She had to phone the assistant superintendent this afternoon. What should she say? If she were to leave, her contract required at least a month's notice.

They drove back to a nearby restaurant for lunch. They were seated at a table in the far corner with a potted plant to one side. She felt confused about Hank's intentions, sad about the break with her sister, and puzzled about what she should tell her employer.

As she ate a toasted cheese sandwich and a Caesar salad Hank said, "You seemed low this morning. Did the walk on the beach bring back memories?"

"Yes, there are a lot of childhood memories on the beach. I used to walk there with my father and jump through the waves with Melissa."

"And your school. You have good memories there," Hank said as he wound spaghetti around his fork.

"That's where I started as a teacher. I was so green when 1 began, but Mrs. Marsden, the principal—she's retired now—was so supportive."

"It would be hard for you to leave," Hank observed as he split a meatball and ate half "Is that why you seem so depressed this morning?"

"That's part of it," Kelli said. "But I'm also very depressed over the fight I had with Melissa last evening. We've had some fights since she was married, but she never asked me to leave her house before."

"The puzzling thing to me," Hank said as he downed the other half of a meatball, "is why Melissa said you had just a slight sprain when you walked into the house on crutches. It doesn't make sense."

"Melissa put her faith in Pam," Kelli responded, picking at her food. "She always has."

"It's obvious Pam was lying. Richard understood that. He told me that it's a problem with Pam."

Kelli ate a small bite of her cheese sandwich. "Pam has always been Melissa's favorite. She's so like Melissa was when she was that age. To recognize Pam's flaws are to recognize her own. She can't face it."

The dining room was filling with men in suits and ties and women in flowered dresses who looked as though they had just come from church. Hank said, "I suppose Melissa identifies with Pam's attempt to marry the rich son of a multi-national corporation owner and rise into the jet set."

Kelli finished her forkful and said, "That's putting it harshly, but I guess it's true. Melissa saw herself as a Cinderella bringing her and her family up the social ladder through marriage, and she sees Pamela doing the same."

"But what about the man Pamela wants to marry?" Hank asked. "Melissa married above her, and she got not only a rising young banker but a nice, caring man. Darry is anything but a caring man. He's a self- centered, selfish playboy who tries to emulate his corporate-raider father."

"I suppose you discussed Darry with Richard too." Kelli felt mildly annoyed.

"Yes, I talked with Richard about Darry." Hank paused to down another large forkful of spaghetti. "But Richard told me that he disliked Darry from the beginning...that Darry was shallow and was too concerned about approval from his father."

"So Richard is ready to get Darry, just like you are. And so is the sheriff and also that horrible Senator Wagner." Kelli couldn't understand why her annoyance was increasing. Did she feel left out by these men in their plans and discussions?

Hank winced. "Why 'that horrible Senator Wagner?' You don't know him."

Kelli was in a combative mood. "It's the way he sneaks around and files a forty million dollar suit for his brother's children. It's a ridiculous amount. And then he conspires with the sheriff to get Darry thrown in jail when he's not there to defend himself."

"I've known Senator Wagner for seven years," Hank hotly retorted. "He's not a man who sneaks around. He's an outspoken conservative Republican State Senator who's represented Custer County for twelve years. I disagree with many of his views but I respect him as a man who speaks his mind and keeps his word. And he's well liked on both sides of the aisle in the Idaho Senate for those qualities."

Kelli backed off a little and asked, "How did you get to know the senator so well?"

"Part of my oral history project," Hank explained, "was to get pioneers in each county to put their memories on cassette tape. I recorded his eighty-five-year-old father in 1962; he had memorable stories to tell of the settling of Custer County. I got foundation support for publishing a booklet on Custer County pioneers and one chapter is on his family. The senator was very pleased with the booklet."

"Why did Senator Wagner file this ridiculously large suit?" Kelli asked.

Hank considered the question. "I don't know for sure. I suspect that any good lawyer starts a liability suit high, expecting the amount to be scaled down in a negotiated settlement or by the court. He certainly wants to set it up high enough to pay for Tom and Lisa's care and education until they are out of college. Then there's pain and suffering from losing both parents. That's worth something. And so is the loss of earning power of Herman Wagner.

"Will Tom and Lisa live with Senator Wagner? Is that another motive for a large suit?"

"That I don't know," Hank said. "They may live with a younger brother and his wife in Colorado. In any case, I suspect a good part of the settlement will be placed in a trust fund for the kids."

"Is another motive for a $40 million suit that the senator wants to get even with Big Mike?"

Hank smiled. "That's certainly possible. Big Mike has hurt Custer County before and he may do it again."

"What do you mean?" asked Kelli.

"He closed a mill where the senator's older brother worked," said Hank. "The brother lost a job he had held for twenty years and got drunk a week later. They found his body in his car at the bottom of a ravine. Another man committed suicide after he lost his job."

"Did Mike close the mill because it was losing money?" "Hardly," Hank said. "The mill never made much money but it was in the black when it was sold. Big Mike bought it because the assets were worth more than the sales price. He bought it with the intention of selling it, and he didn't give a damn about how closing the mill would affect its employees. And I've documented that he's done the same thing to mills in Clearwater, Bonner, and Valley counties." "So you want to get even with Big Mike too?"

"I'd like to see justice done," Hank said with irritation in his voice.

"Are you an expert on justice?" Kelli asked hotly. "From what you told me, I don't think closing the mill was a criminal offense."

"But it's morally wrong. He causes pain and suffering for a lot of people so he can sit in his plush office and make a big profit...a profit he can use to pamper his playboy son."

Kelli was becoming increasingly annoyed with Hank. It seemed to her that he was part of a vendetta against Big Mike and Darry, a vendetta that he had not discussed in advance with her. She asked, "Why are you so down on Darry, so damn judgmental?"

Hank said, "I'd think you'd be down on him too. He put rocks in your pack and rolled a rock down the hill either to hit you or scare you."

Kelli put aside her salad, half eaten. "Putting rocks in my pack was a prank. And a freak of nature may have caused the rock to start rolling down the hill. Or the man on the ridgeline with the binoculars may have accidentally started the rock on its way. We have no proof it was Darry."

How about what he did at the snow slide?" Hank said. "That was no accident."

Kelli found that she was looking for reasons to defend Darry. "That's true, but Darry may have done it on impulse, not realizing 1 would break an ankle."

"But Darry must have realized that a fall into ice cold water would get you soaked and in danger of hypothermia," Hank persisted.

"Perhaps he didn't think of that," Kelli said. "Being dunked in a lake in August in the California coast range is not that serious. And that's where Darry's backpacked."

"But leaving the Wagner family and not getting help for them, that's very serious." The color in Hank's face was rising now.

"But are you sure Darry really saw the boy ... that the boy didn't make it up?" Kelli was playing the devil's advocate with increasing fervor. She wanted to show Hank he was too judgmental and expose the vendetta he was participating in.

"When I rescued Tom and Lisa, I said nothing about Darry and the rest of his party. Tom volunteered that a red-haired man with green ski goggles spoke to him, refused to see his father, and volunteered to get help for them. He never did."

"How do you know that?" Kelli's voice was almost accusing.

"Because the newspaper editor had me talk to Ray Winters of the Clayton Ranger Station. Phone calls are logged in and he never received one about the Wagners. Nor did the other nearby ranger stations. If they had received a call on Wednesday or Thursday from Darry, little Emily and her parents would be alive today. That's two or three people who died because Darry, for some strange reason, never made the call."

"Maybe he tried and the line was busy."

Hank's voice had a hard edge now. "Why are you making excuses for him? He had several hours at Livingston Mill to make the call. If the Clayton Ranger Station line was busy, he could have tried other ranger stations. Jason wanted to make the call at Clayton but Darry said he would take care of it and he didn't. I think Darry was responsible for the death of three people. He should pay for it."

Blizzard in August 181

Kelli was not going to be beaten. "It seems so harsh for Darry to be executed or spend his life in prison for just an oversight. Why is the senator pressing this issue?"

"It's the sheriff. He wants to bring it to the county prosecuting attorney and perhaps a grand jury. A jury will decide if Darry is guilty and a judge will sentence him. Darry will be given a fair trial."

"In Custer County," Kelli snorted. "They hate Californians in Custer County. I saw three cars in Challis with bumper stickers which read, 'Don't Californicate Idaho.'"

"I say he'll get a fair trial," Hank said. "Why is it that you're suddenly so sympathetic to Darry?"

Kelli wondered at that herself. A week ago she would not have defended Darry as she did. "I guess I'm thinking that Pam might marry Darry and he'd become a member of my family."

"Why would Pam want to marry that spoiled bastard?" Hank's voice cut through the room like a whip.

"Because she's carrying Darry's baby." Kelli said lowering her voice so diners at other tables wouldn't hear.

"That's not a good reason for marrying a man."

"You're not a woman," Kelli said angrily. "You don't know how a woman feels about having a baby, about giving that baby a name and a home."

"Did she intentionally get pregnant as a means of getting Darry to marry her? If she did that, I could understand why she'd want to marry him," Hank sounded puzzled.

Kelli's voice softened momentarily. "I don't know. But I really feel for Pam. It's hard being pregnant and not knowing whether you're going to marry the baby's father."

Hank frowned. "Is there any danger you're going to have our baby?" Hank was also speaking in a low voice now.

"No, it was the wrong time of the month." Kelli looked away; she was a little worried but didn't want to show it. Changing the subject, she said, "It may have been the man on the ridgetop with the binoculars I saw. He might have had red hair and a blonde wife."

Hank considered this, eating the last of his spaghetti. "Not likely. I would have seen or heard him if he crossed the stream by my tent. And the outlet stream is too deep to go the other way."

"You've passed sentence on Darry already," Kelli said. "You lack compassion. I don't feel I really know you. You can be so hard and unforgiving...chiseled out of granite...just like the Idaho mountains you love."

She paused. "You feel misled. I do too. I had no idea you were going to be part of a plot to put Darry in jail and stick his father with a huge monetary settlement."

"What do you mean, a plot?"

"Well, you and the sheriff and the senator were plotting as you drove up to Livingston Mill weren't you? And you and Richard Pettigrew were plotting in Richard's study? And you'll be plotting when you meet with Richard's lawyers. And all this plotting will take place when no women are present."

"You can come to the meeting with Richard's lawyer if you wish," Hank said.

"Why should I bother?" Kelli's cheeks flushed red. "You men will make the decision. You don't care how it affects Pam, or Melissa or me."

"I do. I'm doing what I'm doing to help protect your family from a ruinous lawsuit. Don't you understand?"

"But you didn't check with me first to see how I felt," Kelli said. "You should have made no commitments to the senator, to Richard or anyone else without consulting me. After all, it's my family. You don't understand women, Hank. And I don't think I really know you." Kelli was skating on dangerous ice now but she was past caring.

"Are you saying you don't really love me?" Hank asked. Kelli rose from her chair, her meal not finished. "I don't know. Right now I'm angry with all men, you, Richard, the sheriff and especially the senator. I feel put upon as a woman and I just don't trust you. I want to take a nap. I'll think it over this afternoon. Why don't we eat dinner here at six?"

"Do you want me to drive you back to your apartment?"

"Please. And pick me up in time for dinner." She limped to the ladies room.

Hank sat at the table a minute, slammed his fist on the table, and called for the check. After he took Kelli back to her apartment, he would be early to the meeting with Richard's lawyer. He couldn't understand why Kelli was suddenly so antagonistic. He was deeply depressed.

Chapter 44

Los Angeles Area – Sunday afternoon

Hank Barclay wondered what had gone wrong as he drove to the office of Roy Morrison, Richard Pettigrew's attorney. He had been thinking of proposing marriage to Kelli that evening. After the fight they had at lunch he was not sure he wanted to marry her and was doubtful she would accept his marriage proposal if he offered it. But the fight made no sense. He was trying to save Richard Pettigrew's family from financial ruin by getting Pam as well as Ann Pettigrew eliminated from the forty million dollar suit filed by Senator Wagner. Why should Kelli object to that? Why should she take Darry Baltz's side?

Women were hard to understand. Hank thought. Kelli was so touchy about being included in each decision affecting Darry and his father. But she turned down his invitation to attend the meeting. Hank had half a mind to skip out on the meeting with Mr. Morrison and take in a movie. But he had promised Richard Pettigrew that he would meet with his lawyer so he would do so.

At two Hank was ushered into Mr. Morrison's office and sat in a tan upholstered chair. A sandy-haired man with glasses, Ray Morrison sat behind a polished oak desk cluttered with papers and law books.

After the introductions, he got right down to business. "Mr. Pettigrew wants me to deal directly with State Senator Rudolph Wagner. I need to know if he is trustworthy and why he filed such a large lawsuit."

"The senator is a man of his word. You can deal with him," Hank assured Mr. Morrison. "As to his motivation for the large amount, I can only make a guess. He certainly wants to provide for his brother's two remaining children until they finish their education and would like to leave them a nest egg for the future. But I think his greatest motivation is to punish Big Mike Baltz for closing a lumber mill a few years ago and firing the senator's brother and a number of his friends."

"Why does he include Pamela Pettigrew in the suit? She had, I understand, only a minor role in what happened between Darry and Tom Wagner at the Goat Lake trail. I presume the senator is not angry at my client, Richard Pettigrew?"

"I am sure the senator has no vendetta against your client," Hank said. "I think he is using the suit against Pam as a means of forcing her to testify against Darry. He needs a witness who can prove that Darry talked to Tom Wagner. Only Pam can do this."

"Now we come to the crux of the matter," said Mr. Morrison. If Pamela Pettigrew provided this testimony, would the senator dismiss his suit against her?"

"I think so, but I believe you should contact him directly," Hank said. "Can you get Pamela to testify and can you get it on tape?"

"Possibly," Mr. Morrison said. "I understand that Darry is now in Mexico to avoid the draft and Pam has not been able to locate him. If she finds Darry in Mexico, I presume she will want to marry him...particularly since she is now...ah...pregnant with his child."

"I believe the Custer County grand jury is set to indict Darry, and Big Mike probably got wind of it through one of his employees at the mine," Hank said. "I think Darry may also be hiding in Mexico to avoid prosecution. He's now the head of his father's Central American Resort Division with headquarters at Acapulco."

"That's useful information," the lawyer said. "Now, the question is does Darry want to marry Pam?"

"Darry strikes me as a selfish playboy," Hank said. "Someone not ready to settle down, particularly when he finds out Pam is carrying his baby."

"If Darry jilts her, could she be persuaded to testify about whether Darry talked to Tom Wagner and describe their conversation?" the lawyer asked.

"I think so," said Hank. "And Darry may be thinking of jilting her. He has a tendency to run out on commitments when the going gets tough."

"And is more likely to do so if Big Mike is against the marriage," Morrison said. "And I think I know a way to get Big Mike to oppose the marriage. I just need to make a phone call and provide him with some information about Pamela."

"That's your business. I don't want to know about it," Hank replied.

"Fine," Mr. Morrison said. "But I'd like you to phone Senator Wagner right now and introduce me as Richard Pettigrew's lawyer and as a man who can be trusted. I want to be sure of his price for taking Pam out of the suit."

Hank phoned directory assistance and got the senator's home number. After one busy signal, he got through.

"Good to hear your voice," the senator said. "Did you tape Jason Green and Ann Pettigrew?"

Blizzard in August

"Yes," Hank said. "I have a copy of the tapes for you. Shall I mail them to your law office or your home?"

"To my law office, but keep a copy yourself," the senator said and he gave Hank the mailing address. "Did you learn anything new from the tapes?"

"Mainly details of the snow slide and Goat Lake trail incidents. Both Jason and Ann are clear. They did not see Tom Wagner. Darry went back with Pam to identify a noise they heard from the Island Lake trail. When Darry returned, he told them both it was just two trees rubbing in the wind. This was an obvious lie," Hank said.

"I have some information to pass along," the senator said. "The Custer County grand jury will be convened today but I have persuaded the prosecuting attorney to hold off on bringing Pamela's case before them."

"But Darry has fled the country already to avoid the draft and prosecution. He's somewhere in Mexico."

"There's always extradition if Big Mike is not cooperative," the senator said. "We can send someone into Mexico to hunt him down." Hank's mind whirled. What did the senator mean by cooperation? Had he and the prosecuting attorney worked out a deal to sell to Big Mike?

Hank was very uneasy. He said, "I don't want to know your plans. I am in the law office of Roy Morrison, lawyer to Richard Pettigrew. He is a trustworthy man and I told him you are, too. He's ready to talk turkey about what you want in exchange for Pamela to be left out of your civil suit. I'll put him on."

Hank put Mr. Morrison on the phone and listened to the lawyer's end of the conversation, which appeared to be amicable. As far as he could tell from Mr. Morrison's responses, the senator wanted Pamela's description of Darry's conversations with Tom Wagner on tape. He seemed to be suggesting that Pamela place the blame on Darry. He also wanted Pam to describe events at the snow slide and at the caretaker's cabin at Livingston Mill.

Mr. Morrison was smiling when he hung up. "I see the light at the end of the tunnel," he said. "Now I have a phone call to make which you do not want to hear."

Hank shook hands with Mr. Morrison and left. It was a dirty business, he decided when he got to Kelli's car. The Custer County sheriff and prosecuting attorney were working with the powerful Senator Wagner. And now Roy Morrison and Richard Pettigrew were part of the team effort that would try to get Pam to testify against Darry. If successful, the Pettigrew family would not face financial ruin. And the big losers, Hank suspected, were going to be Mike Baltz and his son.

Hank drove aimlessly for a while. He parked near the beach and walked, wondering what Kelli was like as a little girl. He drove by the elementary school where Kelli worked and realized that she had a loyalty that pulled her to resume her work as principal next Tuesday. Perhaps it was better for him to take a plane for Idaho Falls tomorrow and say good-by to Kelli. If he left tomorrow, he could catch a bus for Challis, pick up his car, and be in Moscow before the fall semester opened at the University of Idaho.

But the love that had burned so strongly inside him was far from extinguished. He still loved Kelli, but how much? He saw a mall, parked his car, and walked into the nearest jewelry store.

Kelli had cried herself to sleep after lunch. She didn't wake from her nap until nearly three. Feeling refreshed, she tried to analyze her relationship with Hank. He had many good qualities—his courage, his strength, his skill, and his position as a university professor were important. So was his abstinence from cigarettes and liquor important to Kelli, another abstainer. He had undoubtedly been true to Susan until her death, and, if he married Kelli, Hank would probably remain faithful to her. These were important pluses. Why was Kelli so dubious about marriage?

Partly, it was a concern about her relationship with Melissa. Kelli could reconcile with her sister, but sparks would always fly when Hank and Melissa met. He was so judgmental over what he considered Melissa's obvious social climbing. Kelli was also not sure she wanted to leave her position as an elementary school principal or leave the familiar warm coast of Southern California. Northern Idaho seemed so cold, barren, and far from home. Her mind pictured a land of towering majestic peaks, freezing snowfields, and strong unbending loggers, miners, and ranchers.

Was Hank really ready for a second marriage himself? Had he finished grieving over his wife? Sure, he and Kelli had made love that one night in the tent, but was this sexual attraction or something deeper?

There was one thing she could do, Kelli realized. She could try to re-establish a good relationship with her sister. Kelli picked up the phone in her apartment and called Melissa. A maid answered and said Melissa was out.

Kelli next phoned Denise Panelli, the assistant superintendent who was responsible for elementary schools in her district. Denise was overjoyed that she was back and listened sympathetically as Kelli gave a brief account of her adventures in the White Clouds and her injuries. "Are you well enough to come back when school starts on Tuesday?" Denise asked when Kelli stopped talking.

"I could come back if you need me." Kelli found herself saying. "I will be on crutches for a while and my shoulder will be hurting a little.. .but I could be back in school Tuesday if you want."

"Great! We really needed you last week. I came over for two days and Donna Wu helped out. But Donna's going to have to teach sixth grade this week." She paused. "We need you badly to give direction and counseling to the teachers and handle the paperwork. I know you'll be a bit desk-bound for a while, but we really need you." "I'll be there," Kelli promised. She paused and then asked, "If I did decide to move to another state, how much notice should I give?" "I certainly hope you're not thinking of moving," Denise said with anxiety in her voice. "Under your contract, you are legally required to give a month's notice, but I can't get a good replacement before the Christmas break." She paused. "You're not thinking of leaving are you?"

"Not really," Kelli said. She hung up and wondered whether Hank would ever consider moving to Southern California.

Kelli moped around her apartment the remainder of the afternoon, trying twice unsuccessfully to phone Melissa. She put on a skirt and her yellow Cashmere sweater and waited for Hank.

Hank was early, let off in front of the restaurant, and parked the car, and returned quickly to help her into the restaurant. After they ordered, he excused himself and came back with a dozen long-stemmed roses in a white vase. He smiled at Kelli and handed her the roses. "They're so beautiful. It was thoughtful of you," she said. Hank sat down. "I've come to apologize for this morning. I shouldn't have argued with you about Darry. You and your family are important to me now, not Darry and his father."

"Thanks," Kelli said and smiled briefly. Then she asked, "How did the conference with Richard's lawyer go?"

"Fine. I think your family will be eliminated from the civil suit." Hank paused. "Mr. Morrison phoned the senator and a deal was made. He didn't tell me what it was and I didn't ask."

"And you all sold Darry and his father down the river," Kelli said hotly.

Hank looked sadly at the roses. "Maybe you're right, but I'm not part of it now. The important thing is that your sister and her family will probably not face financial ruin."

Kelli felt her anger rising again, "It was still a dirty deal." "Please, let's not discuss this any more," Hank begged. "Could you come with me to the veranda for a minute?"

Kelli could guess what Hank wanted, but followed him to a table in the corner of the veranda that overlooked the ocean. When they were seated, Hank said, "I love you more than I can tell you. Will you marry me?"

Hank proposed so suddenly that Kelli had no ready response. She asked, "When do you want to get married?"

"I'd like us to start driving north tomorrow. We could find a Justice of the Peace on the way or get married as soon as we reach Idaho."

"But I'm under contract to the school district. I have to give at least a month's notice to leave," Kelli said.

Hank thought a minute. "Well, I could stay a few days and we could get married here. Then you could give notice to your school district and follow me to Idaho in a month."

Kelli shook her head sadly. Hank just didn't understand her loyalty to her family and school district. "Hank, Melissa, Richard, and my parents would want to put on a big wedding. It would take about two months for planning and sending out invitations. And I can't quit my job as principal in a month. The assistant superintendent wants me to stay on until Christmas break until she can get a replacement or train one."

Hank's mouth drooped and he couldn't speak for a minute. "Could we get married at Christmas time?"

Kelli was filled with mixed emotions. She just wasn't sure she wanted to promise to marry Hank, but she didn't want to break off any contact with him. "We might get married at Christmas," she said. "But I have a lot of thinking to do. I just don't want to make a commitment now."

Hank looked sad. He reached in his pocket and brought out a small box. "Open it," he said. "It's not much, but it was the best I could get on a Sunday."

Kelli opened the box, pulled out the engagement ring, and began to cry. When she could speak again, she said, "Hank, you shouldn't have done this. It's beautiful, but you keep it."

Hank was close to tears, himself. "I don't want it. There's no other woman in my life but you. I probably won't ever need it. If you really don't want it just...just....just throw it away." He put his head down on an arm and tears rolled down his cheeks onto his sleeves.

Kelli felt a rush of sympathy for him but did not put an arm around him. She did not want to encourage him. She couldn't promise to marry him now, at Christmas, or any time when her emotions about him were mixed and her life was in such disarray.

After a few minutes, she said. "Let's go back to the table. If you want to get a plane reservation for tomorrow, I'll understand."

They returned to the table and Hank left immediately to phone the airlines, returning to report that he was leaving at 5 a.m. the next morning for Salt

Blizzard in August   **189**

Lake City and then transferring to a plane to Idaho Falls. He would catch a bus and reach Challis tomorrow afternoon.

Hank seemed deeply depressed during dinner and Kelli had difficulty keeping a conversation going. "Christmas isn't forever," Kelli said, as Hank was paying the bill. But he had no response.

They went back to Kelli's apartment. She wondered whether she should try to mend their relationship by offering to sleep with him that night. But what was the use? Hank could just not understand her commitment to her school and to her family. Why was he so insensitive? Maybe most men were that way.

"If I'm going to catch a plane at five tomorrow morning, perhaps I should get a motel near the airport for tonight," Hank said.

"Stay here, you can call for a cab to pick you up in plenty of time to meet the plane." Kelli put on a cup of coffee. "We can watch television this evening and you can tell me about the courses you will be teaching this fall."

They sat awkwardly for two hours on Kelli's living room couch watching television. He phoned for a taxi to pick him up at three in the morning. But Hank seemed too dispirited to say much about his fall plans at the university. At nine, Hank said, "I guess I better go to bed. It's been wonderful knowing you." Close to tears, he added. "I'll slip out at three tomorrow without waking you."

They kissed briefly and then Kelli limped into the bedroom on her crutches. She waited ten minutes, half hoping he would knock on her bedroom door. Then she undressed, put on her nightgown, lay down on her bed, and cried as though her heart would break. She just knew that would be the last time she would see him.

Chapter 45

Challis and Moscow, Idaho – September 9th – 25th

"Did you really kill a bear with a knife?" Tom Wagner looked at Hank with admiration.

"Yes, I did," Hank replied, taking another forkful of beef stew. "It clawed Kelli and bit a hole in the tent." "Show me the knife. Tell me how you did it," Tom persisted.

Hank was tired from his trip to Challis, but Tom was eager to learn the gory details of how he killed the bear. Hank gave a colorful description and then added, "My knife is packed away in my backpack. I could get it out if you really want me to."

"No need," Senator Wagner said. "You must be tired. When you phoned for a ride to your car, I just wanted you for dinner and to spend the night. I didn't want to completely tire you out; you have a long drive to Moscow tomorrow."

"What's a mountain man?" asked Lisa, picking at her acorn squash.

"Why do you ask?" Mrs. Wagner passed Hank the bowl of stew and Hank took another helping.

"Well, the kids in my class say I was rescued by a mountain man. I want to know if this is bad or good."

"Good," the senator replied with a chuckle. "In the old days in Jackson Hole, just a few hundred miles from here, the fur trappers and Indians would gather for trading and a bit of celebrating. These trappers were mountain men —big, strong, brave, and able to survive the terrible winters. It's an honor to be called a mountain man. They're a tough, strong breed; just like your great-grandfather and great-great-grandfather who first settled this county." The senator put a gentle arm on Hank's shoulder. "I'm proud to know this mountain man."

Hank's cheeks flushed. The praise was embarrassing but, for the first time since Sunday afternoon, he recovered some of his self-esteem.

After dinner, the senator took Hank into his library that served as an office in his home. Hank inspected the bookshelves—law books, Idaho legislative documents, histories of Idaho and the West, novels, and even a few volumes of poetry. He saw his History of Custer County Pioneers, pulled it out, and then put it back in its place.

Blizzard in August   **191**

"That history is one of my prized possessions," the senator said. "You know it's not many professors who can write an excellent history and can trudge through three feet of snow to save the lives of two kids. I can't tell you how much you've done for me. I wrote a letter to your President Watkins letting him know what a hero you are to my nephew and niece and to the people of my county."

Hank was touched by the warmth of the senator's feeling. "Thanks," he responded. "I would be pleased if Pam does not have to go to jail and her family is not bankrupt by the civil suit."

The senator smiled, "We have that all worked out."

"How?" Hank asked.

"You don't want to know," the senator responded. "Over the years Big Mike has played hardball and squeezed a lot of good people. It's time that the chickens come home to roost."

Hank went to bed soon afterwards, realizing that the game the senator and prosecuting attorney were playing with Richard Pettigrew and his lawyer was out of his league. The next morning on the way to his car, he asked the senator. "Are you going to call on Kelli to testify?" "No need," the senator said. "Do you think I should?"

"No, it's better to leave her out of it. For some strange reason, she seems to have some sympathies for Darry Baltz and his father." Hank reached Bovill the following evening to pick up his three girls and bring them to their home in Moscow, thirty miles away. Uncle Ted was curious about what happened in the White Clouds and Hank, tired as he was from the drive, provided an abbreviated account of his adventures.

"We were pleased to keep the girls for a few more days," his uncle said, "but I was surprised you needed to go to Los Angeles."

Uncle Ted, Aunt Marjorie, and his oldest daughter, Sara, were standing in front of the wood stove in the living room. Hank stood staring at varnished log walls for a moment, hoping Sara would leave.

Finally, he said, "There was a woman I rescued in the mountains who had broken her ankle. She couldn't drive. I needed to drive her and her car back to her home."

Uncle Ted smiled. "Is she pretty?"

Hank smiled back. "Yes. She's an elementary school principal in Garden Grove." Then, noting too much interest from Sara, he changed the subject.

Hank went to his office the next day to find his colleagues eager for news of his White Clouds adventures. His department head had gotten a photocopy of the earlier news story on Hank from the president's office and had posted it on the bulletin board.

That Friday, Hank was called into the president's office along with his dean and department head. President Watkins handed a photocopy of a letter from Senator Wagner to everyone present.

"This is the kind of publicity I like to see our professors get," the president said. "You saved the lives of the Senator's grandchildren and preserved the contributions of his father and grandfather in your book. He's a key member of the Senate, as you know, and what you did in the White Clouds is worth ten refereed journal articles." President Watkins left his chair and went to where Hank was sitting and shook his hand.

Dean Arthur Federucci and Ivan Kelso, Hank's department chairman, offered their congratulations as well.

"I want to see this get the maximum publicity," the president said. "Arthur, get on the phone with Public Relations and the Alumni Department. Play up the people whose lives Professor Barclay saved ... and get the bear story in. That's an attention getter. When some legislators start talking about the pointy-headed college professors at the University of Idaho, I want others to remember that we have one faculty member brave enough to kill a bear with a knife and strong enough to slog through three feet of snow to save two kids. I think the senator will be in our corner, too, this legislative session."

The dean did the president's bidding and Hank found himself photographed and interviewed.

An article about him was sent to all nine daily newspapers in Idaho. His portrait appeared on the cover of the Idaho Alumni magazine and the account of what he had done was the lead article. Hank, to his surprise and pleasure, had become a hero for the moment.

The letter from Kelli came two weeks later. The Associated Press had picked up the story and condensed it to two paragraphs. The bi-line read, "History Professor Bests Bear." Kelli had enclosed the brief clipping in her letter. She also enclosed copies of pictures she had taken in the White Clouds including a shot of her in her red ski sweater.

All three girls were standing near when Hank opened the letter and showed the news clipping. Joanne thought the mountains were beautiful. Julie wanted to see the picture of the bear and Hank explained that they didn't have a photo of it. Sara was the most interested. She read the article twice and examined each picture carefully.

Pointing to a picture of Kelli, she asked, "Is this the woman you told Uncle Ted you took to Los Angeles?"

"Yes," Hank replied simply.

Blizzard in August

"She's pretty," Julie said. "She looks really nice. Are we going to get to meet her?"

Hank looked down at his shoes. "I don't know," he said honestly.

Chapter 46

Los Angeles – Early October

Kelli plunged into her work as principal in September and found the planning and conducting in-service training sessions a challenging experience. She worked closely with Donna Wu, giving her a chance to experience some of her work. Donna proved an apt learner. She would get her principal's certificate this fall so she could step into Kelli's position next year if needed.

Hank had written a nice, short letter to Kelli thanking her for the pictures. He had enclosed a clipping about himself He closed with, "I still love you."

In the next two weeks there were no further letters from Hank even though Kelli had written twice. She worried about that. Was Hank sick? Was he dating another woman? Kelli wrote Hank another letter—a long newsy letter telling him that Pam and Melissa had been in Mexico searching for Darry for the past two weeks. "When you get some time," she wrote, "could you contact the other people who backpacked into the White Clouds at the time we did? See if anyone remembers a man with binoculars. He could be the person Darry saw."

Then Kelli looked at the calendar. She had marked off the days, anxious about whether she was pregnant. This morning she had learned she was not going to have Hank's baby. She felt relieved, but also sad as if another link to Hank was gone. This was too private to mention in her letter to him.

It had been a frustrating three weeks for Pamela Pettigrew. Her mother insisted that Pam go with her to Mexico to find Darry Baltz and get him to marry her. At first, Pam was delighted with the idea. But the search had proved unsuccessful. They were told at Guaymas that Darry was in Mazatlan; at Mazatlan he was supposed to be in Acapulco. No one had Darry's phone number, and none of the hotels he was supposed to run knew of his whereabouts. Finally, one hotel manager told Melissa he thought Darry was in Paris while another swore he was in Rome.

Melissa was ready to pursue Darry to Europe if necessary, but Pam was fed up with the shell game to which they had been subjected. It was obvious to her that Darry had no intention of marrying her. She demanded to go home and Melissa booked a flight from Mexico City to Los Angeles.

Blizzard in August 195

The next day she visited her father in his office. She sat in a maroon chair staring at the neat piles of papers on her father's desk. She listened as he talked over a loan application with a prominent Los Angeles businessman. My father is an able, decisive man, she thought. He will know what to do.

"Dad," she said when he put down the phone. "We couldn't find Darry. I think he's hiding from me. I don't think he wants to marry me. Maybe he never wanted to marry me ... just have sex with me." Her voice quavered a bit.

Richard Pettigrew looked at his daughter with compassion. "I think you're right. He's a playboy. He has a history of ducking out of things when the going gets tough."

"What am I going to do, Dad? Mom is no help at all. She says I should do the honorable thing, but I think she just doesn't want me to bring scandal to the family." Pam watched her father for a reaction, but his face showed kindness and no shock.

"You have some time to decide what to do about your baby," Richard said. "But you have two serious, immediate problems. Darry will face criminal charges because he did nothing to help the Wagner family after he saw Tom Wagner. You saw Tom Wagner, too. You could face lesser criminal charges."

Pam's mouth tightened in fear. "Could I be tried and put in jail?"

Richard looked stern. "Yes. Unless you tried to persuade Darry to help the Wagners." Richard paused, "And that's not all. You have been named along with Darry as co-defendants in a forty million dollar civil wrongful death suit. Again, it would be different if you tried to get Darry to help the Wagners."

"I can't pay forty million dollars, Dad."

"They would go after me for half that amount," her father said. "Our family would be bankrupt. We'd have to sell our house and our belongings." Richard's voice was quiet but there was an urgency in the way he spoke.

Pam was incensed. "That jerk. He was so anxious to get to Livingson Mill to make that important meeting in LA. His father said he wouldn't be considered for the Central American post if he didn't make the meeting." Her face grew crimson and her lips tightened in hate. "It was all Darry's idea. I saw him talking to that boy across the stream. I didn't speak up then, but I sure objected when we were walking back to Jason and Ann. It was Darry's fault, not mine."

Richard looked at his daughter, his mouth slightly curved. Pamela wondered if he knew she was telling a lie. No matter. Only Darry knew what really happened and he was probably hiding away in Europe.

"Would you be willing to state this on a deposition? That's just a piece of paper which states under oath what you told me now."

Pam hesitated. "Would I be asked to testify in Darry's trial?" "It probably won't come to trial. And if it does, Darry won't be there. He'll be hiding out abroad," her father said.

"And what will happen to me if I sign this deposition?"

"You will be taken out of the civil suit for sure. And I think all criminal charges against you will be dropped." Richard smiled.

Suddenly Pam felt free of the terrible burden around her neck. "I'll sign this paper. Who has it?"

Her father smiled. "My attorney. Roy Morrison, can draw it up. We're going over to see him right now."

Her father now seemed the strong person in her family, not her mother. Driving over in the car, she asked, "What do I do about the baby?"

"Come see me tomorrow about this time," Richard said and I'll take you to see someone who can tell you what your choices are." "And not bring Mom."

"No. And don't tell her about the deposition for a while. She doesn't understand legal matters and it would upset her."

Kelli didn't learn of the deposition until the second week of October and she was upset. Melissa had found out and she had been more puzzled than upset. She called Kelli because her husband's offhand comment about the deposition confused her. Kelli said little. The dirty deed had been done; a legal trap had closed around Darry. It seemed so unfair; Pam had probably lied to save her own skin.

Two days later, Kelli was invited by Rowena Mason to a party at a professor's home near the U.C.L.A. campus. Rowena was the elementary school art and music teacher and she drove Kelli to the party, telling her that there would be some attractive bachelors there. The exterior of the house was white, trimmed with green and the lawns well maintained. Once inside the door Kelli saw a mass of people, most talking in small groups with a drink in their hands. Kelli felt ill at ease; she found it difficult to converse about abstract art or eighteenth century music. She joined one little group in the corner because they had chairs to sit on.

Kelli was offered a glass of wine but asked for a soft drink instead. Kelli relaxed, feeling out of her element, but she enjoyed listening to the sculptor, the matronly musician, the historian, and the sociologist. They talked about their respective fields for a while and then began a gripe session on what the sociologist called "the tenure and promotion game."

Blizzard in August   **197**

"They require too many refereed journal articles for promotion to Associate Professor," the sociologist said.

"And major performances," said the musician.

"Not at the cow colleges," the historian said. "I met a man who actually made Associate on the basis of some published histories of pioneer families in his state. He used interviews and got grant money. He told me he had only one refereed journal article."

"Who's that? Anyone I know?" asked the sociologist knocking the tobacco out of his pipe.

"No, but he's been in the paper," the historian continued, taking a sip of wine. "He's the one who faced down a bear inside his tent and killed it with a knife. And he became quite a hero by saving the niece and nephew of a prominent state senator in Idaho."

Kelli kept silent but the conversation began to annoy her.

"He's a former logger. I read the article too," the musician said. "Probably he thinks a fugue is a kind of mushroom."

The others laughed. "The thing that irks me is that he'll probably make full professor at the University of Idaho on the basis of his heroism and a few more little booklets about pioneers. There are no real scholarship standards there," the sociologist concluded.

"Was it heroism or dumb luck?" the sculptor said. "I could have dispatched the bear with my newest creation, my Roman gladiator with spear. Then I could christen my gladiator, the warrior, and get tenure." Everyone but Kelli laughed again. The sculptor rose to get more wine and filled Kelli's glass along with the rest. Then, the sculpture asked the sociologist, "What would you do if a bear poked his head inside your tent?"

"Run like hell," the sociologist said.

"What about the girl the bear clawed?" asked the historian draining his wine glass.

"Who cares about her, I could always find another chick." The sociologist winked at Kelli. "You'd go out with me wouldn't you?"

Kelli's faced flushed and her drink spilled on the floor. She raised her voice "As a matter of fact, I'm the woman who was clawed by that bear. I thank God I had a man with guts in the tent to protect me. I owe my life to him. He may have been a logger and he may not have many refereed journal articles, but he's got more courage than any man in this room."

Conversation ceased. The sociologist rose angrily and walked away with the historian. The sculptor tried to ease tensions with a sick joke, but no one laughed except himself and he left.

The musician stayed. "You're in love with this man, aren't you?" She put a comforting hand on Kelli's arm.

"I guess I am," Kelli said and tears started to form in the corners of her eyes.

"Interesting. Are you seeing each other? Why don't you marry him?" the musician asked with compassion in her voice.

"He proposed. And I turned him down," Kelli said. "It was after a silly fight. It's complicated. I don't want to get into it."

"Can you get him to ask you again?" the musician asked helpfully.

"I doubt it. I hurt his pride. He's got a job in Idaho and I'm an elementary school principal in Garden Grove." Kelli was in misery, despair tearing at her heart. "I doubt if I'll ever see him again." She stood up. "Thanks for your concern," she said. She found Rowena in the crowd and asked Rowena to drive her home.

Chapter 47

Los Angeles Area – Late October

Kelli was admitted promptly to Richard Pettigrew's office and took a plush seat beside his desk. He looked up from his work and smiled. "It's a long time since you've come to see me in my office," he said.

Kelli remembered the time she'd had feelings for Richard and didn't want to remind him of those bygone years. "I thought Melissa and I would be reconciled by now. I've called several times to ask her how she's feeling, but I just get terse answers."

"Melissa's going through a difficult time." Richard doodled on a yellow pad. "She doted on Pam and now she thinks Pam is going to disgrace the family by having an illegitimate child. She wants Pam to get a quiet abortion, but Pam's totally opposed. Melissa is controlling, as you know, and Pam wants to be free from her mother."

"What do you think she should do?" Kelli asked.

"She should make her own decision," Richard said, drawing a baby on his pad. "I took her to a counselor who described her options, and Pam decided against abortion. She may put the child out for adoption or may raise the child herself. I'll support her in either decision."

Kelli looked at Richard. He was a good father. "Is she going to be facing criminal charges?" she asked.

Richard smiled again. "The Custer County prosecuting attorney has read her deposition and decided that since she argued with Darry to return to help the Wagners, she should be dropped from the case."

Kelli had an acid comment on her tongue but held it back. "And the civil suit?"

"Pam has been dropped from that as well." Richard grinned. "That wouldn't have happened without Hank's help. I suspect you still think the whole process was underhanded, but bankruptcy would mean we would lose most of our possessions and savings. We wouldn't have money to send Pam and Ann to college."

"I do think you were all underhanded, and I guess I thought you men lacked compassion for Darry and Big Mike." Kelli could state her views now without anger.

"We were underhanded in a way," Richard admitted. "But, Kelli, what we all did to place the blame on Darry was not one tenth as improper as what Darry did not do to make sure the Forest Service knew the plight of Hank, yourself and the Wagners. After all, the Wagner parents and their little girl died because he failed to reach the Forest Service."

"He might have tried many times but not gotten through."

"Kelli, he could have informed the mine caretaker. He might have called other ranger stations. He could have had Jason make some calls from Challis, or even stopped at the Challis Ranger Station. Three people died, Kelli. That should not go unpunished."

Kelli felt deflated, too tired to argue further. "What's the result of the deal?"

"Pam will not be prosecuted and will be taken out of the civil suit. Darry will be tried in absentia. But, if found guilty, Custer County officials will not try to get him extradited from Mexico or wherever he is. He will probably not spend a day in jail."

"I'm glad he won't be jailed," Kelli said. "Exile is enough punishment. But what about the cash settlement?"

"Big Mike settled out of court. His corporation is paying ten million dollars to Tom and Lisa Wagner with the senator as trustee until they come of age."

"Is Big Mike's conglomerate going to survive?" Kelli asked. Richard rubbed his chin. "He's taken a hit. The stock of his multinational corporation has dropped by a few points since the suit was announced."

"I feel a little sorry for Big Mike," Kelli said.

"Don't. He's played hardball in a lot of corporate take-overs and won. It's ironic that this time he was beaten by a rural county prosecuting attorney and state senator. Big Mike is moving his headquarters to the Bahamas. There's less regulation there and it's a tax advantage." Richard paused. "Please relay this information to Hank with my thanks," Richard said.

Kelli sighed. "I write him every week or ten days, but seldom get a response. But I will put this in my next letter."

Richard bent forward in his chair. "It's none of my business, but what happened between you and Hank? I had high hopes you would marry him."

"We had a big fight the day after we came to your home," Kelli said. I was upset that Melissa and I were so angry at each other. I wanted things to be the way they used to be with her." Kelli hesitated. "I felt sorry for Darry ... that you were all ganging up on him. And I was angry that all you men were making decisions affecting Darry and Pam without my participation. I felt excluded, as a woman, from decisions vitally affecting my own family, and I placed the blame partly on Hank."

Blizzard in August

"How did Hank feel?" Richard asked.

"He didn't have much of a clue why I was angry. At dinner he brought me a dozen long-stemmed roses. That was sweet." She stopped, remembering that she had left the roses at the table. "He took me out on the veranda and proposed; and gave me an engagement ring. And I turned him down ... even when he suggested getting married and then my working for a month or two until my replacement could be found."

"And do you regret it?" Richard reached across the desk to gently touch Kelli's hand.

"I do," she said. "He is so strong in so many ways. I wish he had compassion and a better understanding of why women hate to be excluded from family decisions." Tears began to form in the comers of her eyes.

"He hasn't compassion?" Richard protested. "He took you in when you were freezing to death and nursed you and stayed to care for you. That's compassion."

"That's part of his strong, inflexible moral code," Kelli maintained.

"That's poppycock." Richard smiled. "Maybe Hank, as a man, feels it is feminine to use the word compassion, but boil down this code of his and you find compassion as well as honesty, bravery, and self- control. He's a strong man, Kelli, a hundred times the man Sterling was."

"But that's part of the problem, Richard. He's too strong. I feel shut out of his decisions." Kelli felt better expressing this deep concern.

"Well, that is a real problem," admitted Richard. "He's a bit of a male chauvinist in a nice way. In a traditional logging family, I suspect it is the man who makes most of the important decisions." Richard paused and looked out the window for a minute and then plunged ahead. "But you're a bit of a feminist Kelli. You're a good professional and I think Hank respects you for it. But you are supersensitive about making decisions. You could easily dominate Hank and that wouldn't be good either. There's a difficult balance that needs to be maintained in a marriage and it requires constant work to prevent the scales from being over-balanced towards either the husband or the wife."

Kelli looked out the window. The smog had cleared a bit for the moment. "I guess your right, Richard. We could overcome this. But Hank wouldn't get along with Melissa."

Richard lowered his voice. "I love my wife, but she's been too controlling for years, particularly towards you. She's abused you, subjected you to her whims, and you always come through for her. It's a bad relationship for you, Kelli." He paused, evidently wondering what to say next. "I have hoped for years that you would escape from this dominance from my wife. It's the only way you can really gain your independence. Leave the LA area. Get out from under her thumb. I'd miss seeing you frequently, Kelli, but it would be best for you and for Melissa. Maybe, after Melissa finishes her therapy and you establish your independence, you can have a healthy, sisterly relationship."

Kelli was dumbfounded. Richard was actually suggesting she leave the area that she grew up in, the area she loved. "But I don't know if I could live in Idaho with Hank," she said. "It's a land of tall majestic mountains, a land of snow, a land of dry sagebrush plains in summer. It's a harsh, unyielding land."

"Have you ever seen the Moscow area in Idaho? Did you do any research on it?"

"No," Kelli admitted.

"It's not like your image of Custer County," Richard said. "Idaho is a very diverse state. Moscow is set in a wheat-growing area, and the rolling Palouse hills are green with wheat in the spring and a beautiful yellow in late summer. A few years ago I attended a two-week institute at the University of Idaho. The campus is green with trees and spacious lawns ... one of the most beautiful I have ever seen. They have summer theatre, music concerts, and a friendly staff. They're located in a small city with tree-lined residential streets and no smog. One of my professors at the institute said the public schools are top-notch and it's a wonderful place to bring up kids." He paused and smiled again. "Do your research on Moscow and the University of Idaho before you form judgments on it. You'll find young, insecure professors there who may gripe and be unfriendly ... but you'll find that everywhere, even in the excellent universities in our area. But I'd think you'd be happy in Moscow with Hank."

A call came in for Richard and he took it. Kelli stood up to leave. Richard interrupted his phone call briefly to say, "Don't let him go, Kelli. He's a good man."

Kelli stepped out into the sunlight. Her first stop was the Garden Grove Library.

Chapter 48

Los Angeles and Moscow – Early November

By the first week in November Kelli had run photocopies of brief encyclopedia articles on Moscow and the surrounding area. It seemed like a place that would make her happy. Sure, she couldn't be a principal there immediately. But she could be a substitute teacher, a teacher, and then, in time, a principal again. But first she would want to marry Hank and start a family.

Kelli began to send newsy weekly letters. She described what she had learned about Moscow from Richard and the encyclopedias. She received one letter from Hank in early November. It read:

"Dear Kelli:

Everything is going well here. I survived Halloween. Lot of trick or treaters at the door. The girls went as witches.

I did some detective work and found out who the man with the binoculars was. You remember the three Idaho State University graduate students who must have camped at Walter Lake. I got the address of Patrick Brown, the leader of the group. He told me that Shawn Muldoon, one of his group, came down from the rim close to three o'clock. He had binoculars and Shawn had been entranced by Pam and may have been doing some girl-watching.

After a lot of calls, I reached Shawn. He said he was mainly trying to find a new way up to the upper basin. He did see a bear cub start the rock rolling towards you. He watched you through his binoculars until he was sure you were all right before returning to his group.

I owe Darry an apology. He was correct in saying he was not responsible for rolling a rock at you. But Shawn was nowhere near the Goat Lake Trail.

We had a beautiful October with lots of red and yellow leaves. But now the leaves are gone and it rains a lot.

With love, Hank"

It was a friendly letter, but not the type of warm letter she could use to rekindle Hank's love for her. She began weekly phone calls to him. They would chat pleasantly for a few minutes and then Hank would find some reason to break off the conversation.

Kelli called Monday night the second week of November and Sara answered.

"Is your father there?" Kelli asked, hoping this would be a longer call.

"He's watching Monday night football," Sara answered, but I think he'd want to talk for a few minutes. Before I get him, I have a favor to ask. I really need help. Dad is such a nice guy but he knows zilch about teen-aged girls and what they wear. Could you phone me tomorrow night at seven when my father is teaching a graduate history class? We need to have a long talk. You seem so nice."

Hank answered the phone. Again the conversation was amicable but brief She had the impression that Hank had lost interest in her. Maybe that's what Sara would tell her on Tuesday night.

Sara must have been sitting by the phone for she answered Kelli's call Tuesday evening on the second ring.

"You said you needed help with selecting clothes," Kelli said, placing a pad and pencil within reach.

"I love my father," Sara said. "He's so kind and he tries to be so helpful. But he thinks of me as a little girl. I'm thirteen. I'm going to start high school next fall. I don't want to wear the kind of clothes that Julie and Joanne wear. You know what I mean?"

"I sure do. I had the same problem with my father. He wanted to keep me in jumpers. But my mother took me shopping."

"You know my dad well. At least that's the impression I got. Can you get him to see that I'm growing up?"

"I wish I was in Moscow to take you shopping," Kelli said without thinking. "But I'm not. You could have a heart-to-heart talk with your father."

"They don't turn out so well any more. Dad is so depressed these days. He just mopes around at home. We've gone on some picnics this fall but they just aren't as much fun because the spark has gone out of him. My best girlfriend moved away and I tried to talk about it with Dad and it didn't work."

"What happened?" Kelli asked chewing the eraser end of a pencil.

"Well, we got alone after my sisters went to bed. I started to tell him how lonely I was and how much I missed my friend. I wanted Dad just to listen and let me get out my grief Instead, he started making suggestions about finding new friends. I could brain him. I just wanted someone to let me cry and talk. Why was Dad so stupid?"

Kelli could empathize. "I think that most men just don't understand what women need in that situation. My former husband was like that too; but he was not a nice, caring man like your father."

Blizzard in August 205

Sara asked Kelli about her life and Kelli reciprocated. For half an hour Kelli enjoyed a long chat and felt that Sara was a very mature teenager. Sara suddenly asked, "You're in love with my dad, aren't you?"

Kelli gulped and answered honestly, "Yes, I love him very much and I think of him every day. I did a terrible thing, Sara. Your father proposed marriage to me and I turned him down. I wish I could take back my words."

"I know," Sara said. "I overheard Dad talking with Uncle Ted and Aunt Marjorie about it. He was terribly hurt. He's still hurting." "I wish I could do something to make him feel better." "You could come see him," Sara said. "You know the picture you sent, the one of you in the red sweater?"

"Yes."

"I had it enlarged and framed for his birthday last week. He stands and looks at it on the mantle for the longest time each morning. I think he still loves you. He thinks you don't need him."

"But I do need him. I need him terribly." Kelli began to sob. She couldn't help herself. When she finally regained control of her emotions she said, "I wish I could see your dad again."

"There might be a way," Sara said. In another few minutes, they had both worked out a plan.

It might work, Kelli thought as she hung up. It just might work.

Chapter 49

Moscow Area – Thanksgiving Weekend

As she reached the parking lot of the Spokane airport, Kelli noticed four inches of snow on the ground. Hank's Uncle Ted carried her large, black bag while Kelli carried the smaller blue one. Ted Barclay was dressed for winter with a bulky, brown wool coat, a peaked wool hat, and logger boots. He was a tall, slightly stoop-shouldered man with a ruddy face and perpetual smile. He looked at Kelli with concern for she had on just a red ski sweater, a blue skirt, and brown shoes.

"Did you bring a wool coat with you?" he asked.

"I've got another ski sweater and a heavy raincoat in the black bag," she said. "Maybe I'd better go back in the airport and change."

They retraced their steps and Kelli emerged from the ladies room with the yellow cashmere sweater over her blouse, then the red ski sweater, and the raincoat as the outer layer. Her top half was warm but as she slid into the passenger seat of the green Ford truck, she realized her bottom half was cold. Uncle Ted produced what he called a "horse blanket" for her legs and feet. It was a nondescript brown, but the wool was thick and warm.

As they pulled away from the parking lot and Uncle Ted paid the fee, Kelli tried to make conversation. "It's a lot colder here then when I left Los Angeles this morning."

"Aye, it's twenty five, lassie. It's expected to go down to twenty tonight."

Kelli was charmed by Uncle Ted's accent. "Did your people come from Scotland?" she asked.

"My father and mother came from the mountains of eastern Tennessee, the Great Smokies, about the turn of the century. But their families came originally from Scotland in the late 1700's. We've been loggers for at least eight generations."

Kelli let him talk on about logging for twenty minutes as he drove into a corner of Spokane and headed south on a snow-slick highway. He was explaining about horse logging in the old days and how, as a young man, he worked on a green chain. Loggers had their own set of terminology and Kelli could understand only part of his descriptions.

"Do you have any white pine in Southern California?" he asked.

"I'm not sure," she responded. "But we do have some giant trees in Northern California called redwoods."

"Aye, and I'd like to measure my chain saw against one of the likes of them," Ted commented.

Kelli was aghast, but was determined to avoid a confrontation on a very sensitive environmental issue. "Your folks must have found a culture shock to move from Tennessee to northern Idaho," she said.

"Not so much. We moved to an area of mountains, lots of trees, and snow in winter. But the logging camps were bigger in Idaho in the early 1900's and there was lots of good white pine to be cut."

Kelli could imagine the big clear-cuts made when they harvested the first-growth timber. Avoiding the subject of logging, she said, "This is a shock for me. It was eighty-four degrees in LA when I left, and there are palms on some of the streets."

This caught Ted's interest and for more than half an hour he asked Kelli about her parents, her childhood, her education, and her teaching career. He had her talk about her first marriage and whooped with glee when she told him how she threw Sterling out when he was abusive.

"Good for you, lassie. No Barclay or Donaldson ever struck their wives. It just isn't done."

Kelli realized where Hank's internal code came from. It was a cultural heritage handed down generation after generation. She explored other aspects of this and found this Tennessee heritage included honesty, truthfulness, generosity, kindness to children, and many other good qualities that Hank had shown. However, Uncle Ted did drink some but he didn't begrudge Hank's aversion to liquor.

"If my father had been killed that way, I wouldn't take a drink either," he said.

"But didn't some of the loggers call him a wimp because he didn't drink?" Kelli asked.

"Aye, and they regretted it," Uncle Ted said proudly. "There was no better man with his fists in Camp X than Hank. Why, once a man came after him with a knife after Hank knocked him down. Hank gave him a hard right to the stomach and then two lefts to the chin that put him out cold. They had to get an ambulance to haul him away and wire his jaw together."

Kelli was horrified. "Hank didn't tell me that."

Ted smiled. "Probably was a bit ashamed. A deputy put him in jail for two nights but he was cleared when the sheriff investigated. Fact was, after talking to him, the sheriff wanted to hire him on as a deputy."

Kelli again tried to move the conversation away from logging. "Were you proud when Hank got a college degree and became a professor?"

"Sure was," Uncle Ted exclaimed. "Imagine a Barclay or a Donaldson as a professor. We used to call them guys pointy-headed professors in Bovill ... but no more. Hank spoke at the high school graduation at the White Pine School last year, and all those Bovill kids listened real good. If he could make it, so could they. And the time is coming when most of them seniors are going to have to get other jobs—the log cuts are shrinking and the mills are beginning to close." Kelli could see now how valuable Hank was as a role model for rural Idaho college students and could visualize the individualized help and encouragement he gave them. She realized that the cultural background of her family was far different from Hank's. Her mother or Melissa would be far more comfortable in Paris, Rome, or Stockholm than in Uncle Ted's world. She wondered how Hank made the transition to the university environment.

"Was it hard for Hank to live in Moscow and teach at the university?" she asked.

"No, but it took him a while to learn to dress the part. But he was a powerful speaker in the classroom. I saw him giving Lincoln's speech against Douglas where he says a house divided against itself cannot stand. Those kids sat with their mouths open and you could hear a pin drop. He gets it from my uncle who was a Presbyterian minister." Uncle Ted asked about the White Clouds trip and Kelli gave him the full details. He sympathized when Kelli went sliding into the frigid waters, was pleased when Hank took her into his sleeping bag, and chortled when Hank killed the bear.

"You got a real man there in Hank. Don't let him get away," he advised.

Kelli glowed. Beneath his rough words, he seemed to approve of her. "I don't mean to," she said, "I love him very much. But the spark he had for me is almost out. Is it because he's still grieving for Susan? Or has he met someone else?"

"It's because you hurt him very much when you turned him down. He's not seeing anyone else. Sara would know it if he was. He misses Susan, but Sara thinks he still loves you. Rekindle that spark, lassie."

"Then you want us to get married. Uncle Ted."

He grinned. "He needs a pretty woman with spirit and education to brighten up his life. I'm voting for you."

Buoyed with this endorsement, Kelli almost missed seeing Moscow. The main street was wide with banks, a department store, some restaurants, a drug store, and fire station and then the highway led eastward past a grain elevator and a cemetery. They passed Troy, less populated than Moscow, ten miles

Blizzard in August

further on, then Deary and finally Bovill. As they drove east from Troy the stands of trees grew more numerous and the snow deeper.

Uncle Ted had talked about the Bovill Presbyterian Church and what a fine minister they had. Kelli made him show her the brown pine church and was captivated by its rustic beauty. As he talked about how much his church meant to him, Kelli realized that this was also part of Hank's heritage. Hank was a product of two cultures—thirty miles apart—but distinctly different. Kelli wondered how she would fit into the two distinct cultures.

Aunt Marjorie met them at the door. The room was already warm but Uncle Ted put in another log in the wood stove as he introduced Kelli to his wife and Myrtle, Hank's mother. The two ladies gave Kelli motherly hugs and Kelli responded. Kelli asked what she could do and was soon set to work mashing potatoes and setting the table.

At six, Hank Barclay walked in followed by his three daughters. His mouth dropped open in amazement when he saw Kelli. He was speechless. Kelli couldn't tell from his expression whether he was pleased, angry, or stunned. Recovering, Hank held out a hand and said, "This is a nice surprise."

Kelli was hurt. She had been imagining that Hank would give her a big hug and some passionate kisses. Instead, he acted as if Kelli was an old, but not close friend who had come for an unexpected visit. Sara greeted Kelli warmly and introduced her sisters.

Hank's mother and Aunt Marjorie served a traditional Thanksgiving turkey dinner with Sara and Kelli helping to serve. Uncle Ted was seated at the head of the table; he carved the turkey and Aunt Marjorie and Hank's mother sat at the other end where they could dish out potatoes, gravy, cranberry sauce, vegetables, and rolls. Aunt Marjorie seated Hank next to Uncle Ted and Kelli beside him.

Determined to ignore Hank's coolness, Kelli was the center of attention. Uncle Ted recounted much of Kelli's adventures in the White Clouds and Kelli was asked for more details. Ten-year-old tomboy, Julie, wanted to hear again how Kelli slid into the ice cold water and how Hank killed the bear. Question followed question and Kelli was vivacious and full of praise for Hank as she described the action. But Hank, the hero of the adventure, was subdued, seldom speaking unless asked a question.

The conversation flowed on to other subjects: prospects for logging next spring; the closing of a nearby sawmill; Uncle Ted's forays for wood for the coming winter, the deer hunting season, and the inevitable questions of Kelli's childhood.

Kelli was asked questions about her nationality and, when Uncle Ted heard her father was Swedish, he heartily approved. "Swedes make excellent loggers," he commented. "You can always count on a Swede."

The girls asked Kelli about Southern California. They wanted to know about Disneyland, surfing, and whether the water was really warm enough to swim in. Sara mentioned that Kelli was a school principal. "A principal," Myrtle exclaimed. She had once aspired to be a teacher and was in awe of a woman who had risen to the position of principal. She and Aunt Marjorie asked a flurry of questions about the courses that were taught and how she handled discipline problems. By the end of dinner Kelli felt the approval and support of everyone there except Hank, the person who mattered most.

After dinner, it was the custom to play games. The adults played backgammon and the girls played cards. Kelli was offered a seat at the backgammon table by Aunt Marjorie, but not knowing the game, she asked to join Hank's daughters. They played hearts and old maid, with Kelli smoothly settling the occasional dispute between Julie and Joanne. Kelli learned a lot about the three girls and felt a growing rapport with them. As an experienced elementary school teacher, she knew how to bring each into the conversation and to subtly praise their strengths and accomplishments. Their spirited conversation and laughter reached the adult table, and more than once Kelli caught a smile from Aunt Marjorie and Myrtle directed at her.

About nine they thanked Uncle Ted and Aunt Marjorie for their hospitality and Kelli and the girls piled into Hank's car for the trip back to Moscow. It had snowed another two inches and the highway was slick. Hank was strangely quiet on the return trip.

Kelli was charmed by Hank's house. It was on a quiet, residential street with trees overshadowing the sidewalks. There was an elementary school a few blocks away. The two-story house was white with green trim and had a broad, old-fashioned front porch, which faced east. Kelli could visualize herself, Hank, and the girls sitting out on the porch, on reclining lawn chairs in the heat of a summer's evening.

The big front room was decorated with matching russet chairs and a couch. The dining room had a large, polished oak table. The kitchen was modern with a four-burner stove, oven, large refrigerator, a double sink and plenty of cupboards. The house was sturdy and much better furnished than Kelli had expected. Susan must have been a good housekeeper and someone, probably Sara, had cleaned the house well so that Kelli was impressed.

Hank brought Kelli's bags into the master bedroom on the second floor and Kelli followed. She noted, with pleasure, that there was a large queen-sized bed, not double beds. Tonight, she would find out what was bothering Hank and they would make-up and sleep together.

Blizzard in August 211

Julie and Joanne shared a bedroom at the other end of the second floor. Hank was getting them to brush their teeth and by the time they were tucked in bed, Kelli had unpacked her bags and selected a seductive yellow nightgown and a chaste blue housecoat. She stepped into the hall to go downstairs but heard heated arguments from the living room, Sara's voice rising in anger. She stepped back inside the bedroom and waited.

"What's wrong with you, Dad?" Sara said.

"Nothing." Hank's lips were drawn up in a tight, angry line.

"I thought you would be happy to see, Kelli. You look at her picture every day." Sara was puzzled, wondering why her plan wasn't working.

"Was it your idea to have Kelli come to our Thanksgiving dinner?" her father said accusingly.

"Yes, of course. But I got Uncle Ted, Aunt Marjorie, and Grandma in on it. They all thought it was a great idea." Sara remembered the fun she had with her Grandmother and Aunt planning the entire dinner.

"But you didn't let me in on it," Hank persisted.

"Of course not," Sara said with exasperation. "It wouldn't have been a surprise if I had."

"I'm the head of this family. Don't I get to decide who gets to sleep in my house?"

Hank looked almost angry enough to spank Sara, but she stood her ground. "Dad, you have been moping around this house, depressed ever since you left Kelli in Los Angeles. You need to see her. She loves you."

"How do you know that?" The question cracked like a whip across the room.

"She called when you were out and when I had a bad problem in school. She talked to me for an hour and, at the end of the time, I felt much better. She called a second time and we had another woman-to- woman talk. I thought I was in love but she explained what love really was. I asked her if she loved you and she said she loved you very much."

"And I suppose she wormed an invitation from you to come?"

"No, it was my idea." Sara stood her ground, her feet planted wide to steady her.

"And how do you think your mother would feel about what you did?" Hank's voice was still hard and tears started to form in the comer of Sara's eyes.

"I think Ma would be delighted. She told me that if she died, she wanted you to remarry a really nice woman. She said you are a strong, brave, and caring man but that you were moody and stubborn and depressed when she went away even for a few days. She said you were good with young girls but wouldn't have a clue how to be a father to a teenaged daughter."

Hank paused as if considering what Sara had said. "And you don't think I have been a good father for you?"

"Oh, Dad," Sara said. "Listen to me this once. You're a wonderful man. I wouldn't have any other father, but you're a man. You don't know that when I come to you with a problem I want you to listen to me...really listen to me until I have talked the problem out. I don't want you to fix the problem. And Dad, I'm too embarrassed to ask you the kind of female questions a daughter asks her mother. Can't you see that I need a mother. And I like Kelli so much. She's like Mom used to be."

"And how do Julie and Joanne feel? Or have you asked them?"

"Didn't you hear us laughing when we played cards this evening? Julie told me she hoped you and Kelli would take her backpacking in the White Clouds." Sara paused, almost out of breath. "And Grandma said you needed someone nice like Kelli to give you back your spark. And you saw how Uncle Ted and Marjorie enjoyed talking to Kelli."

"And so my whole family wants me to marry Kelli and no one has asked how I feel." There was a nasty tone to Hank's voice now.

Sara began to cry. She threw her arms around her father's neck and slobbered into the lapel of his coat. "Oh, Dad, I love you... I love you very much … can't you understand that … I did this because I loved you … and because I know down deep you love Kelli."

Hank was moved and held her closely. "Kelli really means that much to you?"

Her sobs subsided and Sara said. "I want Kelli as my mother. Dad. I don't care if I get a present for Christmas as long as Kelli is here to share Christmas with us." She paused. "You know I've tried to replace Mother since she died, doing the cooking, laundry, and taking care of Julie and Jo. I don't mind it, but Julie thinks I'm bossy and maybe she's right. I'm doing my best but I'm a teenager now and I need to be on my own a little more. Dad, you can't expect me to be the mother of this family forever."

Hank hugged his daughter closely. "You've done a very good job Sara. I understand how you feel. I've asked you to do too much." He paused. "I was so hurt when Kelli turned me down. I've been depressed and angry ever since."

"Kelli told me she feels terrible about how she hurt you. She understands how you hurt," Julie said. "She has something very important to tell you."

"I suppose I could knock on her door before I go to my room." Hank said.

Blizzard in August

213

Suddenly a smile creased Sara's face. "Please do it, Dad. Do it now. Hank released Sara and walked towards the stairs.

Kelli had nearly given up hope. Hank and Sara had been arguing downstairs for nearly half an hour. Suddenly, she heard heavy, male footsteps on the stairs. She straightened her hair and picked up her novel. A knock sounded at the door.

"Come in," Kelli said putting down her book. "I so hoped it was you."

"Sara said you had something important to tell me," Hank said moving towards the bed.

Kelli got out of bed and sat one side. After some hesitation. Hank sat beside her but a foot away. "I have lots to tell you. First I want to apologize for the way I hurt you when we met in Los Angeles. I was way out of line in what I said about Darry and Big Mike ... and I wasn't thinking straight when I turned down your proposal."

"And what do you hear from Darry?" Hank's voice had an edge. "No one knows where he is. Pam testified against Darry, as you know, and the criminal suit was dropped against her."

"Yes, and the huge civil suit against Pam that would have bankrupted your family was also dropped," Hank said, his face softening.

Kelli smiled. "Thanks to you, Richard's family is not bankrupt. I was wrong, terribly wrong to criticize you. Richard thinks the world of you."

"And how do Pam and Melissa feel?" Hank asked.

"Pam is going to a home for unwed mothers in another state to have her baby. Her mother wanted her to have an abortion, but she refused." Kelli paused. "Melissa is having mental problems, I think. Richard says she is in therapy."

"And how do you feel about Melissa now?"

Hank had an annoying way of asking a lot of questions, but Kelli ignored that. "Richard and I had a long talk about my relationship with Melissa. He thinks she dominates me and it's bad both for her and me."

"And what does he suggest?" Hank's voice was curious now, not tight and hard.

"He advised me to leave the Los Angeles area," Kelli said. She picked at her housecoat. "He thinks I need to lead a life independent of Melissa."

"I agree." Hank smiled and the hard lines left his lips. "I thought she dominated you and you were too worried what she thought of you." Kelli hung her head.

"You were right, as usual. And you were right about Darry and Big Mike. Did you know that Big Mike had a heart attack in the Bahamas and turned over day-to-day management of his corporation to his senior vice-president?"

"I didn't know that." Kelli listened for Hank to make a nasty remark about Big Mike but didn't hear it. Instead Hank asked, "What did you decide to do about your contract as principal?"

Kelli smiled. "I love that school, but I gave my month's notice. December 18th will be my last day."

Hank looked surprised. "So soon. Why?"

"Because I love you more than I can ever tell you. I was a fool to turn down your proposal. Richard thinks I'm too much of a feminist...that I want to make too many decisions. He thinks there should be a more even balance in decision-making between husband and wife."

"Richard is a smart man," Hank observed. His lips turned up in a little smile. "Maybe I have wanted to make too many decisions myself At least that's what Sara tells me."

Kelli's face was glowing. There was hope. "There is something else very important I have to tell you. Do you remember the time we made love in the White Clouds?"

"Yes," Hank said warily. "I thought you were safe. You're not about to tell me that you are going to have my baby, are you? That's not why you came, is it?" Hank flushed as if his anger were rising.

"No," she said sadly. "It was the wrong time of the month to conceive a baby as I was sure at the time." Kelli paused and had difficulty continuing. "Oh, Hank, I felt sad when I knew I wasn't carrying your baby. It would be a part of you that I would have always had. If I had been pregnant, I wouldn't have even let you know. I love you too much to force you into marriage."

Kelli's eyes moistened. "I love you. I love you. I want to marry you because I love you. I want to have your baby only if you want me to." She broke down, sobbing uncontrollably.

Suddenly Hank's arms were around her and he was sobbing into her housecoat. They sat, clinging together, without speaking. Then Hank said contritely, "I have been horrible to you tonight. Just nasty and horrible. Of course I want you. I didn't realize how much I loved you. Without you, I have no spark. Oh, Kelli what a fool I've been to let my disappointment at being turned down affect me so. I loved you when I proposed in Los Angeles; I love you even more now."

Kelli was so happy she could hardly breathe. "You mean you might ask me to marry you again?"

Blizzard in August

Hank's mouth turned up in a broad smile. "You wouldn't by any chance have that engagement ring I gave you, would you?"

Kelli looked a little sheepish. Then she jumped off the bed and brought the box from her bag.

Hank opened it and put the ring on her finger. "Will you marry me?" he asked.

"Yes, Hank. I'm floating on a cloud. Yes. Yes. Yes."

When they finished hugging and kissing. Hank began to ask some practical questions. "When do you think the wedding should be?" "Let's get married before Christmas. I can be up here by plane on December 19th." She searched Hank's face for signs of approval and was rewarded with a wide grin.

"I thought people needed two months for invitations and plans," Hank said.

"Oh, Hank. That's when I thought of the kind of big Los Angeles wedding Melissa would like. I don't want that. I just want to be married to you."

"Would you like a church wedding?" Kelli was pleased that all the hard tones were gone from Hank's voice and he was trying to be helpful.

"Yes," Kelli said. "Uncle Ted showed me the Bovill Presbyterian Church and I loved it. But anywhere you want is fine." Hank kissed Kelli. "Uncle Ted, Aunt Maijorie and your mother would love to have us married there. But how would your family feel? The wedding is usually held in the bride's home town."

Kelli smiled. She knew she was losing the kind of wedding she once dreamed about, but it was worth it to marry Hank. "Melissa is in therapy. Pam will probably be in a home for unwed mothers by then. Richard may have to stay with Melissa. My parents aren't feeling too well. Ann is the only member of my family I can count on." She paused. "But it doesn't matter. I've made the decision to lead a new life. I'm going to be a loving wife for you, a good mother for your very special daughters, and we're going to have children of our own."

"You're not going to give up your teaching career are you?" Hank asked with concern.

"I'd like to start our family first just after our marriage," Kelli said. "I'll try for some substitute teaching jobs during my pregnancy and then try later to become an elementary school teacher again. I'll want to keep my hand in, go with you to Phi Delta Kappa meetings, and maybe some day be a principal again. But what I want now is to be the kind of wife you need ... the kind that Susan was for so many years." Hank began to sob again. He lifted his head from Kelli's shoulder and said, "I want to be the kind of husband and father that will make you happy and proud. And if I get stubborn or touchy, just confront me like Sara did a few minutes ago."

They discussed wedding plans another ten minutes; then Kelli said, "I thought of sleeping with you tonight. I'll do it if you want. But with the girls down the hall, it would be better to wait until we're married."

"I can wait. It's only a month," Hank said. He kissed her again passionately and went downstairs to sleep on the couch.

Chapter 50

Bovill – December 22nd

It was nearly time for Kelli and Hank to leave the wedding reception at Uncle Hank and Aunt Marjorie's home. Kelli would go upstairs to change soon, but she wanted a last peek at the wedding presents. There had been a large check from Richard, which Hank would put in a bank in Moscow on the way to a hotel in Spokane. Richard had needed to stay with Melissa and couldn't attend the wedding. There was a silver serving dish from Senator Wagner with a note that his new charitable trust wanted Hank to write a book on the history of Custer County. He promised money to pay Hank and his family to spend the summer in his county and to publish the book. There were presents from some of Kelli's teachers.

Hank came as she examined the presents. "What's this one he wondered? The package is from Paris."

"I wondered, too. That's why I didn't open the brown paper wrapping." Kelli opened the present and exclaimed. "It's from Darry Baltz. It's a beautiful lace tablecloth." Kelli turned to look at Hank, hoping she wouldn't see hard lines form on his cheeks, praying that he could be forgiving.

"It's nice," Hank said without expression. "He must have learned of our wedding from Pam or Melissa." He found a note inside the box and handed it to Kelli.

The note read, "I feel terrible about what I did to you and the Wagners. I'll live with this the rest of my life. But I really didn't roll the rock down at you, Kelli. And I'm changing. I really am. I'm hoping that Pam will join me in Paris this winter or spring, but there's still a gulf between us. I'll probably be an exile the rest of my life. That's my punishment. It's hard but better than life imprisonment in the United States. I wish you and Hank all the best."

"A nice note," Kelli commented.

"I feel sorry for him. I don't condone what he did but I can forgive him." Kelli gave Hank a smile. She was pleased that he could let go his grudge.

Hank went over to say good-by to Ann, who had been the maid of honor, and Jason, who had been an usher. Kelli waved to Ann and mounted the stairs. It wasn't a big, fancy wedding but she felt at home with Ann, Jason, and

Hank's relatives and friends. She had chosen a new life and was eager to get on with it. Hank would be a good husband to her, as he had been for Susan.

But there were times she would have to be assertive and guide him in the right direction. She vowed that she would be a loving wife and there would be a balance in family decision-making. But above all there would be good communication and a lot of love.

Kelli finished putting on her blue suit. She walked down the stairs and hugged each of Hank's daughters and was rewarded with a big hug and tears from Sara. "Be good for your Uncle Ted and Aunt Marjorie," she said. "We'll be back from our honeymoon in three days."

She linked her arm in Hank's and walked out the door to his car.

About the author

Sydney Duncombe, a former college professor, has backpacked fourteen times to the 9,900 foot lake basin that is the site of this novel. He is the author of The Unlikely Candidate, Enduring Faith (PublishAmerica, Inc.) and several recent short stories.